The Arthuriad Volume Three:
The Misery of Morgaine

Zane Newitt

Text copyright © Zane Newitt 2019
Design copyright © Billie Hastie 2019
All rights reserved.

Zane Newitt has asserted his right under the Copyright, Designs and Patents Act 1988 to be identified as the author of this work.

No part of this book may be reprinted or reproduced or utilised in any form or by electronic, mechanical or any other means, now known or hereafter invented, including photocopying or recording, or in any information storage or retrieval system, without the permission in writing from the Publisher and Author.

This title is intended for the enjoyment of adults, and is not recommended for children due to the mature content it contains. This book is intended to entertain the reader, and not to offend or upset in any way whatsoever. The reader should be aware that this book contains adult content.

This book is meant to be educational, informative and entertaining. Although the author and publisher have made every effort to ensure that the information in this book was correct at the time of publication, the author and publisher do not assume and hereby disclaim any liability to any party for loss, damage or disruption caused by errors or omissions, whether such errors or omissions result from negligence, accident or any other cause.

First published 2019
by Rowanvale Books Ltd
The Gate
Keppoch Street
Roath
Cardiff
CF24 3JW
www.rowanvalebooks.com

A CIP catalogue record for this book is available from the British Library.
ISBN: 978-1-912655-24-3

This installment of the Arthuriad is dedicated to the residents of Dinas Maddwy, of Mallwyd, and Dolgellau. A battle lasting three days and claiming approximately one hundred thousand souls occurred in your very hills, creeks and farms: a history-shaping event, both famous and infamous.

Geoffrey of Monmouth moved the Matter of Britain from lovely Wales to Cornwall, desperately hoping to protect your relics, your land grants, your precious documents and sacred tombs from Norman imposition and conquest.

The continuity and integrity of your history, for various reasons and motives, has never recovered from his strategic sleight of hand.

Had Camlan been in America, in England or even in Ireland, coffee shops would have been erected, professional tours conducted, jobs created, history revered and celebrated. Instead, one lonely marker on the farm where the Cymry fell, tattered and worn through the process of time, is the only man-made monument to the fall of your Golden Age… that, and the burial mounds that garnish the countryside; the perpetual reminder of the needless slaughter that divided the kingdoms and allowed the Saxons to ultimately subdue the Isles and create the *fifteen-hundred-years-struggle* that tarries yet today.

There is no mystery as to the location of Camlan, and any controversy about the same is contrived by Academics and Politicians with malevolent motives. It's on any ordinance survey map of North Wales for all to see, just as it always has been. The place is dark, sacred and wondrous, and it belongs to you.

Additionally, this book is dedicated to the Welsh

heroes now dead… Or sleeping. For 'death' is a peculiar word to the Cymry…

Dr. Zane Newitt

Contents

Foreword from the Author:
What Causes War?   3

Prologue I
Authority Obeys the Dying King   10

Prologue II
Merlin Confronts Maelgwn   15

Chapter 1
Keep a Few Drops of That Poison in You, for You Will Need It
There Will Be Civil War   23

Chapter 2
I Will Kill Maelgwn
There Will Be No Civil War   34

Chapter 3
Making a Three-Front Attack a One-Front Attack   47

Chapter 4
Sorting it All Out
Interlude   61

Chapter 5
Stones Do Not Fall From Heaven
No Help From Rome   66

Chapter 6
The Last Lie Ere Arrows Fly 80

Chapter 7
Reinventing the Anglo-Saxon 96

Chapter 8
Undefeated No More
The Battle of Llongborth 108

Chapter 9
Unlikely Traitors
Derfel Gadarn and Alain Fyrgan 125

Chapter 10
No Song for Mordred 133

Chapter 11
Gwenhwyfar Taunts Arthur From
the Grave 143

Chapter 12
Finalizing the Lists
Urien Denied Again 165

Chapter 13
The Summer Kingdom was False, and
You Knew 173

Chapter 14
My Heart Turns to Camelot as the Floor
Around Me Burns 189

Chapter 15
Who's Afraid of Morgaine Le Fay?
Cadfan's Change of Heart   199

Chapter 16
Unarmed and Disappointed   220

Chapter 17
Embrace Your Abomination   235

Chapter 18
Camlan Act I
Alain's Cowardly Retreat and the First
Day of the Dark Ages   249

Chapter 19
Camlan Act II
The Ridge of the Saxons and the Fall
of Cedric   254

Chapter 20
Camlan Act III
Mist
The Misery of Morgaine   273

Chapter 21
Camlan Act IV
The Fateful Division of the Army
and Derfel's Rout of the Silures
and Bretons   283

Chapter 22
Camlan Act V
Elvish Armor and War Dogs   290

Chapter 23
Camlan Act VI
The Fog is Lifting
The Passing of Arthur   304

Chapter 24
Camlan Act VII
The Battle After the Battle is
the Real Battle   310

Epilogue   323

Foreword from the Author:
What Causes War?

Although not approached as a trilogy, *The Arthuriad Volume Three: The Misery of Morgaine* is the natural conclusion to the first Act of the Arthuriad. Volumes One and Two bring Arthur to the scene during the triumph of his rise, capture the difficulties, conflicts and his personal misery in maintaining the *Summer Kingdom,* and conclude with the Civil War. Though there is significant ground to cover after the dread Battle of Camlan, the kingdoms later collectively nominated as 'Wales' afterward suffered sharp declination from which they would never fully recover (indeed, those passionate about the land of dragons and daffodils demark Camlan as 'the fall' and still look for a messianic figure to usher in a time of restitution and return to that short Golden Age and taste of what might be).

This volume is a war book.

While writing it, the constant preoccupation of thought and challenge of view was over and over again revisited and considered. What... or Who... or *Who and What*... really cause war?

My worldview insists that the Elite intentionally cause war for the purpose of creating debt, and debt-bondsmen, thus expanding or sustaining their position over the common people. As James, the Brother of the Lord, says, 'For the love of money is the root of all evil'. In another place Paul teaches us that 'we wrestle against wickedness in high places' – the worldview that best fits empirical, experiential and historical reality is *conspiratorial.*

I assert and affirm this to be the reality. However, preparing the manuscript was an exercise that better equipped me with 'how' this occurs. Some say that 'nothing happens by chance' and that the Secret Societies, Big Brother, the Freemasons or Illuminati contrive, control and manage *everything.* Although this seems credible, when taken to its logical conclusion, it exempts men from their individual responsibility and denies the fallen nature of *all men,* not just the Ruling Cabals. Big Brother may be a Puppet Master, but men are not puppets.

It would rather seem that the Illuminati are specific in their manipulations through impactful isolated events or operations, but that they *do not* manage everything. Rather, they know that mankind is selfish, greedy, murderous, envious, bankrupt of love and lustful enough to destroy themselves, only needing a little cunning and strategic guidance along the way. Indeed they rely upon the truth that man is both fallen and unpredictable. Thus they must rather 'nudge, guide and react' versus micromanaging the masses. Given the right circumstances, regular men will never cease to design and enact far greater evils upon their neighbors than any crusty old banker, CEO of a corrupt Multinational, or

Adept of the Occult could conjure in their vain imaginations.

Make no mistake – the Elite do cause wars.

But so do we.

Had Simon Magus never funded the Saxon Wars, the Four Chords would never have been pulled apart. Lancelot would never have been called away to the Continent where absence would allow lust and resentment to grow over Arthur 'seeing her first', and Arthur never would have been made king of Glamorgan and Gwent at fourteen (placing the much stronger Lancelot in an uncomfortable, subordinate role).

The teenagers may have resolved the love triangle over a fistfight, or amicably, but surely not with twenty years, and then twenty more, of unspoken hurts, strife and cancerously murderous jealousy.

Simon Magus caused the war, and then took advantage of the choices and deeds of men acting freely of their own accord.

Simon Magus is responsible.

And so is Lancelot.

And so is Arthur.

The same extends to the unfortunate circumstances that delivered Mordred into the world. Simon and the king of the Tylwyth Teg selected Gwyar for the Spring Rites, but had no idea what dark fruit their meddling would bring.

Elsewhere throughout the Matter of Britain, the same dichotomy recurs.

Wars are started by the Elite, who are wise enough to intervene periodically, then leave men to do what men do. That is the modification of my personal position and the great lesson this author learned in the research, preparation and writing of the book.

May the reader ponder this opinion and the worthy subject as they navigate the pages and enjoy this installment of the Arthuriad.

'Prince Llew, forced to fight alongside a man whom he raised as his own but revealed to be sired by another.

The Northern Chieftain Caw's favorite child adores the South and is historian and scribe for the very Throne he would usurp.

Urien strains to slay his own brothers and kinsmen, else turn on the king.

Maelgwn to take arms against the man who slaughtered his love, and in so doing ally with the man whom his love loved.

Gwyar to avenge Gwalchmai's death, but in doing so cause another son to fall; else to watch her brother perish.

Roman Catholics to fight their rivals, but join with heathens.

The Church of the Britons to see the burgeoning yoke of Rome break, but the tax is joining with Druids and Witches.

King Arthur of the Cymru to protect the Tribes from splintering into two weak principalities, ceasing to be one nation. And then, once weakened by division, ceasing to be altogether; for the Long Knife is rested.

One more traitor to execute, one more villain to fell.

To kill a third son, or to see tyranny consume the Land.

With such impossible conflict, does it not become needless? With so many weeds and entangled loyalties and deceptions, ought not they neutralize and cancel one another, revealing another way to find reconciliation, or restitution?

But alas, evil men have struck the spark, and mortal men must burn in their desires to make war over one another. Thus Civil War for the Cymru is embroiled.'

Dr. Zane Newitt
Fall, 2019

'The Strife of Camlann in which Arthur and Medraut fell and there was plague in Britain and in Ireland...' Annales Cambrae

PROLOGUE I
Authority Obeys the Dying King

Markings glowed, a flashing ember of mystical letters upon the hilt. From Eden to Avalon, through time itself, it sang haunting warnings to its wielder. *Cast Me Away. Cast Me Away!*

"Fling it not! Yield to it not! Stay it within thy hand!" Morgaine of the Faeries: a visage of loss, a mask of pain, eyes as a well whose bottom was filled with grey stones and speckled gold, only bereft of water. Face once as olive, now as phantom; the pain of both the North and the South, the woe of the ruin of Britain, centered and balanced as a great winepress upon one little grape. One slight Faerie. "Bedwyr!" she beseeched. "Fling it not!"

She labored in contested strides through the waters until the depth overcame her. Then she swam. At other times she appeared to run upon the face of it. Her cries continued; pleading, begging cries.

Suddenly her cries were arrested.

Morgaine had come unto the midst of the pool. She beheld first the fingertips, red and full of youth, sparkling. The fingers were forming a loosely-held fist, as though it were holding an invisible sword. *Or waiting to soon catch one most real and visible…and near.* Next she saw the wrist; lastly, the forearm of the silver-skinned Breton. That unmistakable armor adorned in white samite.

It was the rising, silent call of the Lady of the Lake, outstretched and ready to accept Excalibur. Ready to accept the passing of King Arthur.

"Mother, no!"

The awesome and awful power of the rare appearance of the water spirit now passed, silence broke. Morgaine pressed past the gilded arm protruding from the sacred waves, resuming her way towards the knight standing despondent and bleeding, wobbling in the watery reeds, near the shore.

***

Bedwyr.
The loyal.
A friend closer than a brother.
The joy in a time of mourning.
A fabled and unfailing knight.
One deserving of twelve bards' songs.
A survivor, one of scant and few, of bloody Camlan.
Bedwyr the True.

Yet twice he had disobeyed his lord. But now, the third time…to be true.

Even so, he paused. His eyes closed tight; bile and clotty black blood from his liver had climbed his throat and escaped. The nature of his wounds murdered dignity, and he vomited out the blood with violence, giving no regard for cleaning himself after.

His eyelids flittered in osculation.

How can it be? How so that Llyn Fawr is undefiled amongst the desolation of our cursed isle? Have I passed into the hereafter?

Bedwyr long gazed at the lake as he reflected upon these things.

By chance, a faulty latch had caused his armor to fail at Camlan. Early in the first day a Saxon battle-axe had found his guts and gashed them. For the sum of the clash, which had lasted three days, his insides desperately sought to escape to the light of air and bring him the mercy of death. But Bedwyr had work to do ere he yielded to his spirit's now constant effort of exodus and release.

Bedwyr pressured the gaping wound with his right arm, the nub of his missing hand a seal upon the canyon where his seared bowels swam.

Yet he tarried, though he knew he would soon unseam, and perish. Tarrying, relishing the waters that served as an aromatic footstool beneath the highest peak in the most mountainous region of the tribal kingdoms of the Britons. Tarrying perhaps to capture but once a glimpse of the damsel to whom he had been sent, and bask in the mystical peace of her sacred abode. A moment of peace, covered neither in soot nor char, an air of happy fowl and innumerable flowers generous to give their musk. A moment of remembrance of the Summer Kingdom. *Maybe I have already crossed over, and will be granted rest in Llyn Fawr always,* he thought.

He stood upon the very spot where a

Pendragon, King Meurig ap Tewdrig, had retired and returned his sword to the Lady. And it was here where the Sword of Power she had loaned to the Merlin, who passed it to a sandy-haired boy, that he might be king. The greatest of kings.

And now that very king, forty years hence, lay in a small chapel at Aberdaron, near the shores of passage to Isle of Apples at Porth Meudwy, surely soon to die. Too lame to journey to Glamorgan, and even were that not so, too damaged to walk into the waters and return the symbol of his virility and vitality to its source. Thus Bedwyr was charged by proxy to the task.

Twice he had ridden from the north. His saddle was now as red leather, the whole of his horse as dipped in crimson dye. Twice the sword had been brandished high, only to be withdrawn again. For he could not, though the sky had broken and the kingdom fallen. No, he would not. He would not fling *hope* into the lake, casting away the time of his Iron Bear forever.

But Bedwyr the True had found his resolve once more.

I will not forget the authority of my slain lord. He is my king and my friend; how can I dishonor him at last?

"A day will come more dire than this day," the king had said.

"More dire than the End of the World?" Bedwyr had mused, cradling his king. Bedwyr had ever used humor, during each of the Twelve Battles, even upon the lines at Mynydd Baeden. "By definition, that cannot be."

There was a medicinal comfort from the

smiles Bedwyr wrought. And it had worked then as well.

"The world's end is not nigh; be not deceived, old friend. Now, heed me, for my breath thins and my light goes."

"My lord?" Bedwyr had harkened.

"A day will come more dire than this day. At the hour of Cymru's greatest need, a king shall come, and the sword will rise. Take. Return to her. Be not thrice untrue. Go!"

Bedwyr had seen that look, that authority divine, that real and just power; he recalled it now, and his resolve doubled.

The knight clasped Excalibur by the tip and reared to cast it away.

"No! Must not! Cannot!" The witch was upon him, and stayed his hand.

"Gwyar," asked Bedwyr, "how came we to this dreadful end?"

PROLOGUE II
Merlin Confronts Maelgwn

The Pictish strait called Miegle is shaped as a flexing forearm divided by three wanton and puffy veins, three crooking creeks. Although the unbearable freeze was most intense near the waters, Mordred would cling to the banks; for the veins would lead to villages, and the villages to harbor, and harbor to escape.

Mordred.
Whelp.
Coward.

Which of the three creeks would he choose? The one most expedient of terrain, for he was a soft man and would choose the easy path.

Thus Maelgwn made for the northernmost, leaving the drama of the crumpled corpse of Gwalchmai, cradled in the arms of the raging Pendragon, and the dismembered queen, whose fresh blood cried from the icy blackened earth: one hundred—now five hundred feet behind.

Maelgwn immediately sensed that he was being followed; the pursuer himself pursued. He stopped abruptly. Then he dipped his shoulders to the left but in the same motion jolted hard to the right, ducking behind an overgrown ash tree for cover.

Hoarfrost and not a few shifting grimy rocks betrayed his would-be attacker, whose weighted approach was near. Soon Maelgwn, fastened as a shadow to the trunk of the tree, could see, and feel, the breath of his follower billow; a misty cloud in starless pitch. Closer he drew. Again closer. Soon they shared obverse sides of the same tree.

A weapon was drawn. Maelgwn either felt or saw this. A weapon was swinging—*Making for my head!* The skill of the strike was advanced; a professional killer. Maelgwn avoided the blow by the most narrow of margins. In withdrawing and dodging, he retreated from the tree and backed up hard, crashing into a third participant.

But I sensed only one attacker!

The two attackers were not two. They were seven. The silence by which all save one of them had earned positions on Maelgwn bewildered and disoriented him, and the foe he had crashed into shoved him hard to the ground. When he rose, he was surrounded by a perfect circle of knights. A circle of perfect knights.

He was in the center and they as seven sunrays. Each of them diverse in their armor.

A red knight.

A green knight.

A yellow knight.

A knight of light blue.

A violet-clad knight.

A white knight.

Lastly, a knight from brow to toe-tip in a metal skin of black.

Each knight's long sword in color corresponded to the knight to his left, so that the Black Knight's blade was white and the White Knight's blade was violet, and this was the pattern throughout the company.

Maelgwn found his balance, and his battle dirk, just as the seven began to orbit, swords held in an overhead but parallel position. In perfect concert, the swords were all erected into an overhand striking pose; the spiral closed and they were upon Maelgwn, soon to overcome and slay him.

"Enough! Return into him, else flee to another place!" The command of the Merlin of Britain pierced the night and rattled the forest.

Seven helms turned as one to acknowledge the bark, then disregarded it. The brief pause gave Maelgwn a moment to look closer upon the multi-colored troop. A glimpse into their forms, a glimpse into their eyes.

It cannot be. They are all…they are all ME!

Resuming their pose, each of the seven colored knights fixed again upon Maelgwn and made ready to deliver.

"Have you had quite enough? Assemble thyself. Quit you like a man, Lancelot!"

Ancient words followed the castigation, delivering a spell that caused the warriors to disintegrate, becoming a sparkly dust; a dust of red, and yellow, and light blue, and green, a shiny sand of violet and white, speckled with flakes of black.

A mild rush of wind finished the task, and Lancelot lay alone.

Alone with Merlin.

Eye to eye on the barge to Broceliande, eye to eye in the makeshift tabernacle of the Council of Nine, eye to eye in the guesthouse ere a stumble redirected history's course.

These heroes had shared much peril together and normally found a fondness in looking level at equal eyes seven feet from the earth, a fondness born of rarity and equal stature. Both were weary of stooping to greet men, else giving salutations upon balding crowns.

But this time, Maelgwn was consumed of haste and hate, and desired no reunion, least of all with the *other* tall Briton. And from Merlin's eyes emanated an authority, a hot white urgency that made the whole of his face shine as an avenging, angry angel.

Maelgwn made a strong fist about the bottom of his battle dirk with his left hand, a loose fist about the top with his right.

"Excalibur cleaved the spike of Lancelot. And yet I behold it whole."

"My mother restored the steel of both Titans, only mine privily." Maelgwn postured, somehow becoming as tall as the frozen trees that compassed them. "That when we stand together again our arms would be equal."

Merlin suffered not one more word, and brought the tall tree low, disarming the Bloodhound Prince with the fluidity and grace of a Cymreig maiden spiraling in frolic at festival or feast. In one move the dirk had changed hands; in the next it whistled, lost in the dark of the thicket; the third move put the head of the walking stick of the old druid upon the neck of Maelgwn, now shifting his throat that he could not speak. Or breathe.

"The Lady of the Lake mended the weapons of Lancelot and Arthur that they have peace, forever retire AND NEVER REPEAT such a sorrowful day. Grace and love in the stead of the seeds of strife. For they are a vine that choke upon your soul. She mended metal as symbol of your reconciliation — she did not forge instruments to renew your division, thou fool!"

Merlin released the staff, and then continued. "I bade you do one thing above all else. Tell me, if your lust gives way to reason and your envy gives place to recollection, what was the thing?" demanded the wizard.

"You charged me watch over my son above all else." Maelgwn answered true.

"When you were conducting pretend searches for me, watched you over him?"

"My mother would have been executed as a murderer, as YOUR murderer, had one found you out."

Merlin disregarded the retort.

"When you swam in self-pity and bathed thyself in the blood of boys, watched you over him?"

"That was MY Giant to fight!"

"Always an excuse — always towards yourself, never towards the good of our kinsmen." The rebuke intensified.

"The Cup of Christ took my son, our future High King, and none of my failings could have prevented that, neither the new Merlin." Maelgwn shoved the old man, or ghost, or devil, or invention of Maelgwn's shattered mind.

This appearance of Merlin, however, was no

shadow. The druid stood, and brandished steel of his own.

Maelgwn was not impressed. "That dagger has breached my loins two score. Again, I fight myself and no man."

Where Merlin the apparition would pierce the warrior in bloody reminder that passion would beget death, Merlin 'the actual' presented the weapon's edge, and opted for a different tactic.

"Lancelot. See thou the tip?"

"Aye."

"Galahad perished due to the treachery and manipulation of the Dynion Hysbys. Gwalchmai is slain due to the folly of mighty men, the failing of princes. The Healing Balm and the Hawk of May — dead! There is no clear heir. Arthur's brothers and uncles are pledged to the Presbytery, and your Ravens are pretenders! The land is desolate. Children starve, cattle are walking ribcages." The blade's edge was presented to the very tip of Maelgwn's perfect nose. "The Long Knife has new children reared to take up axe and shield. And the Council of Nine plots their ceaseless apocalyptic designs on these Isles. The survival of Cymru rests upon the edge of this knife."

Merlin's magick presently caused a large snowflake, ornate, spectacular and fragile, to light upon the blade. "When it comes time to do that which you would do, for Cymru's sake, I beg you, do it n—"

Maelgwn pinched, causing the snowflake that was Cymru to evaporate in a prick of blood. "I did not do that which I would, and now she makes her grave at the snout and paw of dogs! Her blood begs for vengeance, and I swear it, she will be avenged."

"Will freezing men fight for lust? And the starving lend their battle axe for adultery?" Merlin made a final appeal to the *Unreasonable One* with reason.

"The hosts of Maelgwn Gwynedd will fight for the Sons of Cunedda and to right the calamity wrought by the Silures. No other reason need they."

Seeing that Maelgwn's delusional justification was set in mortar, and his intention as brick, Merlin gave a great sigh, its puff of frustration filling the icy dark.

"You would be in league with the Traitor that bedded your true love against the man who executed your true love?" The Merlin allowed for no reply. "But you murdered the brother of the Traitor you would support. Putting you in an impossible strait, for Morgaine will not succor you, and may remove you from the plane of the living."

"Neither will she suffer her brother the king to kill *their* son." Warm spit left the snarling prince's lips, freezing as a trail of anger and hurt upon his marble chin. "My own counsel will I keep with regard to whom I lend my Hosts. And those to whom I lend them — they will be the victors. The Sorceress has no power in warfare, as demonstrated during the Saxon Wars. Let her kill me in my chamber; the outcome will not be altered."

"That *Sorceress* is amongst your very best of friends, from the time of your youth. Have you forgotten, in the Madness of Maelgwn, that she has ever loved you?"

"Nay, I've not forgotten." Maelgwn recovered his dirk from the thicket and fled. Turning, he added, "I've not forgotten. I'm counting on it."

CHAPTER 1
Keep a Few Drops of That Poison in You, for You Will Need It
There Will Be Civil War

The desolation growing within Arthur was filled, nay, distracted, by the reunion of all reunions. The long-dead resurrected, the longing and cureless woe undone.

The library seemed to revert to brighter days; the very countenance and composition of the room was glowing, reminding the embattled Britons of the glistening times when the Boy with the Sword and his Merlin were invincible.

Arthur rose, snatching up the wizard's coned cap. A slap of dust. And another. Somewhere high above the lofts and shelves a barn owl shrieked, protesting that it should share in the night's discourse. Arthur approached the figure filling the doorway with folds and folds of robe, wave of white wavy hair, yet more dust, and splendor.

"A strategy." Arthur smiled, absent of judgment. "What counsel givest thou to me, wizard?"

Arthur's tact in treating two decades of dearth and disappointment as vapor, twenty years of bearing a heartache, of not knowing, as a parenthesis that never happened, disarmed the Merlin, who was set to give what answer he could.

"We will speak of strategy, of method and aim—soon, my lord." A lump and a rasp. Merlin himself could not calculate how much he had missed the king and the power of his presence.

But by saying nothing, the student had become his master. Arthur's pause was endless, his gaze all awe and no gall. The power of silence compelled Merlin to give answer where no query was made.

"I was dead," Merlin stated plainly, then followed it with crypt and riddle. "But death means many things to we Britons, and many more to we Woeful and Sorry Damned."

The Pendragon remained silent, his beam constant, eyes fixed upon his mentor, his counselor, his friend.

"It was for me to serve you in bringing about the Summer Kingdom, and not for me to serve you in governing it. I forfeited seeing you bring rays of Heaven to earth, and for missing it, I am truly sorry. You did beyond all we who love mankind and cherish peace could ever have hoped for, Little Bear. You did it."

"You speak of summer. You talk of heaven." The smile fell. "But the whole of Glamorgan is beneath winter. The sum of Gwent buried in Hell. The great red dragon I could neither prevent nor contain." The tall druid stooped, his eyes finding the marbled floor. "You were *dead*, and by my very soul, 'twas by men and motives foul. Who wounded you unto death? This Mystery of yours, did you discover the meaning of it?"

"Let the secrets and peculiarities of wizards remain veiled; his ways are not our ways, his days not likened unto ours." The owner of these words spake with authority not unlike that of the Merlin himself.

"Dyfrig, old friend!" Merlin turned to see not only the bishop but Arthur's father as well, carrying themselves as two overbearing parents interrogating a young man with endless questions three minutes removed from being left by a damsel.

Loving but annoying, and now there be three of them. Arthur collected his poise, and reverence. "Three old Wise Men and a young prince," he mused. The context and scene were not lost on him.

"At four years and five decades, you are not so young, my sovereign." Dyfrig bowed, chuckled, and bowed again.

"Any jest that renders him aged renders me ancient!" Meurig contributed with a huff. "Let Arthur of Caerleon a lad be, and let him ever a lad remain!"

By imposing upon the discourse, Bishop Dyfrig had achieved what he sought – distraction and delay. He did not so soon want Merlin in the king's ear, with his heretical views on ending ecclesiastical orders and rendering meaningless the sacerdotal rites of baptism and tonsure. Though the land lay in ruin and the rotting smell of bloodlust and rancor was as a pungent cloud sprinkling the Tribes with constant fear, the politics of religion were still paramount for the old bishop. And, though Dyfrig and Merlin were friends indeed, the bishop was glad for the Christian Bard's long absence.

Thankfully, as the dread of recent events and the end of the kingdom were at hand, the distraction worked well, and the four men were onto other subjects.

Subjects far less comfortable for King Arthur.

"In pursuing the traitor Mordred ap Cynfarch, your wife, his captive, was accidentally slain, and no bard will sing of it otherwise." Meurig was resolute, the just and jolly retired lord advocating lies for his firstborn.

"No." Arthur looked upon the three wise men. Three grey beards that loved the Cymry and shared in the greatness of her Golden Age. Arthur knew that his fall from grace would represent their defamation as well; for all heroes of the age would be recorded *as Arthur*. "A dishonored king executed judgment upon a traitor caught in the very deed of plot, the very act of overthrow, under the very candlelight of two witnesses. In this case, there needs be no counsel; I acted in accord with our most ancient laws."

"All things are lawful, but not all things are expedient," said the Merlin.

"Yes," Arthur acquiesced. "I brought no honor to our nation, no glory to Cymry; rather, only suffering and loss for a love oh so unrequited."

"Sometimes love is as a poison rather than a clear spring, my Son. I am so thankful for your mam, and so very sorry for your long years governing with a troubled heart. Whatever comes next, whatever you need, I am here for you, to the ends of the world."

"You are very fortunate to have never supped from this chalice," Arthur responded—an acknowledgment of admiration, and not a little envy.

"The poison will pass." King Meurig continued to offer consolation.

"Let it not pass." Merlin surprised the assembly. "The battle dirk of Maelgwn Gwynedd that punctured Gwalchmai was meant not for the Hawk of May. It was meant for YOU! The Whelp surely makes for Eire, or worse, to appeal to the Long Knife, and the son of Meirchion is a cancer upon the Continent. Your enemies in the North will feast upon calamity; for the loyalty of a man is limited only by his opportunity."

Arthur groaned at hearing all these things. "Despair reigns; add no more words to what is plainly seen with the eye. For all men see everywhere that the sky itself shatters upon us."

"Despair reigns not." Merlin increased his stature and, with a puff of dust, approached the Pendragon, as he had but presently done upon the Bloodhound Prince. Only, this time, the Merlin stooped. "*You* reign, Lord Arthur." The druid took the cheeks of the king into his hands, paternally and with great authority. "You can still save us. But in order to do so, you must abandon mercy, you must suspend regard."

"We cannot become that which we oppose, Merlin," the bishop offered.

Merlin ignored his colleague of old, continuing his plea. "From the days when our accord with Rome shattered to now, we have labored to prevent what will now surely come to pass." The wizard panned the room, still holding the head of the king as one talks to his mates in the kitchen whilst holding a hot kettle. "There will be Civil War." His words were both a boom and a razor. "Our enemies are not just carnal; the Devil himself would rule this land to fulfill his wicked purpose. If we are to mitigate great slaughter, even the passing of our diadem from this Island, we must commit deeds never imagined. Only terror can arrest a war in its youth; only deeds that bring nightmares can create hope to end war before it, in earnest, begins. There are dark deeds necessary to end the night and allow for the birth of a new day."

Merlin the Orator has returned to us indeed! thought all collectively.

Meanwhile Arthur's right hand clasped the wizard's left, whose fingers still coiled about his face. Merlin used to fasten upon the Iron Bear's cheeks in this manner oft when giving ill tidings, else a hard lesson. *Merlin the Teacher. Merlin the Sage.* Arthur knew he had grieved these twenty years, but he had mis-measured the depths, until present was his friend. Arthur allowed himself to escape the despair, to free himself of the hurt, surrendering all heady weight into his druid's hands. Merlin granted him the moment, suffering the weight of twenty years of ruling and the misery that accompanies great men. Whilst the people rejoiced and reveled in freedom, Arthur the Saxon Killer, the Giant Slayer, the Executioner of Treacherous Children, the Cuckolded Husband, and the Just Man, had had hard years.

"The Northern kings will be in league with Rome, and with Rome's Church. This will be a match of gwyddbwyll, and the clay game pieces will be heirs. We have peered down the corridors of time; we have proactively anticipated this very day. By placing southern princes in the north and begetting children with allegiances to both, we have positioned this generation to retain and respect their Tribe but to venerate the People over local differences. We have created a generation of children with so many conflated and complex alliances that they are forced to be truly Cymry, less so Silure or Ordovice." The men listened. Merlin released Arthur's face, and continued.

"But, nevertheless, the Houses of Caw and Cynfarch Oer have young candidates in the persons of Mordred's sons by Kwyllog ferch Caw."

"What claim has Cynfarch to the sons of Mordred? For Mordred is—" Dyfrig found not words to finish his question delicately.

"For Mordred is *my* son," answered Arthur, "and your grandson." Meurig did not like hearing these words, neither Arthur in posing them.

"Llew ap Cynfarch has claim to the line of Mordred by marriage to your sister, Gwyar. The House will decry the intrigue and claim beguilement, or even ignore the fact that the children are of the Pendragon line. Else, they may claim to put forth a son of Mordred in the guise of unifying the Tribes with one born of both great Houses."

"There are a few candidates for the High King that could trouble us," Meurig agreed. "But this has ever been the case, the unfortunate circumstances of Mordred's beginnings notwithstanding. This is politics, and no cause for terror."

"Mordred's sole existence is fixed upon killing the man who killed the only thing he ever loved—" Merlin started.

"Two things—" Arthur began to interrupt.

"Son, stop, I beseech you."

The Iron Bear raised his hand, staying his father. "As I said afore, no more secrets, as they are the canker that eats at the soul of the Cymry. This empty creature Mordred adored his *brother*, Amr. And did see me visit justice upon the lad. This happened during Merlin's sleep of death, and though the Bard knew much, and divined more, this he saw not."

"Double the reason to hear me." The revelation only strengthened Merlin's perception of the first maneuver in the coming war. "Likewise, Maelgwn's sole existence is fixed upon killing the man who killed the only thing he ever loved."

Assuming the conclusion, Dyfrig and Meurig protested in unison. "Maelgwn will NEVER take up arms aside the Whelp!"

Merlin pressed on. "Mark's sole existence is killing the man who deposed his father of all possession and title, causing Mark to be born in Cernu, a vagabond and an outcast with no land. Which of these," the druid posed, "is most dangerous to Arthur?"

Meurig thought on this for a great while. "Mark," he finally answered.

The Merlin smiled. "Why?"

"Mordred's is a motive of jealousy and passion and unbalance. His danger comes only from those who would make use of him. He is a puppet."

"Brilliant," Merlin approved, "and the other?"

"I was Pendragon for many years too, Bard." Meurig poked at the rib of the tall druid, reminding him that retirement had not robbed him of his skill in statecraft. The poke was soon followed by a smile and embrace between the two heroes of old.

"True, true, King Meurig." Merlin gave a crinkle-nosed grin. "And the other?"

"Maelgwn is dangerous, to be certain. If his Hosts really do engage us, the task will be formidable. But his is a motive of jealousy and hurt, and he trusts not his own judgment. He is as unpredictable as he is dangerous."

"Agreed!" contributed Arthur.

"And he may not survive the fortnight, having killed a son of Gwyar. Who can fathom what wrath he hath begotten in her?" Dyfrig added.

"Mordred and Maelgwn are both lethal threats, but Mark the greater on account of the truth of *recency*." Merlin the Teacher may as well have been at pulpit or in lecture hall, ushering his truths and views with fluid form. The living dead man truly most quickened when teaching.

"Though the former enemies," it pained Merlin to nominate Maelgwn so, "may have borne malice for years, the recency of the act that pushed them to war is fresh. They are imbalanced and illogical. By contrast, Mark has been under the mentorship of the Council of Nine," Arthur shuddered as Merlin revealed this, "plotting and cultivating his hate for decades—raising an actual army for years."

Merlin went on to draw the men's attention back to the sons of Mordred, tying a perfect knot before delivering his decree. "Arthur's greatest threat was wrought of our mercy. He was created because we were kind. If we are to truly spoil this insurgence, and utterly stamp out the rebel Mordred—" Merlin paused.

The moon cast her blue light through the highest windows, bending it into a funnel that lit upon the Merlin. He continued in silence until at last Arthur commanded him to speak. "Mordred's heirs and mercy upon Mark's father—what, Merlin? What is the connection?"

"When you slew the painted queen, did your pain and hurt rush out of you? Is the hole now filled? And the heart mended?"

"What has that to do with—"

"Answer you me, little Bear. Did it make things better? Or for the worse?"

"I thought that by taking her breath I might have a surety that she'd not share her bed with others, or know that at any moment that she looks upon another in the way I desperately longed for her to look upon me. I thought it would be over."

"But the poison remains?"

"Yes, Merlin, the poison remains, that it would overcome and drown my soul." The anguish of the king emanated forth, seemingly an actual substance that greyed the blue light resting majestically upon the resurrected druid.

"I want you to heal, but that will be far off, my lord." Now Merlin delivered the decree. "Save some drops of that poison, suspend conscience. Order the death of the immediate house of Mordred. His deceased first wife's children; male or female, young or grown. Put to the sword animals, and whatever of his estates the comet spared, raze. There will be no second coming of Mark the Mad in the person of Mordred's seed. Order this, and then get thee an army to the Continent."

"We must do this?" Meurig whimpered.

Now Merlin clasped the cheeks of the Senior King, as he had but presently with the younger. "There will be Civil War. I am of a single mind to lessen the souls it sends to the Underworld." Merlin turned to Arthur, uttering thrice more, "There will be Civil War."

The nobleman and the aged bishop understood the Bard's reasoning, but whether they could perform their charges, they knew not.

CHAPTER 2
I Will Kill Maelgwn
There Will Be No Civil War

Gwyar ferch Meurig and Llew ap Cynfarch Oer presided over the interment of their son, the famed Round Table Knight Gwalchmai. The body was borne from Pictish land whence Lancelot had killed him, through dreadful winter and broken roads.

The Tribes in the South West of Deheubarth had made Gwalchmai their Prince, and he had adored his little village, Castell Gwalchmai. It was meet that he should be buried here. Though his coastal village was now an ashy grave covered thickly with ice, having nine of ten trees uprooted, else reduced to ringed stumps, and though dark billows were perpetual as Illtud's choirs, the corpse caused an array of light and beauty to shine about the whole of the region. This caused the bards to sing, *'Even in death doth the Hawk of May bring the Sun to woeful Deheubarth. Year after year, the Green Knight shall renew us.'*

Where the river Peryddon met the western sea, beneath the shadow of a little stone house of prayer Gwalchmai favored and lodged in oft (especially in the times he had buckled under the shame after his defeat to Lancelot), was Gwalchmai laid to rest. *Yet not the whole of him.*

Llew insisted upon a proper Catholic burial. To this did Gwyar consent. The funeral rites were somber but celebratory, honoring and full of love, and even the Sorceress appreciated the grandeur of the Roman customs. His burial chamber was ornate, a deposit well beneath the earth filled with yellow plaster and bricked with gold-speckled black marble. Two of his steeds joined him in the ground, along with his shield, and his twin curved swords, of such smithmanship that they were suited only to his form. Additionally, there were placed with him five treasures of Cymru.

The Hawk of May himself was clothed in silver skin, shined and without blemish. His wild crimson locks were tamed, a simple torque about his neck. He looked perfect. As the young soldier, unblemished, transfigured to the early years of the Saxon Wars.

When was finished the Catholic ceremony, little Gwyar rose and approached the body, which had not yet been wrapped and lowered. Llew stood betwixt the Witch and the Hawk of May, appealing with both palms.

"We have an accord." Gwyar's four words reminded her disaffected spouse that she had agreed to a Christian funeral and that bartering with the Fae was without repentance. He gave ground.

One of Gwyar's Nine Maidens presented the Lady of Avalon with the helm of Gwalchmai, which she placed o'er the head of her dead son.

Her tiny fingers clutched hard upon the plume—and then her dagger flashed.

"Sirs, please lower him. Bring the Sun to the hereafter until the end of days when you will rise again, and reign with Arthur and his kinsman and companions. *You are the Summer Kingdom, my son.*" A fount of tears spilled from the Lady as the body was lowered. She erected herself and turned to the assembled guests.

Gwalchmai's brothers, all present save Mordred, surrounding the shoreline mound, saw it first and gasped with great hurt.

The helmet containing the head of the massive curly-haired warrior was wider than Gwyar's chest, and she struggled to hoist it. At one point she nearly dropped it, then recovered, and, at last, with dagger in left hand and head in right, proclaimed: "For as long as Cymry do rule the Blessed Isles in the Sea, the head of Gwalchmai ap Llew ap Cynfarch ap Meirchion ap Gwrwst ap Ceneu ap King Coel shall be paramount amongst all the relics in your place of worship, be it heathen or Christian or whatsoever label future men may apply to their false religions. Never shall it suffer corruption, and year by year shall it renew, that it be a reproach to all men, a reminder to men throughout all ages that Lancelot did wound the innocent and that passion did kill justice. Look upon it and marvel, look upon it and fear, for soon Lancelot's head will give my son's company, only on a spike!"

Gwyar was taken by full consummation of the Primal Witch. She levitated from the ground, her eyes set aflame, a wrathful glare upon Llew. "There will be no Civil War. I will find Maelgwn

Gwynedd the Manslayer and Adulterer, and I will kill him."

***

The weather increased in violence. Gwyar and the Nine Maidens could not return to Ynys Enlli, but Caerleon was less than one day's ride from Castell Gwalchmai. Thus, she sought lodging there. And to be near her brother. Though the burial arrangements had been made in haste and it was not uncommon for friends and kinsmen to make pilgrimage to the resting places of the lost in their own timing, it concerned Gwyar that the king was not there. Perhaps it was out of respect for Gwalchmai, knowing embers kindled between the Pendragon and King Llew over the revelation of Mordred's paternity. Or perhaps Arthur was in too much disrepair over the loss of his Gwenhwyfar to make public pretenses. Whatever his motive, Gwyar worried after her brother, and hastened to Caerleon knowing not in what state of mind he might be.

Arthur, however, was not at home in his burnt city; neither Bedwyr, neither Cai, neither Cadoc.

Gwyar perceived a sense of withheld communication and half-truths from those who received her but dismissed it. *Even with Cymry reduced to rubble, boys are off politicking.* She did look in on her mother, Queen Onbrawst, who—like all Britons, blasted by the Comet, the knowledge of Arthur's bastard traitor, the execution of the Queen, the death of the Hawk of May and the brooding and moaning of the Land itself—paced without purpose in cold halls, or remained in bed all day succumbing to deep depression.

"It is the last day of December." Onbrawst sipped at her tea, sitting up in bed. Gwyar sat upon a couch pulled up hard to the post, her hand upon her mother's forearm. She anticipated the humor that was forthcoming, for she knew her mother well. "By Caesar's reckoning, tomorrow is the new year."

"We are a full fourth into the year by our reckoning," Gwyar responded, and paused with a smile.

"Let the Romans be right for once, that the year five hundred and thirty-seven be better than thirty-six."

"Aye, we will give them this, only that the days will be better." Gwyar appreciated the Senior Queen's hope, lip-service as it was, for both knew that only darker days coiled as a snake at the door, ready to strike and kill them all.

"My little faerie. Woe is me that I offended the Sovereign of the other realm, and that the Fair Folk have punished you so. I was a horrible mother to you, child," Onbrawst lamented.

"You loved me enough to see me reared by own kind, Lady." Gwyar was gentle, full of grace to the mother whose only mistake in an honorable life had been rejecting the advances of a Devil. "I'm hard to love," Gwyar chuckled.

The changeling witch and the pious Christian sat for a long time at tea, speaking of all things save politics and religion. Onbrawst drifted back into sleep whilst there was yet daylight (though day and night were hard to distinguish, as Caerleon had been impacted most by the Red Dragon, and was day by day in its shadow, else covered by a yellow gas), and, against her judgment, Gwyar felt drawn to go outdoors and walk. Drawn to the spot where Cymry fell. Drawn to Mordred's Thicket, the Field of Malevolence.

Llaniltern was untouched by the apocalypse that made of Caerleon desolation. Gwenhwyfar II's dwelling was intact, clean and beautiful. The pitch yet green. No snow, neither ice, neither soot. As if cut upon by a butcher with cruel, cruel humor, the place of ongoing and perpetual adultery and betrayal was spared.

Gwyar, knowing not whether to curse God or Arddu, shook her fist at the firmament, shouting imprecations at both, and wept.

This is my fault.

I traded long-term peace for temporal happiness for my brother. For Arthur. I let him have his whore that his night terrors lessen and his great quest for love like our parents' be fulfilled, though it were false fulfillment.

To cover for a lie, or to not speak against a lie discovered, is to be part of that lie. I am a liar, I am an adulteress, I am Mordred and Gwenhwyfar. I spared the king and killed the country. And I killed my own son! My Gwalchmai…

A generation has not known war, not known rape, not known raising revenues for armies that ought to be raised for art. A generation has enjoyed the liberty to argue about God and gods, the freedom to wrestle about baptism and tonsure. An entire generation was spared the Saxon Axe because of my concealment. I protected Arthur, and he did above and beyond all that could be expected of fallen Man! And, at that, with Giants preying upon the hills and crooks!

Was it worth it?! My head says yes but, dear

Gwalchmai, my heart is an open sepulcher – my bosom says no!
   Mordred.
   My son.
   A twig to the womb at sixteen would have the Kingdom saved!
   A swig of herbs and an hour of rough issue would have my brother's honor preserved!
   But for a mother's love, I could not kill you then.
   "Neither can I yet kill you," she said aloud.
   "But you will slay the Lancelot, eh?" The Elf was behind her, then at once twirling in the center of The Field of Melwas. "A lovely spot to cast a circle and dance, wouldn't you agree? So pristine, so undefiled." He mocked the Sorceress, consistent with his nature, though he wrested with it as he could.
   "No, I cannot." She loathed the Faerie King's presence but had no will for the banter, no joy in the joust.
   "Blind passion and the illogic of a mother's love. From even before the Flood, you possessed a love of your children, though they be abominations and monsters. Break your cycle, or Cymry will pass into shadow and Germans will rule this dirt."
   "I will not kill him, neither will I suffer my brother to do so." Gwyar had once accepted that Arthur would defeat and execute Mordred, but time had changed even that. She supported Arthur, but she would sue him for mercy. *Banish the man, imprison his family, but murder the last of his line, and lose another son, the Priestess could not.*
   She set about to scold the Elf for his imposition

but alas, he was gone, a circle of stones left in the field.

This is my fault, she reiterated, but nevertheless sought out Maelgwn that she might kill him, and after this Arthur, that he may not kill Mordred or his heirs.

***

January
AD 537

The Julian New Year began as the old year had ended, with a lethal freeze. Though the sense of the Kingdom was that *it was at war already*, none would fight in this blister. *Wherever Arthur and his Companions are going, I do hope they are warm.* Gwyar had no Sight for the matter, and mused within herself that she was too cold to practice divination. Rather than magick, the Faerie used deductive reasoning. *Maelgwn will pursue Mordred, the lover of his love. Perhaps to make alliance, perhaps to eat his soul. In either case, where Mordred is, there will Maelgwn openly be. None will pursue him until the curse of this winter thaws – if it ever thaws.*

What she reasoned was so. *For women know things.* Making for the ports and traversing the sea over to the Continent (and to his ally, Mark) was not possible. But rousing fellowship and followers amongst the Gewessi was obtainable. By following the river south to Aberhonddu into the kingdom of Brychan Brycheniog (the old but virile chieftain who was son to Arthur's aunt, Marchel) the Traitor could find like-minded men, as a cell of the rebels of Eire had settled in these parts, sharing lineage with Brychan.

Marchel, aged, had affection for Mordred and would give him haven, food and rest. And with rest, rejuvenation, and with rejuvenation, recruitment. Queen Marchel had learned the darkest of occult arts amongst the Dynion Hysbys, and amongst the secret druids that rejected the good news of Padraig (thus *a few snakes* remained in Ireland) in her husband's lands in Eire. A conjurer and a meddler, all done under the absent nose of her late husband, the very pious, very Catholic and very poisoned-to-death Prince Anlach. Ceridwen the mother of Taliesin had taught Marchel about herbs, and she took advantage of and corrupted what was received.

History and legend would later call Marchel *Queen Morgause, aunt of Arthur and friend to Morgaine of the Faeries.* But Morgaine and Morgause were no kindred spirits. All that Morgaine did was for the sovereignty of Cymru and the survival of liberty. All Morgause did was for Morgause. In this regard, though beyond years and lacking strength to pose a serious threat to Arthur, she was a perfect help for the fleeing, scared and desperate Whelp.

The sub-kingdom of Brychan was not far from Glamorgan and Gwent. Every one of Brychan's twenty-six children and grandchildren were loyal to the Pendragon, but he was not; neither were the rank and file of his men, as they were given wholly to the Popish denomination of the Christian faith. Because of King Brychan's disaffection towards Arthur, especially towards

Bishop Bedwini and old Dyfrig, he could be swayed to help Mordred, whether openly or privily.

Thus, once again, both the radically religious and the radically devilish stood against the High King, whose friends were druids and the old Church, who didn't much like one another.

Mordred was hiding in a barn, cowering behind the stalls as a dog that had taken the meat from the master's table instead of waiting patiently for the scraps. Slithery, sneaky, and warm with a full belly.

By chance, Maelgwn Gwynedd, who was alone, and Morgaine of the Faeries, with her company of Nine Maidens, reached the double hinges of the barn door at the same time.

The night was far spent and Marchel was not found, but looked down upon the scene from a tower room where she sat by a giant iron cauldron, scrying both night and day.

A heavy log that lay across two iron hooks separated Maelgwn from the door that led to Mordred. No sooner had he lifted one side of the log from its hook did it slam back down with a violent crash. The mighty man could not cause it again to budge. He turned. Bewildered, he looked round, then down.

Nine torches suddenly helped him discover the invisible door-locker. Surrounded by priestesses, he sensed that his comeuppance for Gwalchmai was at hand.

Mordred fixed ear to barn doors, but did not present himself.

"I saved you, I healed you, I brought you back from the realm of the dead, only for you to replace yourself there with my son!"

"Would that you had suffered me to perish, Gwyar. But your brother has slain my—"

"Your what?" Morgaine growled. "Your wife? No. Your sister? Nay. Maybe your mam? Again, no. What was she to you that you would put your spike in my son's back?"

"She was one my true love, and Arthur must die." Sorrow now absent, the burst-bubble version of Maelgwn's self manifested; the greatest warrior of all time versus the Primal Witch engaged.

The bards do not agree upon whom attacked first, but Maelgwn lay quickly in a pool of his own blood. Lightning proceeded from the fingertips of Morgaine, inflicting sting after mystical sting upon the invincible Son of Cunedda. From his crumpled position, his dirk swung low, severing her dark blue coating at the midriff, but reaching no flesh.

He found his feet and sought an overhand strike, blocked by her little dirk with fluidity and minimal effort. He stepped inside her strike and brought the hook of his spike down her shoulder blade. Hoping for a scream, she lent him only laughter, recoiling and examining her wound.

"I am no stranger to blood, mine or that of adulterers. Why must men cheat? Why must men betray?" The bolts came with ferocity now, bringing Maelgwn to his knees, his black curly hair now grey, now white. Jaw broken, his eyes rolled to back of the skull; the full weight of the oak of a man fell. And yet would not die.

Twenty more times, as a demoniac scorpion, she stung him.

"Why won't you die? Die!" She screamed this until her voice became hoarse and exhaustion overtook her. Then her screech became a whisper and a whimper. "Why won't you die?"

"For the same reason you cannot use your powers in an open field of battle. Was it not the same in the Saxon Wars?"

"What means this?" the most powerful of the Britons sobbed.

The king of the Tylwyth Teg traced his crimson fingernails along her tiny brow, collecting and then sloshing the sweat off. Then he brushed back her raven's hair. "It means Cymru *is* officially at war. The Creator will only let our kind punish men unto death, yet we can kill them not. A rehearsal for our role in the End of Days. His glory we are not to subrogate." The Elf embraced the slight Faerie. "We faeries live under peculiar laws and peculiar ways, daughter. An actual *man* must kill this fallen hero, and moreso the coward that watches beyond that door."

"What was the act of war in the Christian God's mind? The two armies lining up and arguing at each other ere the Adder was slain? Surely a cattle raid is more akin to a war than that! Why cannot we save lives with our gifts, or curses, or whatever they be?" Morgaine was shaking.

He continued to hold her. "His ways are not our ways, my child. I am sure you can still kill"—he laughed—"simply not in the context of battle." He lifted her chin. "Besides, you love him; some part of you wants him to live; let us not blame God for that." He pointed to a large stone. "If I am wrong, smash the Lancelot about the head with that stone."

Morgaine knew there was truth in the Elf's words, lack of timing or decorum notwithstanding. She offered no response.

She did not open the door, did not force her Mordred to conjure the courage to face her. Instead she spoke through the door. "My son. I do love you. I will beg of my brother to give you mercy. See that you do nothing to add to these troubles, that your days drawing breath in this life might be multiplied."

Marchel was lurking, and Morgaine knew this.

"Gather him up and give him your herbs if it pleases you, Crone."

The Nine Maidens marveled.

They and Morgaine vacated the place, seeking King Arthur.

CHAPTER 3
Making a Three-Front Attack a One-Front Attack

Mordred ap Llew possessed a *hundred* (a division of land within a cantref) in the northern kingdoms ruled by his father. His first wife (who was taken ill and had been deceased for several years) was a kind, godly woman and had founded a chapel that the bards would, after her, call Llangwyllog. And her chapel, along with a humble dedicatory shrine, were revered by the people, and located within his hundred.

Though he was ever absent from his estate — for before the manifestation of his great sin he was ever at Caerleon or Caermelyn, exercising his forked tongue and flattery to make a reputable name for himself, whilst simultaneously and perpetually defrauding the king's bed — Mordred's sons and daughters maintained a pious, warm and lovely home. Each of these were in their teenage years, the firstborn being Melou, and had been reared by Mordred's cousins, bards and steward.

They were all home when the mounted soldiers arrived. Home, doing what the rest of

Cymru was about—staying warm. The comet had not damaged this cantref, but the air was foul and the cold extreme.

Thus, while Gwyar sought her brother in the south, desperate to have audience and make appeal for leniency upon Mordred and his immediate House, Arthur was north, directing his men to deliver a steely message devoid of mercy.

Arthur had two hundred and two score soldiers, the Merlin, Taliesin, Bishop Bedwini, and Meurig in his company. Bedwyr, Cadoc, Amwn Ddu and Cai were present as well.

"Our most ancient customs will demand an answer from the northern tribes, should we see this strategy fulfilled," Bedwyr reminded Arthur. And Bedwyr had no pun nor humor to add. Even he whose role was to lighten the mood bore a burden too heavy.

But Merlin would suffer not this downtrodden disposition amongst the men. He was the real architect of the twelve major battles (and sixty smaller besides), his resolve unlike any other man's, save perhaps that of Maelgwn Gwynedd. Merlin would see Mordred uprooted, and he would not risk hesitation or withdrawal.

He spake on behalf of the Iron Bear. "The Red Dragon that smote our Island is as a gnat upon the beard compared to the death that organizes itself from all sides against justice, and hope, and liberty, and the Round Table itself." He then pointed at the Pendragon with his staff, dramatically. "And against our Hope himself!"

Merlin took Arthur aside; he puffed his pipe, then chewed upon its stem as if he were angry with it. "The poison, Bear: some yet courses through thy veins, yes?"

"Much." But Arthur did not look upon his beloved wizard. "I see no northern tribes, neither their princes. Bedwyr," he hollered, "where is Caw? Or his tempestuous robber sons? Why is not the House of Cynfarch here to stand in the gap for Mordred? Where are these Mighty Ones of the Old North who ever boast that they can rule better than we, but would put us under the yoke of a State Religion? I am standing here in the open, and we number but a few. Come! Let us stand together!" he called at shadows. In challenging the list of all of his domestic foes under heaven, he failed to enumerate Maelgwn or his hosts, the most dangerous of all Ravens— and the lack of mention was noteworthy.

Arthur himself was compelled to wait in the chapel, and not to look upon the execution of his grandchildren. He stared long at the shrine of the daughter-in-law that never had been, imagining for a moment sitting at tea with her, or showing her the golden city of Caerleon. *I am sorry, daughter; sorry I begat, and you married, a monster. Sorry for the monstrosity that must needs be.* He gave the formal order, then put himself behind the chapel doors, and stood with arms folded in prayerful contemplation before the altar.

Merlin joined him.

"There will never be another 'Mark uprising', and the terror of your ferocity and resolve will slow this war and, peradventure, end it."

Arthur's eyes were bloodshot and his countenance bleak. Thoughts of the Traitor's spouse brought a rush of thoughts about his own. Involuntarily, his mind fixed upon Gwenhwyfar II. He could see, taste and smell her being passionately used by Mordred. In the twinkling of an eye he was again looking down, his massive war dogs feasting upon her. Lastly, he relived Maelgwn's declaration of coming war. He withdrew from daytime visions and fixed upon his wizard, in exile during *heaven on earth* but now returned, full of passion and verve, when hell reigned over Camelot. Merlin always knew what to do, and now he *was here.*

"We have never visited such terror, even upon the most barbaric Germans." Arthur voiced one final reservation, one last protest. "But should it give Mordred pause ere he raise an army—should it cause his knees to wobble and turn him away from seducing the Gewessi of Eire against us—let it be. Only…never speak of it again."

Merlin bobbed his head a few times, listening, understanding.

"Bring me the lad Iddawg ap Mynyo for to be our herald, please," Arthur requested.

***

The Noble Round Table Knights brought slaughter upon the children of Mordred. Dreadful, unparalleled slaughter. No beast survived with beating heart, nor manservant, nor maiden. Such was the desolation that the wailing reached the western sea, the weeping unto the southern tip of Britannia.

The bards referred to the tragedy as 'The Tremendous Slaughter of Cymru' and sang long songs of the ordeal; some used it as a warning against treachery and commended the Round Table Companions, while others condemned the same, calling the brewing conflict 'The Foolish War'.

***

Iddawg ap Mynyo, selected to lead an envoy for the court, differed little from any of the Silure lads that had come into their twenties during the Summer Kingdom.

The Round Table Fellowship had drastically reduced the size and scope of the military, ensuring that no central power would be tempted with corruption to leech the people of resources, gold, cattle and freedom. Ever at long study of the histories of fallen empires, and apt to heed their failings, the Cymry recognized that most governments turn on their own people in times of peace and devour them. And armies are the brawny arm of governments, puppets of the rich and powerful that control them.

Tyranny must be checked, but defense of the Islands was still paramount. Professional soldiers were employed at the borders and ports, and the web of fortresses that guarded the kingdoms of Glamorgan and Gwent continued on, manned at all times.

Training and readiness remained, but training for a battle can never simulate the reality of *real war*. Thus young men were left to strike upon wooden shields with dulled swords, their verve and passion fueled by aged living legends teaching them and telling tales of old. *And by their loins, for boys must fight.* Four thousand lectures about the horror of confronting the Saxon invasion could not convince a growing boy to pray for peace, nor focus more upon the plow than the buckler. Young male minds see only the glamour of the triumphant return of shining skin, a procession of flowing banners; young male imaginations are filled at all times with the fight, hearing betwixt the ears trumpets blasting sounds of victory, cymbals and drumbeats of glory.

Only those who have never warred covet war.

Behind metal faces are broken minds, and beneath metal skin shattered souls. Fractured knuckles that calcify and will not heal, disjointed shoulders that slip in and out of socket nightly, never allowing full rest, nocturnal sweats, bowel irregularities and nervous fits are the real spoils of war. But of this, the peacetime youths cannot be convinced.

And Iddawg was a peacetime youth.

He wanted to see Arthur wield Excalibur in person, burned to witness Urien and Owen as rapiers thrashing their foes. Sought just once to view the sons of Gwyar and Llew, or Cadog or the Black Knight, or any of the famed warriors engaged but once in *Vivien's Dance*; to view the perfection, fluidity and skill of the Briton warrior.

Iddawg was amongst those who cared not for what had happened between Arthur and his witch-sister during some heathen rite four decades ago. Those given to reason knew that the birth of Mordred was either by happenstance, misfortune, or political intrigue. What Iddawg cared about was the harvest, the freedom to keep the fruits of his family's land, and giving the allegiance of his sword, if ever required, to a local chieftain that defended justice and regarded the poor. Though the harvest had failed Arthur, Iddawg (as with most common men in the south) clung to the promise that Arthur was the best hope to restore the land over which he had so long reigned. And reigned so well. That Mordred would raise an army, kidnap the queen, betray the Sovereign and join with criminals and worse, Rome, caused the lad to *want war,* if only to see Mordred bend knee and give his head for his crimes.

But the articulate speaker, who had learned diplomacy and decorum at the feet of both Taliesin and Illtud, wore none of these predispositions upon his visage, giving neither Arthur nor the Merlin pause in deploying him to communicate with the Whelp. Heralds were not to be harmed, and their words considered proxy for the king himself.

Arthur bade Iddawg find Mordred and communicate with somber grace and calm temperament that traitors would no more have heirs to corrupt the Cymry, that the woeful example of Mordred must deter the debased and the haughty.

Moreover, the king instructed his herald to be direct, with unmatched clarity of communication. *If Mordred will forthwith withdraw claims to a throne upon which he will never sit, and should he halt to stir the North, should he end the provocation of the urges of starving and desperate men. If he no more lures them to enraged ambition and folly in chasing after the false promise of the spoils of supplanting the Pendragon. If he wholly abandons his course instantly, then will*

Arthur let Mordred live out his days under the house arrest of his mother, Morgaine of the Faeries.

Then would the Civil War end ere in earnest it began.

"Finding Mordred will be impossible; he is as a thimble in a wheat field. If only we had one with the Sight, for to seek the enemy out." Arthur smiled at the lad, looking up at his wizard.

"I cannot." Merlin could feel Arthur's disappointment.

"My Christian druid." The Iron Bear now fully understood that, whatever Merlin was, surely he was changed. "We will find another way. Have you objection to others practicing such things?"

"A man is at liberty to do as he wills—"

Arthur was honored that the great orator would borrow and cite his proverb. The men said in concert, "Only that he doesn't kill his neighbor for it."

Iddawg was charged to search the land to make the declaration of the king. Others would investigate and seek to find the Whelp, by whatever means, and fortnightly meet the messenger with reports of progress, potential and leads.

Meanwhile, Arthur would sail to the Continent.

Unlike Mordred the Coward, he did not fear the winter sea. Whereas Arthur would follow the next step of Merlin's strategy to the letter, the Traitor remained in stealth, hiding with Marchel until which time he could present himself to the Gewessi that occupied the hills of the Brecon Beacons. It was most unlikely that Brychan Brycheniog would war against the High King, but if it came to it, he would surely discreetly feed the rebels of Eire, and provide arms and aid to the bastard son of Arthur. But if indicted regarding Mordred's whereabouts, Brychan in full and intentional ignorance would remain.

***

Caermelyn. The golden fortress whose halls had housed Merlin's invention, the Round Table, was rubble. So too the table formless shards, chunky blocks and snapped bolts. The calamity from the heavens had rent the spectacular castle, even defying nature and melting white marble, which in parts were now mixed with soils in the foundations and ramparts.

"We don't go to a fellowship hall; we *are* the fellowship. Our capital is laid low, yet we endure." The resolute king, adorned in his dark blue and crimson, gathered his knights, their regal wives in gowns fair and hair jeweled. And the bishops and notable of the Church of the Britons besides.

Resilience personified assembled. In spite of the assembly's resolve of spirit and defiance of the cold, regardless of their grit and defiance of the dire strait and collective focus on seeing the dark days through to a morning light that must surely, and soon, come, there was great and audible lamentation at the absence of Rhuvan, Maelgwn and Gwalchmai. Two empty chairs and one missing Champion. The twenty-and-six now twenty-and-three.

Moreover, the resurrected wizard was not in attendance.

"You scourged both the Roman Church and

the Dynion Hysbys over a murder that, well, may or may not have even occurred. I am a distraction, a source of suspicious wonder," he had confided half an hour before the assembly to the Iron Bear.

"Rome threatens the liberty of all men who would exercise the freedom of conscience in worship. And the Dynion Hysbys were bewitched by our enemy. Our *actual enemy*. The leader of your Order." Arthur did not covet this uncomfortable conversation. "When we survive this and the land is healed, I will mend the Dynion Hysbys; I will loosen my grip and encourage those who revere the old ways to restore their rites and worship as they will."

"Former Order." Merlin flipped his hood upon his head. "And until we chop the head of the hydra, and his peers or superiors' heads also, our sovereignty of these Isles will not endure."

"Peers? Superiors? Whose ill whims command the Masked Priest but the Devil alone? Surely he tops the stairwell."

"Everyone answers to someone with greater authority than themselves, even he," Merlin replied. "Everyone but the Emperor, Lord Arthur ap Meurig," he grinned. "Now, unto your assembly go, and explain why you must take the battle to Mark, why you must leave."

So Merlin kept some distance from Court, and Arthur convened the Round Table Fellowship.

The strategy had two preliminary objectives.

First, strike terror into the Silures' would-be opponents by exterminating the line of Mordred. The blood-bathed warning would slow, if not fully arrest, any faction, especially those in the north, from action. Arthur was renowned for carrying out the strategies of Merlin and Illtud to the smallest detail, possessing unmatched gifts of execution, having fearlessly executed risky maneuvers in his twelve victories against the Saxons. This time infamy might replace fame, and he might rather be called a tyrant or a terrorist in place of a hero.

But if the strategy worked, and if the land recovered, heating cold lands and cooling hot heads, then the bards would well record that his harsh act saved thousands of lives – and spared a nation from the mental, moral and spiritual consequences of war.

Saxon Slayer, Giant Killer, Executioner of Rebel Sons. These were his monikers, and he wore them willingly that the people enjoy their twenty years of summer. With the hope of yet a few more to come.

Secondly, Arthur would take three ships of one thousand soldiers to Brittany. These were soldiers, some of old fame but for the better part new, that were volunteer reserves. Farmers, pig and cattlemen, artisans. Leaving their homes, whether huts or fortresses, was a hardship on their loved ones and livelihoods, and the sacrifice great.

Cai and Bedwyr personally lent their celebrity to asking the Tribes to raise troops, and this act, the *asking for lives,* made it finally feel like the Times of War had returned. Having spent the sum of their youth in perpetual conflict, the two famed knights liked not the feeling.

The three thousand would serve a subordinate role, lending muscle and support to King Hoel and Amwn Ddu, who were flanked by Mark's confederacy. Due to the season, there was not currently active fighting, just encampments and positions and empty negotiations laced with real threats.

Merlin would have the Silures pick a fight with Mark, and drastically reduce his numbers. And then back unto Caerleon. If the first strategy faltered and Mordred did activate an army, then he could be taken on more directly, Arthur having crippled a supportive front. If the first strategy was successful and none of the kinsmen of the Cymru took arms, then the play upon the Continent would serve to position Hoel to at last defeat Mark, and subsequently the Merovingians, and end what was now becoming a slow-bleeding and protracted war.

No army in the history of mankind has ever, neither can they, win a war contested on two fronts. The risk was material that Arthur would have to conduct, or rather endure, a three-front war; from the Continent, from the North, and from Irish raiders embroiled by Gewessi.

Frighten the North into staying home and pummel the encamped enemies in Brittany, presently warming themselves, layered and snug under many skins, in their pavilions.

Kill Mordred's children, punch Mark directly in his mouth.

Make a three-front war…one front.

What Maelgwn Gwynedd would do next was unknown. The biggest threat, the least discussed. Although the slaughter of Mordred's house would deter Caw and Llew from giving supplies and men to Maelgwn, it was unspoken and self-evident that he was viewed separately from his northern kinsmen. There was no calculating whether he would be holed in some cave for a hundred years, or present with his Hosts to crush the Silures the very next morning. Merlin encouraged all to plan around what was known, not to fret about what was unknown. If Maelgwn did represent a type of fourth front, the whole of Cymry would fall anyhow.

This was Merlin's strategy.

The Round Table Companions, the loyal chieftains, the noble ladies, and those of wealth and repute, along with the bishops and druids, received Arthur's words and understood with great clarity his course.

Shivering but proud, and cleaving to the hope that three thousand souls, even if lost, would yield peace for above one million, they bade Arthur Godspeed. At this, the prologue of the Civil War officially began. All prayed that the early operations would abridge the tome, and that the days would be shortened.

Urien and Owain, Cadog, and Cai were notable amongst those who would join the Pendragon himself in Less Britain.

Meurig, feeling virile and spry despite his age, would serve in Arthur's stead (and he jested, making all to know that he might not yield back the throne to his boy, causing levity and the medicine of laughter for all).

Bedwyr would stay behind, being principally accountable for seeing that Iddawg was successful in locating Mordred and delivering Arthur's decree, and secondarily receiving Gwyar, as it was reported that she sought the king.

Rhun ap Maelgwn not only supported Arthur but was given charge of a ship, one third of the men.

This, and so many like scenarios, continued to bewilder many who could not conceive of Maelgwn clashing with his own son, whom he loved exceedingly. The whole Matter of Britain simmered with madness and boiled with calamity, but simmered nevertheless.

Seeing the final ship leave the port and find stride in the icy, deadly waters, then fade out of range of vision, Taliesin the Bard murmured, "Who can sort out this foolish war?"

CHAPTER 4
Sorting it All Out
Interlude

Before King Arthur departed he tended to his cough with honey, tea and herbs. Merlin noticed the complaint and harassed him without ceasing, beseeching him to spend time round the fire pits and avoid the decks and the winds at all costs. At fifty and four, Arthur still looked a young man, especially to a paternal old wizard.

Also the king spent a precious few moments with Gildas, the chief scribe of the court, and the youngest son of Arthur's enemy, Caw.

Gildas was twenty and had been in every way Arthur's foster-son for half the lad's life. The historian was deeply troubled and implored the king not to slay his older brothers should they meet upon the field. The Pendragon desired the injury of no Cymry, even the base rogues of the House of Caw.

"Do you feel that the judgment brought to the sons of Mordred will cause my brothers to unhand spear and stay home?" Gildas asked.

"Merlin believes it will engender both shock and awe amongst them. And that they will indeed stay home. But even if they do, Mark and his confederacy of the disenfranchised grows like a cancer. There will always be angry men from every tribe, and every kindred under the heavens. This is the nature of man, my son." Arthur enjoyed mentoring Gildas. "Though the unhappy and the discontent, and those who worship themselves above their neighbors, will always be with us. What is different about the threat to our kinsmen in Brittany is that disenfranchisement has become organized. Periodically villains come about, bring very bad men together, and covet our liberty and our very lives."

"Can Mark defeat the Round Table Companions?"

"No." Arthur answered a plain question plainly. "A professional army of long-haired Salians hailing from the Rhine River in Germania have united with Mark." *And not by happenstance,* thought Arthur, his mind going to the Masked Man who embroiled the nations. "Thus, even were we not beset by Civil War, we would have to fight on the Continent to defend our friends, and ourselves."

"Were we not divided, we would crush those Franks with no more effort than an eager winebibber crushes a grape!" Gildas recognized that disunity alone might change the future of his world, being of a younger generation, and that a far different Cymru might lie ahead.

"Yes!" Arthur smiled. "You are wise — perhaps the next Merlin?"

"None are as smart as he," Gildas countered.

Arthur roared with laughter, still less popular

than the celebrity druid. "I have important charges for you ere I go."

"Lord?" Gildas nodded.

"Get thee to the monastic cells in Neath. They are safe, and reports indicate unharmed by the Red Dragon. There, draft a register of my lineage to Noah. Of the sons of Cunedda to Noah. Of the sons of Llyr to Noah. Of the landholdings, weddings, guests of weddings, grants to any ecclesiastical body, and of the noble women to Noah as well. Add not opinion or bent, nor narrative."

No explanation was required. Before all the Bear of Glamorgan exuded only calm confidence; kingly, stately, comforting. But this confidential charge was the act of a realistic sovereign who recognized that the line of his people might be wiped from the Earth, the request of one who hoped that a scroll or parchment would be the stuff of future study. That Arthur might clearly live by the ink and scroll of Gildas, who loved nothing more than to write of the famed king and his fabled companions.

A register of Neath to record the times of Arthur.

***

"Foolish strife, to no good end. Foolish war," Taliesin reiterated four, now five more times. Chastising the air. Frustrated, disgusted as the last ship left the reach of his perspective.

The Chief Bard pondered how any could sort out who would stand against Arthur, and why, and who would yet keep their fidelity to the

Pendragon, and why. In his mind did he start to list the principal actors in the coming folly.

Llew ap Cynfarch Oer will stand against Arthur.

As for Urien, Llew's brother, for Arthur. And Owain ap Urien for.

Mark the brother of Cynfarch and uncle, though with fewer years, of Urien and Llew will stand against Arthur.

Gareth ap Llew for Arthur.

Ogyrfan (not that Giant, but rather the youngest son of Gwyar and Llew, whom history would record as Aggravaine) for Arthur.

Mordred the Traitor, son of Llew by marriage and Arthur by blood, against.

Geraint ap Erbin for King Arthur, but Caw ap Geraint against.

Gildas ap Caw for King Arthur, but Hueil the Cattle Thief, most violent of Caw's sons, against the High King.

And the remnant of daughters and sons of Caw, devout saints all, divided in their allegiances to Arthur versus their father.

The Chieftain Brychan against his kinsman Arthur, but Cadoc ap Brychan for.

The myriad of children by Brychan's three wives for Arthur.

In Powys the youthful prince Cynan Garwyn against Arthur, by reason of jealousy of the men of Gwent.

In Dyfed, Gwerthefyr against Arthur, as he burns with envy that Gwalchmai rules in his cantrefs.

In Rhos, Cynlas Goch, who serves as captain of cavalry and is tip of the spear for countless wedges made of human skin with silver flesh shielding the Iron Bear himself, will favor his cousin Maelgwn against Lord Arthur.

Bedwyr for Arthur.
Peredur for Arthur.
Cai for Arthur.
King Hoel Mawr of the Bretons for Arthur.
Amwn Ddu, the Black Knight, for Arthur.
And Rhun ap Maelgwn for Arthur.

The High King of the Picts, Drest, though offended at Maelgwn for his fallaciousness and murder, knowing his tribes do worship the Bloodhound Prince, will align against his friend, King Arthur of the Silures.

And Cedric of West Saxons against the Briton who gave him mercy.

And I, the Merlin-Taliesin, along with my Merlin, do fight for Arthur always and always.

And Maelgwn and Gwyar, what will you do?

CHAPTER 5
Stones Do Not Fall From Heaven
No Help From Rome

February
AD 537

The devout, faithful Catholics in Rome began to wax furious against their leaders, who continued to demonstrate extreme and overt dereliction of duty, open corruption, and utter disconnection from their parishioners.

The two great Islands in the sea had been wasted, first set ablaze and now becoming as a glacier of ice, by an astronomical catastrophe. Rome and Greece were mostly unharmed, suffering unusual cold and some change of composition in the winds. The damage to these storied nations was, for the better part, inconsequential. Their "cometary disasters" were the Visigoth and Ostrogoth hordes, now matured into fully functioning 'states'. They had split the old Empire in twain, and plunged the indigenous Italians into an ongoing Gothic War.

The Long Knife that had invaded the Britons with neither mercy nor rest, until at last repelled by Arthur at Baedan, had even more vicious kinsmen in these, who were known as the Wild Boar. The undefeated Cymry had not yet faced these conquerors and masters of North Africa, vast tracts of land above the Rhine, and much of Italy besides. *Neither did they want to, hearing of what brutality they had visited upon their conquered hosts.*

Downtrodden and exhausted, and shackled by religious bindings, the people of Rome had acquiesced to foreign rulers upon the throne and puppets in the Holy See. For their brothers and sisters in Christ starving to death over in the Isles, they demanded that the wealth and generosity of the Church be engaged; yet She engaged not.

From the shadows, Hormisdas, or *Simon* Magus, who *was* the Adept of the Council of Nine, installed his own son, Silverius, as Bishop and Holy Father of the Church of Rome. Hormisdas controlled King Theodahad of the Ostrogoths and bade him consecrate Silverius Pope, against the will of the Church and the people. Magus did this to create unrest, chaos and resentment.

He controlled the Visigoths and Ostrogoths, and the Merovingians, and the Cymreig traitor Mark ap Meirchion. He caused schisms only to resolve them, wrought confusion only to replace it with false clarity, created debt and desperation only to bring about the stability of slavery. He embroiled the western world, making up for the time lost when Madoc, the brother of the Silure King, had penned him in Caledonia for so many years. *And a Golden Age had blossomed with the Illuminati High Priest bound.*

Now the mighty ones of the Earth were his pawns—save King Arthur, whom he had hoped aforetime to control through contrived wars, then through his druid, and now through his sins. The world itself would at once turn on the coveted isles and their legendary king, and he would rise from the calamity as Nimrod of Old, the mighty hunter and world leader before the Lord.

Else the Merovingian would put Arthur the Tyrant's head on a spike, and that mantle take.

But the rising protests of the faithful, which amused Magus, were overwhelming Silverius, and had to be dealt with as the immediate imperative.

The Britons had given Rome tin, copper, silks and grains throughout their tempestuous relationship. They had also loaned the diminishing empire heroes, leaders and souls. There never was a *Roman Britain,* nor were the Britons ever conquered by any nation. Rather, like oil with water, the two endeavored—through treaty and politics and not a few blood-soaked fields—to share the same bowl, but never mix. Finally, Eudaf Hen had chased the Romans away for good less than two centuries ago. But relations remained. Sometimes for ill, ofttimes good, and primarily ecclesiastical.

The primitive church of the Britons and the Popish Church ever conducted Synods, Councils and Conferences, always seeking to scratch itching ears, perpetually yearning to hear some new thing. Debate, chest-pounding, pride and the desperate need for white-haired men to be something above their fellows and to bask in the cheers and claps of their own preaching fueled the connections between the proud nations.

As Christian men under the headship of the same Savior, regardless of seasons of hate or hours of affection, they always fed one another. When Rome suffered draught, the Britons gave food and clean water. When a diseased calf spread its malaise, killing the herds of three cantrefs, the Roman Church brought relief and meat unto the Cymry. Whatever squabbles of state, or border, or Scripture caused the leaders and the elite to burn towards one and another, the churches of both the Romans and the Cymry lent charity unto the poor, be they of another race, or even amongst the heathen.

But Silverius the Stingy was breaking this custom. Breaking it dramatically.

Although neither aging Dyfrig nor Bishops Bedwini and Illtud sought aid from the Roman Church, many of those with Catholic leanings did. Amongst them was Dewi, whose renown as an orator and influential saint was on the rise. Though he suffered willingly, choosing that path of punishing the flesh for the benefit of the spirit, the same imposition he wished not for the flock, nor for any person in the cantrefs in the southwest. He and others throughout the whole of the island (save the Silures) sent letters to Rome, beseeching her to send food, undamaged and dry woods for burning, pelts, blankets and fats. The letters moaned and sang of the suffering wrought by the Celestial Judgment. The Comet was described as a volley of so many stones, showered from heaven.

The answer Silverius gave was made on theological grounds.

"Heresy," he directed his emissaries to write. "Rocks do not float in the heavens, and the only stones of fire are upon the Mount of God Himself. And if the Cymry tribes fancy themselves worthy of God Himself wasting the stones of His garden upon them, they are guilty of pride and arrogance, and if not, then lying outright."

"They are not proposing an atheistic explanation, nor stating that the stars are rocks, only that the luminary encasement becomes as rock when it enters the horizon of the first heaven," came the collective protest by the emissaries, wanting not children and the elderly to perish over the mysteries of the construct of the cosmos and the prattling over words.

"Rocks floating in the heavens is an absurd insult to the created order of our God. Let them suffer that they may not blaspheme. This is my decree; answer me again not in thy insolence."

And so the public Pope gave the words that the dark Pope in the shadows uttered, and the freezing Catholics in Deheubarth, in Powys, in the spectacular knolls of Brecon, in the midlands, in Gwynedd and in the Old North would receive no provisions from the wealthy coffers of Rome. Empty barges would screech and halt upon the ports, transporting scant people and even fewer supplies throughout the sum of February.

However, the compulsion for tithes from the parishioners was not relieved.

"Father, will our refusal to help the *Walles* not cause them to turn against our Bishoprics there, and bring about unwanted reconciliation with the Silure Bishops?"

"Let them grow a little more desperate yet." Magus assumed his educational voice, coupled with his Italian laugh. "When Spring is yet cold, else comes not at all, we will forgive the ignorance of their claims and offer a bargain of charity." The sinister laugh was chilling, even to his own seed, who recoiled. "At the first, the Saxons preferred greatly to emigrate to Britannia as guests, conscripts, and subordinate barbarians to their advanced Brythonic and Gaelic superiors. Our gold caused them to imitate and, over time, *become* a monster for the lust of it. 'Twill be the same for the tribes that adore the Faith after the Roman customs—only we will buy their allegiance with blankets and cheese, with lard and biscuits, rather than with gold. They will pledge their fighting-aged men to us against the Round Table Companions, or the carrion will feast on frozen *Walles* flesh."

After he gave these icy words, Magus made for Brittany to look in upon the Merovingians and Mark's confederacy, wanting to evaluate their progress in harassing and, if possible, displacing the Cymreig sister-cities.

The twenty years of waiting and goading had passed. Many young Saxons had grown to fighting age; the Cymry were wearied and tattered from Giants, from unnatural beasts, from scandal, and the deep, growing hurts of unrequited love poisoning the breaking heart of their celebrated king. And, above all, from the flaming pestilence wrought from above.

Childibert ruled Orleans and Paris. He

wielded a magical spear with Biblical connotations, had a Blessed Lady to guide and balance him and remained a lovely alternative should the line of Meurig ap Tewdrig fail. He lusted to rule the surreal and magical twin of Caerleon upon the Continent, the famed Lyonesse. Gwythyr the Just and Hoel the Good alone were as a great wall of truth and warmth against the serpent and the door—the tribe of Merovee.

When Rome grew disgusted with the Church, and the Church's chief bishop, the Wild Boar would take pretended offense that their appointed Pontiff was so despised, and crush Rome. Then they would lend allegiance to Mark and Childibert on the Continent to do the same. A Holy War would erupt, with the pretender Christ's children the victors.

But the pesky Bretons, who shared the undefeated pride of their Silure cousins, were a key cog. And thus Simon would see for himself how best to eradicate their position.

He knew not that the Iron Bear too was visiting his Breton kinsmen.

***

Arthur and his select three thousand were clad in grey leather with light mail and black helmets. Nothing about their attire brought undue attention, calling them out as the famed warriors from the Summer Kingdom in the Blessed Isles.

They were subordinate by design. There to help and to hack, discreetly.

Gwythyr and Hoel's men wore dark blue checkered silks atop their metal skin, the former with a red horsehair plume and serpent-finned helm. The headwear of the leader. Arthur was glorious because he was not jealous of, but rather filled with joy over, the success and achievement of others. He grinned from ear to ear seeing Hoel ap Budic II of Kerne direct the men.

Mark's army were encamped in the border forests of Bro-Wened, but two hundred yards from Kerne, which formed a natural buffer between the invaders and Leon.

King Hoel's personal bugler blasted the trump of warning to the enemy, proving the Breton sovereign's honor. It was a surprise attack in winter, but no cowardly ambush. Hoel bellowed out warnings that the Confederates should dress, should bathe, should eat, should organize their women and their infirm—and then leave expeditiously. Else be scourged by men simply protecting their homes, their loves, and their lives.

A space of three hours was given.

The Confederates of Mark feigned surrender and organized a retreat, claiming that they would return again at Beltane to renew swords, and to stand together yet again with the Bretons.

But just as the protectors would relax and return to hearth and home (or in Arthur's case, to the extravagance of Gwythyr's lodging in the sides of the north in Leon), a line of four hundred rushed upon the Bretons.

Calm, regal, and stoic, Hoel was not fooled. "Side volleys, and see that our ranks move not to flank."

This skirmish, or minor battle, was in an open field at the edge of a forest and the area demanded a traditional 'line versus line' battle. The army that earned a flanked position, or better yet double flanks, would win the day. There was no high-ground position to be gained.

Instead of hastening to earn a flank, Hoel divided Mark's lines into three by lobbing arrows near the middle right and middle left. Because Hoel knew he had Arthur and Urien and Rhun's men at the ready, he favored an unconventional tactic and created three separate 'circles of men' fighting. Rather than an elongated battle earning a flank, at much loss of life for both sides, Hoel desired three quick 'surround and surrender' scraps.

Cymreig bowmen are the best that history has ever produced. Precise, artistic, lethal. The average bowman could draw and loose three ere his enemy could string one.

"Slay not our disgruntled kinsmen amongst them; imprison the Franks, kill the Danes and the Geats, grant no mercy to any tribe of the Long Knife," Hoel instructed.

Arrows showered down, fastening some by foot to frozen tundra, clipping others in the neck. Some found shelter beneath wooden shields and were filled with mortal fear at the whistle, thud and stick of some many hundred missiles as angry hornets upon them. Many lost the contents of their bowels; some broke the line and sprinted into the forest, taken down as a stag during the hunt by Cymreig arrowhead.

Hoel signaled unto Urien, Rhun ap Maelgwn and to the Pendragon, each of whom rushed upon the three divisions and rapidly encircled them.

Simon Magus's carriage presently arrived. A

servant helped him to a footstool, and then to the ground.

"Where be Mark?" he asked of no one in particular. A young soldier who spoke Latin with moderate skill and low intelligence answered.

"We are ambushed; he is not here this day." The lad searched for proper words. "But the long-haired ones are here, they have charge of the men out there." The boy pointed towards the Tribes of Merovee, receiving a harsh lesson in Silure and Raven steel. *For the Cymry cannot be defeated when unified, cannot be overcome when fighting as one.*

Simon Magus approached. Closer. Closer still. Yes, his assumption was soon validated. *Could these be Arthur's men? Arthur's men these are! And their form is as if twenty years were but a fortnight. Even those with greying beards are swifter than the youthful Long Knives.* Simon was as a man looking through an enchanted mirror back through the corridors of time. A witness to the fighting spirit that had birthed and protected the Summer Kingdom. *Though they starve and freeze and their halls are filled with sin and scandal, the spirit strives and thrives. They are not yet broken.*

Simon witnessed Urien mercifully let five run into the wood, disarming two more, now sending yet four more retreating to the pavilions. The objective was to defeat Mark, not to send more Cymry souls to the Underworld — to see the Cymry traitors, discouraged and without hope of victory, abort their cause and return to farm or cattle, and forsake the sword. The honor and grace of the Cymry granted to their own, but in equal measure withheld from men of other tongue and tribe, engendered an idea within Simon, one that he would hide in the storehouse of his mind for later withdrawal.

Could the Silure himself be amongst them? Could he be providing live training to his younger men under the guise of supporting the Bretons? Magus looked through the clamor and clank, looking for King Arthur himself.

But King Childibert had found him first.

The fighting was diminishing, as the final few minutes of the fire within a cooking stove: a few final wisps, then silence. Three circles of Britons and Bretons fully surrounded three circles of confederate rogues. The fighting had ceased, the incursion assuaged.

The Merovingian had given no heed to the trumps of warning and preparation offered by King Hoel and rushed to the fight late, in only kingly winter robes in flattering red leather boots and feathered frontlet. Thinking oneself a god provides confidence, and confidence seems to beget luck. He thrust himself without worry into the division where Arthur discreetly made combat. It would seem that royalty knew its own.

"Your bards say you favor disguise. And that you can take the form of a bear, or an eagle." The pompous Merovingian spoke in a deep, intentional Latin. "I believe the former; the latter is part of your mythos. Am I correct, Arthur son of Meurig son of Tewdrig?"

Friend and foe gasped. That celebrity might be amongst them seemed to slow time and heat up the field. Arthur, found out, kept his helmet low, eyes fixed upon the dirt.

A loud, bellowing and celebratory laugh

diffused the mystery. "Of course he is King Arthur. And he is my kinsman and best of friends!"

"Hoel." The Iron Bear quickly stood erect, with shoulders brought back and chest squared. "This is your day—not mine, not ours." He looked to his Round Table Companions. He locked eyes with the Breton. They laughed together, relishing the moment. Another victory.

"It is *our* day, and your discretion let you do your surgical work so well. Perhaps I should come and lead your armies in Caerleon in Cymru?"

"Please do!" Arthur cared for results, not glory.

But the Merovingian understood none of these principles.

"Why would a god hide? Perhaps for the shame of your house?"

And here King Arthur the Pendragon stood eye to eye with King Childibert the Merovingian.

Magus was petrified but could not reveal himself, lest Arthur slay him instantly upon discovery. All of his wagers were upon one chariot, all eggs cooking in the same pot, with none in reserve. Both of his Anti-Christs upon the same field! A name-seeking youth with a dagger, an ambitious, zealous archer, a duel, a fall, a misstep. Should one perish, both would perish. *And my life's work perish. By Lord Lucifer, these men were not meant to meet on this insignificant field!*

Magus prayed that Arthur's character would outweigh Childibert's guile, that grace would outweigh provocation, that kindness would subdue arrogance. *Let everything I loathe win the day for a space of five minutes, that my Merovingian might leave the field alive, and free.*

Arthur did not bear Excalibur in this battle, lest the Sword of Power be identified and distract the men. But, symbolically, Excalibur stood face to face with the Spear of Destiny. The Briton and the Frank. The one who adored Mary against the one who claimed descent of the same.

Hoel, Rhun, Urien and the others had overwhelmingly won the day. The message was ringing and clear. Kerne and Leon were not to be won. And Arthur did choose honor, and mercy.

"Put some clothes on; this is a field of a battle, not a festival dance for those that favor young boys." Arthur then drew up his authoritative *kill voice*, causing his proud opponent to tremble. "Live today, to give Mark MY notification. Leave these lands; disband the Confederacy, or when Spring hath come and blood and skin has warmed…the armies of Hoel, the Ravens of the North, and mine own Silures will return, and crush him." Arthur paced three steps closer, looking up at the taller Frankish Lord.

Dark Lord, no, let not Arthur run him through! Simon prayed.

"And I personally will crush you," Arthur concluded. "Should you or he find in your blackened souls a love for life and the sparing of men, come and face me, or any of my Fellowship, in single combat to determine the outcome of this pathetic invasion. I will lodge with Gwythyr ap Greidawl. You or your herald will have safe conduct. Take this message, and take your leave, *king.*"

Magus sighed a great sigh, and became as the shadows of the Wood.

***

Arthur rested for three blissful weeks in the dreamlike manors of Lyonesse, and then a messenger arrived.

His messenger.

"Iddawg. Lad. Welcome! You have discovered the hiding place of the Whelp. What tidings?"

The boy did not give direct response to the inquiry of his lord but rather skipped salutation, handshake, embrace or nod.

"Arthur, you must return to Caerleon at once! At once!"

CHAPTER 6
The Last Lie Ere Arrows Fly

March
AD 537

The three weeks before Iddawg presented himself in a frenzy at the manor gates of Gwythyr were a calm and desperately-needed respite for King Arthur, with one exception.
The nocturnal apparition had returned.
That Gwenhwyfar II had never loved him, never been true, was ever an opportunist, and had defiled their bed with his own son tormented Arthur. That he must slay his own son, *another son*, that tyranny might not shackle the remnant of the Britons bent the Iron Bear's iron will to the point of breaking.
But King Arthur cannot be broken. And the ongoing company of true friends was good medicine.
Walking the shoreline alone was good medicine too. Cai looked on from a defensible position and a small troop of awe-stricken children with wooden swords interlaced his legs. This was as *alone* as the king could be.
Lyonesse was second only in beauty to

Caerleon. Indeed, the twin city was as a twin, only the seaside views were of deepest blue instead of the greens and browns of the Usk River. *Maybe this Caerleon is fairer than mine,* Arthur marveled; then his mind saw the golden roofs, the banners, the markets, the amphitheater, the wild horses ever at play, guarding the city below with their whinnies and mirth from Lodge Hill. He could almost smell the springs and feel the baths. *Almost as fair as mine.* He smiled, forgetting for a moment as he breathed in the blissful ocean air that his Caerleon was now as a wasteland from the Biblical apocalypse. The seahawks seemed to sing to him in the Breton tongue, and retirement in a simple hut was a heavenly proposition to the embattled Sovereign.

A fortnight and a week to rest, and then again to the lines.

Arthur and Amwn Ddu were greatly concerned that Danes and Geats had joined with Mark's vagabonds, contrary to Greidawl's reports, but remained confident that the Britons and the Bretons would crush the insurgents at the next go, stamping out the threat upon the Continent entirely. Arthur would go unto the land of Beowulf and beseech him for an audience, imploring those tribes not to join their Germanic cousins in donating their blood to Britain's shores. These Germans could be reasoned with and were not like unto sons of Hengest and Horsa, having only yellow hair and blue eyes in common.

But Mark continued to attract traitors and debased men of every sigil, with every pelt, under heaven. His nomadic nations spoke above five languages and had taken lands in Eire, in

Corneu, and on the Continent. A radical Catholic in charge of radical Arians (else heathens who worshiped the gods of Valhalla), the lot of them were a mixture of oil and water, new threads with old, spotted cattle with single fur, a monstrous rolling rock gathering moss.

Thus far, none of the house of Hoel, nor Gwythyr, had betrayed their Silure allies and joined to Mark. Only treachery or intrigue of that sort or some other could defeat the Round Table, whose three thousand, combined with thirty-and-five thousand of Hoel's own, would force Mark out of the field and down deep into the Broceliande Forest and thoroughly defeat them.

Like unto the days preceding Mynydd Baedan, a policy had to be designed and planned on how to administer the victory.

Mark would be beheaded by Hoel.

Most Saxons would be killed and buried in collective graves, their princes' and mighty ones' heads sent as a strong message that Cymru would not soon suffer another wave of Saxon invaders after twenty years of external peace.

Geats and Danes, prisoners to be used in preventative negotiations.

The Gewessi confederates whose swords belonged to Cedric, arrested and made to travel back to the Isles to be dealt with in West Saxons.

The Cymry traitors, seven years' penance above the wall in Caledonia (for the Britons were yet tired of bloodshed, most of all of their own.)

Unlike at Mynydd Baedan, there were no nauseating all-night debates about who would baptize, how a conquered foe would become part of this census or that flock, and who would get to claim which soul. Arthur was allied with the Primitive Church of the Britons, and with the remnant of druids that held to the old customs, but had no part with the Dynion Hysbys sects. Twenty years of politics and scandal and the *murder* of the Merlin had at least made those lines clear for the king.

Instead, the three weeks were of pleasant discourse, focused strategy discussions, much continued grieving and a deep inhalation of cider, shellfish and harp before the next move in the infant Civil War.

If Mark could be truly rooted out on the Continent, his cells on the Isles would be as gnats. And if the unspeakable judgment visited upon the House of Mordred caused the Ordovices to keep sword in sheath and Arthur's other rivals and enemies to bite the tongue and stay home, then would Cymru be saved—and given space to heal.

***

None of the three thousand brought to aid Hoel and Gwythyr were slain in the winter attack. None received even a scratch. Their *carve with arrows and circle smaller divisions* strategy was executed with precision. No battle rust shown by legendary and aging warriors, no fear or impulse by the new generation of knights.

Not one drop of blood spilled, save for that of King Arthur, who gashed the top of his left hand wrestling with his beloved war dogs but two nights removed from the victorious romp.

A hundred men sat at meat in Gwythyr's

palatial hall, and a hundred men jested with the king as a droning chorus over this. "We fight the perfect battle, with nary a turned ankle, our unblemished record as marble, only to suffer one casualty — and that our own king by a pup!"

The whole of the hall laughed and laughed, as did their Pendragon, who also coughed betwixt ciders and reveled in insults at his own expense.

These men loved Arthur, and he they. Failed harvests and Grail rituals gone awry and which fellow put his member into which lass did not remove from that love by neither jot nor tittle.

Enter Gwenhwyfar.

Gwenhwyfar ferch Gwythyr, heiress to Lyonesse and, to the reckoning of many, the whole of Brittany.

Gwenhwyfar I was tall.

Gwenhwyfar II was as slight as the Faeries.

The daughter of Gwythyr was of average height for a woman, a median of the former two.

Arthur was sitting on a simple stool at a long bench, taking the drubbing and goading of his men, gulping the scrumpy, and coughing, when her hand was suddenly upon his. She was standing and had stooped down, fresh wrappings and a chalice of an herb concoction being negotiated and balanced with her free hand.

"Boys will jest and revel while infection sets in, else whilst our High King bleeds out." One lock of dark brown hair disobeyed her hairnet, which was made of thinnest silk and silver thread, and ran freely down her crimson cheek, fully hiding one of her eyes, which were regal and happy.

Arthur, ever attentive to others, respectfully

pushed the cascading lock from the lady's face, and their eyes met—directly.

Gwenhwyfar of Lyonesse had seen him but a few times, and a few times known she was smitten. Now eye-to-eye enamor begat love, and love begat true love. A transcendent love that surpasses physical or romantic attraction is heavier than the fondness of mind, or the welcomed comforts of shared interest. Nay, this was a spiritual, deep, once-in-four-thousand-lifetimes, never-to-be-repeated-or-replicated, one and true love. She looked upon Arthur more intensely than Queen Onbrawst on the old King.

Periodically the bards wrote of this kind of love, and most dismissed it as mythology. Even the Cymry, who dwell amongst faeries, wizards, wandering beasts, monsters and flying things, rejected and mocked to scorn the notion of such a love as possessed Gwenhwyfar for Arthur.

For all of this, the sandy-haired king noticed her but as the daughter of his ally, the poison of his recent betrayal too fresh, his heart closed; in the way he needed to see her, woe to Arthur, he was blind. But friendly nonetheless: he was gracious for the attention to his wound, and to his cough, which had agitated his throat and made it sore.

He took his rest early, thankful for sleep. But his sleep was disruptive, and, as the equinox of night and morning came, so too did the female apparition so much part of his years as a younger man.

Gwyar and he had shared their *theories about it,* then let it pass into the corridors of fog as a lost memory.

Is she reaching out to me? In vengeance? My manhunt for Mordred and my rage for Gwen resulted in the death of the Hawk of May, and then the act of war upon her grandchildren, guilty only of proceeding from the loins of the Whelp. Does she now hate me? Or need me?

The visitation was not lustful, nor sensual. It did not consummate in ritual and taboo acts as before. Rather, the night-witch embraced Arthur with four perversely long vine-like arms, drawing him close as a spider does with a woven and rolled fly. Aware but unable to move, in the clutches of the paralytic grasp of his uninvited bedmate, he called out "Morgana, Morgana—Gwen—!" and awoke, sure that the incident had been real and unable to find again rest for the sum of the night.

And this was the pattern every few nights for the course of his respite from the victory on the forest borders of Kerne until the arrival of Iddawg the Emissary; pleasant days, strategic planning and splendid camaraderie with the men in the evening, early to bed, and Gwyar—else some devil—sharing his sheets and pillows at night.

Gwenhwyfar ferch Gwythyr created every reason to steal a moment with King Arthur during those days.

None of Mark's men, nor Childibert's, nor any of the Saxon Tribes answered the Silures' challenge and offered their sword in a single match of champions. Thus the drums of war continued their low rattle…

***

As a hunting hound that will jump over a cliff or run upon a frozen pond for his master did Iddawg pursue Mordred to deliver the king's decree.

His primary method was to have a standard bearer wave the red dragon of Arthur overtly and openly in the streets, along with a bright yellow flag that indicated *neutrality.* Neither hot nor cold, yellow was the lukewarm color of messengers. Iddawg was ambitious and full of verve and chased down every lead and whisper, most of them false.

At last the chieftain Brychan, fully aware of the fact that Marchel lodged the lad (and fearful of hiding this truth from Arthur, whom he feared but did not favor) discreetly made Iddawg aware of the barn where dwelt Mordred.

Marchel, ancient and mischievous, was a person who meddled and enjoyed strife for its own sake. She carried unspoken bitterness for being married off to the Gaels for the sake of *war prevention,* received little accolade for her role in securing peace for the Summer Kingdom on countless occasions (for the raiders of Eire were both at once friends with, and desirous to rob the cattle, gold and land of, the Cymry), and she had been systematically oppressed by her late husband's religious overreach. Thus, in the boredom and jade of life's twilight, she feared neither noose nor axe, and quite reveled in the opportunity to rebuild The Monster Mordred, though it would be direct treachery against her brother Meurig and her nephew, King Arthur.

Thus the bards would call her Morgause of vile villainy against Two Pendragons.

Her dark arts and the knowledge she stole from Cerridwen (the mother of the second Merlin, the bard Taliesin) gave Mordred an artificial bravery and recovery of purpose, though she could not exorcise his petrifying fear of the man he had cuckolded. Marchel employed a smith, doubling his compensation to labor for long nights, restoring Mordred to his Mab the Dive Child, helm and taut armor, though this iteration was dull silver enameled with blacks and greys in the place of its gold-plated predecessor.

He received Iddawg, not knowing the ill tidings that had befallen his children, manservants, livestock, and property.

The emissary, full of verve and patriotism, had rehearsed Arthur's sentence hundreds of times. He ate the words and slept with them upon his brow. When he bathed, he bathed in them, and when he dressed they were his trouser, and his shirt.

But being face to face (or rather face to masked face) with the *Judas Iscariot of Britain* caused anger to supplant duty, and the fantasizing of battle to replace reason.

Mordred exuded arrogance. He *was hubris.* Iddawg beheld the man, and hated him.

The messenger of the king did not want Mordred to live a life of exile; being fed, reading, exercising, seeing the light of another day. Such was the temptation that Iddawg perverted the king's sayings, baiting the snake to emerge from the hole.

"Travel without arrest or harassment under my banner of peace to Llangwyllog. The High King's own guard will conduct you. Inspect the status of your home. We will meet there in three days' time, and I will provide further instruction."

Of course, none of this was authorized by Arthur, Merlin, the bishops, the Royal Tribes, or any person of authority. Iddawg should have communicated the somber news about the execution and then offered a life of house arrest, and an end of the rebellion. Instead, he goaded and poked upon the Traitor.

"And if I stay here, choosing rather the protection of the beacons and the cauldron of my great-aunt to nourish me, what then? Will father Arthur come and crush me?"

The response came. A direct lie; the err of answering evil with evil.

"Arthur will crush you in any wise. The army readies now, sharpening skill, using live action against the son of Meirchion to ready three thousand elite soldiers, all cavalry, in Little Britain. And a thousand thousands to be raised. The message is found at your estate in Llangwyllog. And it is a portent of greater judgement to come. There will be no pardon. Sue not for peace. Go you, Sir Mordred son of Cynfarch Oer, inspect. And give me answer that I might give your response to our Lord."

Mordred juddered but mustered a question.

"Sure you are, lad, that these are the king's words?" For messengers are usually of a neutral tone, careful to interject not emotion, nor vigor, nor tone in their delivery. But Iddawg emoted these all.

Nevertheless, dishonesty reaches a point where reversal is impossible, and the foolish

Iddawg had exceeded the juncture where reason could be regained—and lives saved. "The message of King Arthur ap Meurig ap Tewdrig to you, Mordred son of Cynfarch," again intimating that no matter the Whelp's lineage, he was no heir, "has been delivered by my authorized hand. And now, farewell."

At this time, Iddawg relished his lies, believing fully that Mordred would raise some men—after all, his *golden tongue* had seduced some—and be dispatched quickly by Arthur or his Round Table Fellows. Mordred the Traitor would perish, and the boy's small provocation prove inconsequential; nay, helpful.

But Maelgwn, who *was* the Lancelot of the Court of King Arthur and his famed twenty-and-four, convalesced also in the same household (save that he was brave and did not hide, rather resting in the same abode as Brychan, accepting herbs and salves of Marchel). The perceived hubris of Arthur by the mouth of Iddawg reached Maelgwn, and every sown seed of rage and anger and hurt was nourished threefold.

And then tenfold when Maelgwn, who followed Mordred and his conductors to Llanwgwyllog openly but from afar, witnessed the place of slaughter.

Mordred was prostrate upon the muddy, freezing dirt for hours.

Maelgwn observed.

This is so much overkill, thought the war veteran. *Were it not for the herald's words, I would think this is a terror to deter, and no military action. Arthur's madness over what we saw in his bedchamber lingers long; he will murder Mordred, all the whole of the northern princes, lest I stand against him.*

But Mordred had been the lover of Lancelot's love too, in the same person of Gwenhwyfar ferch Ogyrfan Gawr. Having no present desire to speak with the bastard son of the king, Maelgwn instead sent one of his bards.

"Rise," the bard beseeched Mordred.

"Yes, rise, and give response." Iddawg was on the scene, the allotted time period having fulfilled its days.

Mordred was prepared to surrender in the face of so much devastation. His wanton lust and abyss of empathy had resulted in the loss of all.

Of Gwen…

Of his sons and daughters…

Of cousins who resided at his estates…

Of property and livestock…

Of freedom of mobility.

Though his lungs were filled with air, he was dead, his time borrowed, the debt soon to be recompensed.

The empty brain-pan of a father's son will cause such a pause in ambition, the blood of his daughters painting warnings and curses upon the side of the barn.

Maelgwn's bard spoke instead. "Mordred will repay and revenge. Let Arthur his war paint apply; Maelgwn will champion the North, and the armies of Mordred."

Iddawg was numb. He had overstepped. Knowing not that the Lancelot and the Traitor would so soon converge paths, or even ally at all, he had hoped for a skirmish, a brawl, a two-hour burst resulting in Excalibur buried in the chest of the Pretender, with his curly metal locks.

What now but to give the message, and hope

that one legend from his youth would best the other?

That the Bloodhound Prince and his Hosts (the chief of all warriors amongst the Cymry; ferocity and skill exceeding even that of the Silures) would fight for him gave Mordred courage. And courage fed revenge.

"Suffer me two days more, lad," he said.

"To reconsider the hasty words by the representative of Gwynedd?"

"Two days, I beg of thee." Mordred gave fake courtesy, his tone sneaky, reptilian. "Get you back to Caerleon, else to Caermelyn, and I will come unto you with the response that I desire you, on your honor, to return to your king, my father King Arthur." Mordred's eyes saw Lancelot atop his steed, two or more feet taller than his company, the shadow of dusk outlining a god amongst boys. "Travel south, and take thy rest, and we will congress soon."

Maelgwn did not want an end of Cymru, just an end of Arthur. Neither an end of the Summer Kingdom, just a change of who held the diadem—*For he killed my true love and wronged me too grievously.* His ideal scenario involved drawing the Pendragon into singular combat, felling him, and ending this madness. Though he had never coveted the throne, and hated politics, the greatest warrior in the world would occupy the seat until some young lad would rise; be him a son of Cunedda or of the house of Tewdrig, no matter (although Mordred would not reign). Maelgwn was wrestling his demons to find honor and reason, and all evidence presented to him, on account of the false words of Iddawg the Herald, suggested that Arthur had switched roles, becoming as Maelgwn had been for so many years.

Mordred had darker designs.

Due to the countless years at court, either to bed Gwen or to posture and politic, he had become an expert on the terrain, access points, lesser-known streams and hidden roads in Caerleon. He knew Gelliwig better than the locals. Deception and *the adulterer's sneak* beget expertise.

Thus, the effort was minimal for Mordred to conduct fifty privily into Caerleon.

Firstly, he traveled openly, a *defeated foe traveling to the Court of Arthur to surrender to the Herald of the absent king.* Or so he pretended. Openly he presented in Caerleon with ten.

Secondly, he hid the other forty, blinded even from the eyes of the watchful hillforts. For treacherous and devious Mordred knew how to hide; and to hide men.

***

As night fell, having but twenty-four hours until Iddawg was to convene with him for to hear his response, and see it borne to Arthur, Mordred and his fifty were upon the doorstep of the humble cell of Gwenhwyfar I, the retired queen, the lovely Lady and Honorable Mother of the Blessed Isles in the Sea. A stone circular structure with a hearth that served as a pole and a thatched roof that looked like unto a floppy wizard's cap. The humble dwelling of a stately woman who, in the years when she ought to have thrived and flourished, toiled in solitary brokenness and despair.

A humble dwelling, too easy to breach for creeping criminals.

Mordred's men butchered her chickens. Drowned her cats. Speared her great fish. Abused her dogs.

She was as a monk, yet a dame, and alone most of the time. But three guards were at the watch, diligently minding her home in nearby quarters of their own. They launched a fiery missile into the Cymreig March night just as arrows filled their bosoms, pierced their throats, impaled the soft tissues of cheek and thigh and, as they turned to fall and die, their hindersides as well.

Their alert brought ten quickly, who were overcome by Mordred's numbers.

The slaughter matched, by intention, that which had been visited upon the Whelp's children.

Vicious, violent, murderous, wrathful.

Entrails and bone.

Unnecessary slices, unneeded thrusts upon those surely already at the door of death.

Mordred himself found the former High Queen, who was yet queenly.

She knew what he was about and flinched not, drawing the authority of her former husband; in grit and valor an *Iron Bear too was she*.

He abused and used her, and she filled him with gaping gashes that would never close in return. Each of her fingers snapped and dislocated in protest. Her nails were torn away, left in the chest and shoulders of her assailant. Resilience never abandoned the *real queen*. He put the blade to her throat and finished her as he finished inside of her.

"Now I have had BOTH Gwenhwyfars." He drooled, crimson spittle dripping upon her pale cheek. He tugged on her locks as a maniac tears at a grasshopper. "Gwenhwyfar the Black," another yank, and a proud admiration of the trophy now in his hand, "and Gwenhwyfar the Red."

"Flesh becomes dust with the passing, but the Spirit transcends all. And the Spirit of Britannia is Arthur's. Arthur *is spirit*. We are all Arthur. And you but flesh. My husband's only misfortune is having spoiled, awful sons! And glad am I that he killed them all." Her eyes pierced the villain, speaking of him as though he was already dead.

She then, or perhaps from its inception, separated her mind and soul from his assault upon her body. No matter the depth of his evil design, her dignity remained intact, for he could not rob her of it. He was not her equal, and her disposition in the final moments of life defeated him all the more.

Gwenhwyfar I here passed into glory, murdered by the cowardice of Mordred.

The Whelp etched his crude response in her torso for Iddawg to find.

The self-same day, Queen Onbrawst, who had long battled illness, gave up the ghost, and died.

Thus the Cymry lost two Elect Ladies. And weeping and gnashing of teeth was great throughout the land.

CHAPTER 7
Reinventing the Anglo-Saxon

Iddawg congressed with Arthur privately, giving false report that exile had been offered and rejected by Mordred, with avarice and hubris. After hearing the lie, Arthur was anxious to receive a counter-proposal, or new terms, from his rebellious bastard son.

"You have done well, lad." Arthur handed the young emissary a wooden cup, brimming with the sparkling cider of the Bretons: made from varieties of ancient apples blessed by the water faeries, and by Giants, and rivaled in quality only by the sacred orchards on Bardsey Island, which is Avalon.

Iddawg accepted the offer, and drank hastily, wanting courage, from any source, to help him through the thorns and thistles of the lies he'd sown.

"Hand me the letter, please." King Arthur was ever polite, treating the man who cleaned the pigpen with equal respect as the high-ranking knight, and he who minded stables as an Archbishop.

"Parchment and papers have I none." Iddawg trembled.

"A verbal response then? Proceed."

"The response *was* written, my lord."

Seeing Iddawg shake, but not knowing that the tremors were of what his deceit had wrought and not just the weight of the matter, the king attempted to calm and steady the boy.

"You are distressed and confused; sit." Arthur assisted him in sitting at a small round table in the king's chamber. "And I think I know why." Arthur scratched at his chin, proud of his deduction.

"You do?" Iddawg's eyes were as wide as two great moons. *A poor liar assumes; a good liar waits.* Though his lies were the layered sort of youth and verve, he was the kind that waited, rather than revealing more than what was known by uttering one sentence beyond that which was directly required.

"I think so." The king's face looked beyond the boy, into the memory of his own youth. "When I was your age, the Merlin bade me deliver a decree, penned by the Lady of Llyn Fawr herself, to Bishop Dyfrig. The Church and the druids were, of course, debating this point or that point." Arthur laughed, recalling when the harvests had been full and men fat and merry, hungering only to gnaw upon one another regarding gods and mysteries of the afterlife. "It was of such import that my wizard pleaded with me to deliver it to the old bishop personally. Cai and I rode late into the night, until exhaustion overcame us. We stoked a small fire and warmed ourselves on spiced mead. Finding ourselves overslept, fogged and grogged the next morning, we hastily packed our horses and continued our errand."

Arthur crimsoned, even now, upon the recollection.

"I presented myself to Dyfrig and his disciples at Llanilltud, proud and stately. And under a barrage of pulse and stab, a ferocious headache secondary to the mead, reached into my cloak—nothing! Then the side pouch—bereft. The antepocket where I hide important trinkets, scrolls, and medicines—void." Arthur's cheeks were as crimson as his famed cloak, and so hearty was his laugh that both hands clutched a corresponding knee as he bent at the waist, shaking his head. "Vivien looked as though she was going to turn me into a toad or repossess Excalibur when Merlin made me ride all the way back and tell her in person what I had done!" *Many rumors surrounded the Lady of the Lake. Many disturbing reports, conclusions and assumptions. But Merlin had returned; why not Merlin's peer and partner? Why not the goddess who had once commanded the Tribes? Arthur greatly missed the squabbling of his Christian and pagan friends.*

"You lost the document, didn't you?" A conciliatory smile remained. "These things hap—"

"No; the reply was not misplaced." The space for delay was no more and Iddawg battled a fainting spell, which was tugging upon his neck, his shoulders, and his consciousness as a great iron anchor. Candor and brevity remained. He shared how Mordred had invaded Caerleon with a small company of men and exacted dramatic revenge.

As he listened, King Arthur was transported back through time. Before his days as peacetime leader, or the legendary protector against Giants and foul beasts. Before the dawn of the Summer Kingdom. Prior to all of these things, from the time he was fourteen, Arthur ap Meurig had been *the War King*. A man with a resolve as marble, a constitution as granite. He had seen things that no person ought to be made to see, and he had seen them a hundred times over.

Teeth spiked into bark.

Brain matter splattered on the ferns.

Fingers and toes garnishing the ground as mushrooms upon leafy green dishes.

The jelly of the eye.

Hearts exploding, painting men in fresh, bright red blood.

And more.

The War King did not flinch when the dread and woe visited upon his kinsmen, and upon the wife of his youth, was described. *The strategy has failed. Mordred answered terror with terror. His bravery we have miscalculated. Merlin and I must adjust.*

Arthur had just one query of the boy whose lies had embroiled the kingdom in Civil War. "What was the record carved in the flesh of our Queen Gwenhwyfar?" This he asked in that authoritative tone known across the Isles, o'er the breadth of the Earth.

"War," Iddawg replied.

***

"Your three thousand superior warriors tip the balance here; we can end this phase of the war, my lord!" Hoel was visibly upset, scurrying about, trying to stop crates and barrels from being loaded upon the fleet. Ships were returning home.

"Mordred struck at the very heart of Gwent." Arthur was filled with compassion, yet not sufficient unto the changing of his mind. "O, Hoel, would that we could stay, but our capital and the center of our hill fortresses are at risk." The Pendragon could not help but glance at Rhun, who busied himself loading and organizing faster than his men, distracted, bewildered and sad. "Especially if the Maelgwn has joined unto him."

Hoel pleaded, as did Gwythyr, his daughter Gwenhwyfar on his arm.

"I love you, Hoel. You are my greatest ally. And my kinsman. I beg of you, hold the line against Mark and Childibert. Distract them, delay them, earn but a draw to buy time." Arthur now looked upon Gwythyr, doing all to impart the confidence and influence of real leaders. "And I will return to Brittany, and you will defeat Mark. This I promise."

"You cannot be convinced elsewise?"

"I cannot."

Like Arthur, King Hoel ap Budic II was a legendary, remarkable man and chief. Selfless, wise and full of grace, knowing that a protracted conflict similar to the Saxon Wars lay upon his doorstep, he ceased from negotiating and did the opposite of what most men would have done — and exactly what Arthur would expect of him. Having less, he offered more; having little, he gave.

"We will defend Brittany. Moreover, if

Mordred gathers numbers more expeditiously than you can resurrect the armies of our old Summer Kingdom, we will send all that I can supply in men, in horse, and in steel, to support you."

"May we sack him quickly and your men remain." Arthur's face full of thanksgiving. He then turned to Gwythyr and embraced him. And lastly, to the stately young woman who carried herself amongst men, emanating her presence as an equal (for their equal she was), but having mastered the grace and technique of not usurping the delicate pride of men, none of whom know how to respond, let alone relate to or with, a strong woman. But in her was no manipulation or seduction. She was regal. She was stately. She was strong. She simply possessed the temperance to wield her strength humbly and in good timing, like a mirror or counterpart to King Arthur.

But she felt neither power nor strength at this moment—only sorrow and longing. *I love him, and he sees it not, and but barely does he see me. But now does look upon me!* Sorrow and longing, combined with the helplessness of rushing skin and tumbling insides that accompanies falling deeply in love, vexed the damsel.

"The Lady of Lyonesse. Will you take care of these men for me while I ride forth with Excalibur once more, crushing villains and saving Britannia?"

He boasts in a jestful tone to garner my approval. Perhaps he dotes upon me yet knows not yet that he dotes! Yes, that is it! Gwenhwyfar ferch Gwythyr possessed the wisdom of Gwenhwyfar the First and, like unto her, *women know things.*

"Tend to thy cough, and to the wound upon thy hand, and come safely to thy home in Lyonesse as swiftly as the arrows loosed by our Cymreig longbow, my Lord."

Arthur had suffered both of his wives murdered, and gruesomely so, in a span of three moons. His heart was a thousand shards. The light within guttered and wilted like the last wick curling ere the candle has no more wax to give and becomes nothing.

Yet Gwenhwyfar the Last's words bound one or two of the slivers, added wax, stoking the candle with just a bit more light. Arthur *saw* Gwenhwyfar, his anguish heretofore having blinded him of her beauty: a beauty that surpassed Gwenhwyfar the Adulteress, for its source was deep within the soul, and one with her composition. *She is rare and wonderful! There is hope for Cymru's future with heroes, and heroines, of whom the bards have not yet sung! Her husband will be most fortunate,* was all that Arthur's brokenness allowed himself. "Nay, dear friend. As swiftly as a Silure arrow, for our missiles are faster than any of the other Tribes."

The vaporous moment of levity vanished, and Arthur made one final request of Hoel.

"Iddawg will travel with our company. Will you please conduct envoys to Caerleon, informing the Merlin of our course?"

"What is the aim of thy vessels, if not for the Severn, or the Usk, lord?"

"We will sail around the horn of the Isles, then up north."

"For an assault? Your numbers are so few!" Hoel was bewildered.

"We will establish a beachhead with our three thousand, and then make ongoing targeted strikes, slowing his build of an army whilst purchasing time for us to do the same. Tell Merlin we make for Llongborth. Bid him make haste to send for warriors from the North."

Arthur would use a *pincer strategy*, attacking a beach from *below* and then bringing five thousand men from *above* in Rheged. Urien's men. He would use Ravens to fight Ravens, continuing to hope that soldiers from both sides would see the folly of such an enterprise, and discard blade and axe.

"I will see it accomplished," said Hoel, comprehending the king's design.

***

Though the comet had devastated Cymru, the loss of life and land to the east, in Lloegyr, was much worse—fivefold. Whole tribes had been removed from the face of the earth. The remnant, neighbors with the Cymry by blood and the Angles and Saxons by geography, did something unprecedented.

Within ninety days of their *apocalypse,* the Lloegrians conferred with Cedric—the vassal king given permission to live, and to rule, with generations of constraints and accords that kept the once invaders, now immigrants, in check and controlled—to make a proposal.

Cedric's lands, known later as West Saxons or *Wessex*, had suffered much less, causing the Saxon poets to cry that *God himself wanted the Celts destroyed*. This they boasted privately, that none of the mighty Britons might hear them. Still, the trauma of the catastrophe, and the strength that yet remained amongst the Silures and their allies in both the Midlands and the southwest, resulted in Saxon people having no appetite for war. Certainly none for finishing off a helpful people that would provoke the unifying of the Cymry in response.

Instead, both Lloegyr and Saxon took a different course. A monumental shift.

Cohabitation.

Saxon men were given unto daughters of the western and southwestern Britons. For survival. That any blood might remain of the original stock and that children be born native to the Isles to work the land; lest a Boar mightier than Cedric and his predecessors march upon the shores and easily wipe out the woeful and downtrodden inhabitants.

Grandmothers who had, in their youth, been raped and used twig or herbs to rid their wombs of German seed now willingly permitted the fair daughters of Boudicca to lie with men who were not their own. The catastrophe had created an air of gentleness and respect, and life surpassed bloodline. Cedric's Saxons and Gewissee matured in this crisis, laying aside their barbarism and treating the Briton girls as goddesses worthy of worship, respect and adoration. And from this moment the Iceni, the Catuvellauni, the Cantiaci and the Trinovantes, whose capital was Londoninium, began to integrate with the Angles, the Saxons, and the Jutes, becoming a new people—the former fading from history.

As for chief Cedric, if forced to choose between

the upstart Mordred and the long-reigning High King, Cedric would cast his lot and sword with Mordred. Arthur had demonstrated a *cold grace* to the lone surviving liege of the confederacy that was comprised of *all of Germania* that had failed to overcome the Cymry, the sole surviving chieftain of Baeden. Rather than slaughter his tribes (who were diverse and numbered greater than twenty), Arthur let them exist. And for this, Cedric was thankful.

He did not hate Arthur for his deeds, nor did he care about the marital affairs, usurpers, conspiracies or schisms over the proper way to bow down before the Roman god, Jesus. If he hated the famed king it was for this: that he *was King Arthur, and perceived a better man than Cedric.* On account of this, Cedric had, for two decades, coveted a rematch. Though Mordred repulsed the Germanic noble and Maelgwn was an unstable man of fluid composition and no character, they were the catalyst to an end. An end that might give Cedric's blade one more go at Excalibur.

***

Arthur and Cai in their ship, and Urien and Owain in another, and Rhun ap Maelgwn Gwynedd and his one thousand Ravens, sailed for Cymry—the long and slow route round Kerneu, to attack what army Mordred could raise on the beaches in the north.

Learning of this, and knowing that the Sea Master Madoc ap Meurig had ventured to seek out new lands—and that the ports were no longer a vault of iron due to the loss of lives and resources—Simon Magus wagered that he could send a troop of spies, small in number, to bring message and instruction to Cedric (whom he *owned* by reason of gold and silver) in advance of Arthur's arrival.

Finding a scribe who could write in Latin amongst the brutish barbarians from the Rhine (and finding one surprised Simon, given the ignorance and illiteracy of the Saxons, who by practice refused to learn the tongues of other men, or conversely lacked the aptitude to do so), he instructed:

The Walles destroy themselves.

The Shining City on a Hill that gives light unto the world teeters upon the cliff, ready to plunge into the abyss. Sin, deception and immorality burn the nostrils as brimstone, avarice and corruption as sulfur.

Rome could not conquer them, having to govern by treaty and endless prostration and the kissing of Silure arse to trade and to engage in enterprise. Your kinsmen, the sons of Hengest and Horsa, the offspring of Odin himself, were made as a city of grave mounds before the longbow of the Celt.

They were the height of civilization until vanity was found in them. And now their enchanted island, worth more than any mortal could be made to grasp, is yours for the taking. The damage cannot be reversed if we but conduct the next campaigns with wisdom.

And herein is wisdom:

Let the Saxon change.

Let the Saxon start to become the example of grace, and literature, and art, and religion and civility, and let the Celt be as the barbarian.

Learn therefore the Christian Religion as packaged by Rome; and use it as your cloak of righteousness, discarding it when the objective be fulfilled.

Form orders and guilds. And make your most promising men as their bards.

Heave your black leathers and your wooden lacquered shields into the sea and make unto yourselves metal skin that shines with pride and craftsmanship.

Learn mercy.

When the Walles falls before your Long Knife, give him quarter. Bid him go in peace.

The moral authority is ready to shift unto a new people.

Mordred took their honor, Maelgwn their constancy, and Arthur showed rage in the place of justice. He is no god, and the people will fall to you not on account of your strength of battle, but rather because they see in you what once was.

One thousand years hence the Britons will be remembered as they are now rather than what they were, and the Saxon as you will become rather than as you are now.

Do these things, become these things, though only in pretense. Do them! And at last the Boar's tusk will have run through the Red Dragon.

- S

CHAPTER 8
Undefeated No More
The Battle of Llongborth

In the middle of March, five hundred and thirty-seven years after the Lord, Arthur's fleets achieved the shores of a beach in North Cymru in the region called Ceredig ap Cunedda, between Tresaith and Aberborth, upon the sands of Penbryn, next to the mansion recorded by the bards as *Llanborth*.

The landscape featured hilltop waterfalls that poured directly into the sea, long strips of beach, small hills and several pools of stagnant waters.

Maelgwn's Hosts, the best warriors in the world, numbered twenty-four times twenty-four, minus Rhuvan and Rhun. They calmly watched the three thousand arrive, studying, absorbing. Ready to move up the coast and engage upon the Bloodhound Prince's charges.

Maelgwn pulled his curly white hair, which had been made so in an instant by Morgaine the Sorceress, tight at the brow and then braided it with leather, and with gold. His jaw was yet misshapen on account of the selfsame encounter. For this cause, he abandoned his custom of ever presenting his youthful, chiseled face waxed and clean and now favored a wild, bushy beard, which was also white. With Rhuvan deceased, the mantle of *most handsome alive* had reverted back to Maelgwn, who was fifty years and six. He chose snow-white silks and capes to pair with his foster-mother's skin-tight, lightweight silver armor. His men chose what sigils of the Ordovices they would and he flew a black and gold dragon banner, making wavy protest that legitimacy as High King was no longer valid.

Twenty-four bards plus one hundred and nine trumpeters and drummers were configured at the base of the waterfall, making the music of war that motivates or terrorizes the hearer, depending upon perspective and battle line.

Continuing steadfast in the view that Arthur had entered into a state of madness without redemption, both against the late queen and the offspring of Mordred, and hoping to prevail by isolating and killing him whilst preserving life, Maelgwn gave specific instruction to the men.

"Injuring strikes only. Where possible, kill not. Where mercy is available, avail it! No arrows to be loosed, neither spear flung." Maelgwn grimaced, tears and wrinkles ruining perfect blue war paint. "And harm not my son!"

Mordred's upstarts numbered about five hundred. Most of his company were Picts who were still bitter over Maelgwn's use of their lands and the innocent blood spilled for his selfish lust. But fear swallows harder than gall. They feared Maelgwn as a god, imputing him into their pantheon of gods (though many had converted to the Christian faith), and thus aligned with Mordred.

Hueil ap Caw ap Geraint lent two hundred. Llew ap Cynfarch Oer gave one hundred and fifty more, as he prepared his constitution to stand against Urien, his brother, and his nephew Owain. These northern ravens formed a straight line upon the beachhead, and would be first to meet Arthur's armies straightaway, with no deception or trickery.

Hueil the Cattle Thief and Llew the captain of the Old North first, then the Picts; last of all, Cedric and the Long Knife as a third wave.

And Maelgwn would engage surgically when and as desired.

***

King Arthur's instructions nearly mirrored those of Maelgwn.

Avoid mortal strikes.

Seek opportunities to extend mercy.

Look upon thy cousin, and father, and brother who bears shield and axe against you, and beg him reverse his aim, and make peace.

This Civil War is not one battle. It is three hundred thousand individual moral contests. Try first to win your personal assignment by imploring your opponent to simply drop his sword.

All of this wisdom and more gave he, but as rules of engagement for the Cymreig combatants alone.

The Saxon and the Pict slay, reminding them of our past glory, and their present position, for they will fill burial mounds here at Penbryn by the score, and by the hundred score!

Arthur and Urien expected no reinforcements above their present crew. For the Silures and her allies simply had not the time, nor armaments or supplies (for the Comet had destroyed many armaments, and many blacksmiths besides) to prepare a proper military force.

However, Arthur's choice to attack the beach in the Ceredigion region was not rash. It was swift, but not impulsive. Similar to Mark's scuffles and minor strikes on the border lands, Arthur's purpose was to establish a base. A place far from the ring of fortress hillforts, which served as protective eagles o'er the whole of southeast Britain, where the Silures could block supplies, replenish traversing troops, and tactically initiate minor conflicts meant to diminish the will of Mordred and *the others* gathered against him.

Though I wish Excalibur was in mine hands, that it might bathe in Saxon blood today! he complained.

"What is the boy-king without his famed steel? We would not want the bards to have to write into the tale details which did not of a truth occur! Yes?"

Suddenly a very tall druid cast a shadow from behind the Iron Bear. Although his wizard had randomly manifested over the years in visions, in dreams, in whispers and as a phantom upon the lakeshore, his voice never ceased to both startle and delight Arthur. Cai was in front of the king, looking up, beyond and behind him, grinning an unquenchable grin.

"Merlin! How?" Arthur exclaimed.

Turning, he saw. A fourth vessel, much

smaller than the other three, had used the former as cover, and slid ashore as a swan glides from mere to soil. It was one of the platform-topped longboats designed for waging battles upon rivers, large pools or lakes. The commander of this longboat was none other than Geraint ap Erbin: an old ally who, in his youth, had been called *Geraint of the South* because he had been transplanted to the north, that royal houses might survive in the generation following the Night of Long Knives.

So long associated with the Old North was Geraint that he was now known as *Geraint of the North* (and so it was with many chiefs and elders at this time), or, more frequently, *Geraint father of Caw*.

So it was that Geraint came to join Arthur; both men at arms against their own sons.

Geraint was a master at sea and possessed many fleets. He had apparently sailed south, gathered Merlin, Bedwyr, Taliesin and other necessary men, and then returned back north to Penbryn in the same amount of time that Arthur and his captains made but one journey. His speed and skill amazed Arthur, who greeted him with accolades.

"Let us gain the beach and peradventure the cantref, and no more."

Geraint nodded; the two statesmen were of one accord.

But what does Merlin think of this maneuver? Arthur wondered.

He did not wonder long.

"I agree with your decision to suspend support of Hoel and poke the Whelp here in the

North," the resurrected wizard encouraged the High King. He then cast a glare upon Iddawg the Emissary. "That Mordred did not place tail betwixt legs and disappear amongst the Picts, else Eire, befuddles me. You are sure you gave him the words *we gave you to give him,* lad?" The glare, ancient and searching, persisted.

"The very words." The lump consumed the circumference of the boy's throat; he swallowed four or five times, struggling to breathe, and withdrew amongst the men, looking *busy.*

Merlin doubted.

But the battle was at hand.

The wizard and the Pendragon surveyed the scene together, dispatching Urien and Owain to congress with Hueil and Caw concerning terms ere the battle commenced. They both noted that the Saxons carried themselves differently than afore; dignity in posture, discipline in alignment, an air of professional soldiering about them. And improved skill upon horseback, it appeared.

Meanwhile, Maelgwn's drums beat.

Thump. Boom. Pause.

Thump. Boom. Pause.

Coronet in single squealing note.

Repeat.

The peculiarity of the matter would have befuddled even the most creative bards. The Saxons in professional garb, calm with neither drool nor growl, helmets plumed, silks clean. Rough and callused Caw and his troop of traitors and lechers the same.

And there was Mordred, in his god mask, flying a golden dragon atop two red chevrons – borrowing from, yet perverting, the ancient sigils and symbolism of the Silures.

Against this *majestic force*, in this inverted and perverse moment, were *the invaders.* Freshly come from supporting Hoel the Great in discreet black and grey attire, the three thousand Britons looked more raiders and pirates than celebrities and demigods from the Summer Kingdom.

None of this strangeness was lost upon the mentor and the student, the counselor and the sovereign — the two great friends.

"Which would you prefer, Bear?" The nose crinkled and the pipe puffed. "Fish that looks good," puff, "or fish that tastes good?"

Arthur chuckled. "We used to taste *and* look good," he countered.

"But does any fish *smell good?*" Bedwyr contributed, ever adding brevity at just the right time.

The three heroes enjoyed the moment, the overly cold March winds howling in protest and sometimes in concert with Maelgwn's drums and horns.

"Lo, Urien returns." The tenor returned to gravity and the mood snapped back into focus. "What terms given by Hueil and Llew?" asked the Merlin.

"We have instigated a military threat to the Ordovices and all men of the Midlands and northern Cymru. And are to return at once, else perish."

"I am amongst the *all men of the north,* and I stand with King Arthur Pendragon!" old Geraint the Sea Commander screamed, his war blood elevating above a simmer, en route to a boil.

"Archers?" asked Merlin.

"Withheld," came the answer.

"Prisoners?"

"Yes, save for those who were present at the —" Urien did not need to finish describing the deed accomplished against the House of Mordred.

"Pious for one who betrayed the throne for untold years and would usurp the Round Table Fellowship." Arthur gave scathing rebuke, his *authority voice* building, thunderous.

"Bishops and priests?" asked Merlin.

"Unharmed, safe conduct."

"The dead?" Merlin again.

"To be buried where they fall, unless our attendants can bear them away under threat of sword and spear. And the lads we have are fighting today, not cleaning pot, dressing wound, or fetching water." Urien looked upon the Saxons, assembled several hundred yards off, clearly separated as an additional *wave* against Arthur. "We will ensure *they* are in separate mounds, apart, from our Britons who may fall here."

"And may that number be few," Arthur concluded.

"Be there any warriors, excluding the Hosts of Maelgwn, that we should mark for exceptional skill or fleet of horse?" Merlin made his final inquiry. Perfect planning prevented poor performance, and the Merlin used to gather extreme amounts of intelligence; patterns and predictions, variables and dependencies, on individual infantry, cavalry, archers, hurlers, spearmen, commanders and notables amongst the enemy. The battle was over before it began on account of Merlin using information to drive decision-making and indicators for the course of strategy.

This, coupled with the valor, leadership attributes and mystique of Arthur and his famed Companions, resulted in an undefeated, invincible force.

But Merlin had been long in abeyance and could not apply the methods on this day.

"Mordred has found a champion that forms a vault o'er the coward at all times. He is called Eda Elyn Mawr. Mark him—note him. My son Owain grappled with him in sport and always seeking advantage by trickery is Eda Elyn Mawr."

"And he is a radical proponent of the Roman way, giving his sword to the Bishop of Rome over any *temporal* chief," contributed Owain ap Urien.

"Other?" Merlin pressed.

"Derfel ap Hoel ap Budic II, and his kin Alan Fyrgan, have deserted our beloved friends on the Continent, lending their sword to Lancelot," Urien said, pale at having to answer.

"So, the insanity of this war has crept into the houses of Brittany as well?" Arthur was crestfallen. "Amwn Ddu and Hoel must be grieved unto the sinews. Derfel is an honorable boy, his fame flowering. His likeness is as one of our Round Table fellows from the Saxon Wars."

"The women swoon at his appearance and his spear has no equal save the battle-dirk of Lancelot, who also makes war against us." *Boom. Rattle. Thump.* The Hosts of Maelgwn taunted with haunting horns. Urien was disheartened.

"Be of good cheer, brother. May the day conclude with his capture, that we might reason with the lad." Arthur sought to comfort the man who surveyed the lines.

All agreed, for Derfel was a noble and powerful young warrior.

A final threat. "Leave these shores. And see to it that you leave now. Tyrant! Oppressor!" Caw bellowed. "Hop a-boat, and take my father with you!"

"This is my land too!" Geraint's retort matched the anger, exceeded the volume.

The clash began.

Arthur was as brilliant at the Battle of Llanborth as ever in his youth. Speed; grace; perfect counterstrikes. A complaining knee and a loose shoulder joint had no impact. He felt in top condition; he led by example, defeating twelve men in as many minutes, slaying none.

But something was *amiss* with the rest of the men. Mistakes were made; hesitations begat poor defense. The older warriors were *old*, and the younger men's inexperience threatened to undo the band.

Nevertheless, such was the might of the black-clad Silures and their allies that, by a narrow margin, they outlasted the Ravens, winning the first wave. Caw and Hueil retreated. Mordred never engaged, preferring to hide behind his *champion.* Fifty Britons broke bonds with Mordred and reunited with the Round Table confederacy. Derfel was brilliant but withdrew when the cause was lost.

The death count was less than five.

"They are in league with the Saxons and with the Picts. But, God be thanked, they are not commingling and combining the forces.

They yet remain in well-defined, and separate, compartments. The Saxons come next," Bedwyr observed, breathed deeply, resetting his lungs. "And now they do come."

The second engagement was of a far different disposition.

The Saxons possessed the advantages of high ground and mounts (for though Arthur's armies had traveled oft with their steeds, very few had been taken with them to Brittany, on account of the bitter cold and the nature of the engagement). This was unfamiliar territory for the Britons, and a reverse of the normal scenario where a small number of mounted knights could best a large number of foot-soldiers.

Fortunately, Geraint had brought a *few horses* with him, giving them to the choicest knights, hoping to sway the balance of advantage. Cadog, Cai, Bedwyr, and Gareth cheered when they received stallions; they quickly saddled and rapidly clashed with the approaching Saxon, *horse rider to horse rider*.

The Saxons had improved.

But not enough.

Soon they were dismounted; next, harvested like wheat. Arms and brain matter decorated the beachhead. Entrails fed the birds.

"Do not envy thy brother's steed, lord." Geraint beamed, jesting with the Pendragon.

"Can it be?" Arthur's smile was as the noonday sun, as the infant being surprised with his first puppy.

"The old wizard made me bring him, saying: 'Bards sing of swords and armor, men are immortalized in ink and lore, but every soldier knows 'tis the horse that wins the war'."

"My Chief Strategist turned Poet." Arthur embraced *his horse*, Hengroen. Time ceased for three seconds, as did the drums, as did the Germanic screams, as did the precise instructions and commands in the language of heaven, which filled the air. *The High King, Excalibur in his right hand, bridle of his horse in the left, was twenty-three again, cunning and quick, the savior of his people.*

If Merlin was a poet, then on this day Arthur was an artist; a painter with blade in the place of brush. *And O, how did Excalibur paint the shores red in German blood!*

The Britons were handling the Germans with ease. Then the Picts entered the fray, favoring slingshots and three-balled clubs, sprinting headlong into the lines.

The Ravens fought with great skill and order. The Saxons had improved, their motions and strikes similar to the Cymry. But the Picts were sloppy, dirty. Their chaos was their strength, their lack of apparent strategy *was their strategy.*

Harassed by the painted fellows from the side, the Saxons fully retreated — to the chagrin of Cedric, who was unable to get close enough to Arthur to even see him, let alone make a crying challenge for the opportunity at glory — and the Bloodhound Prince slashed in from the other.

Arthur's men struggled to execute their charges where combat with their kinsmen was concerned. The kingdoms had degenerated into a Civil War in word and decree, but not in the heart. Maelgwn's men were a degree better. Their movements swifter, their power strikes more effective. Exercising mercy in obedience to his instructions, they but clipped their opponents. When Arthur or Urien's men fell, they were swift to help them aright, only requiring that they disarm.

The Picts slew a few of Arthur's men but in the confusion of battle, when a Pict raised club or axe against Rhun's troops, Maelgwn himself put battle-dirk to Pict, shouting reminders that his son was not to be harmed.

Where Cedric failed, the Lancelot succeeded. He did breach the Silure defenses and was upon King Arthur himself—the one target to whom no quarter would be extended.

"You fight shoulder to shoulder with Saxons. Traitor! Forever traitor!"

The words pierced Lancelot, running him through with greater force and precision, and pain, than the sharpest tip of the spear. Then the voice of Merlin, who was rushing to the place where Arthur and Cai stood—readying weapons to fight an unwinnable fight—but was well outside of earshot, whispered that familiar verse, as if it were added to Scripture itself: *"When it comes time to do that which you would do, do it not."*

One of the Lancelots in Lancelot considered the words, and his weapon began to lower. He did not speak. He could not believe himself on the side of Saxons, from whom he had saved Cymru. *Would you deliver Caerleon into the hands of the sons of Hengest and Horsa? Would you replace Vortigern, becoming the chief of treachery?*

Cai's club disrupted the introspection.

Maelgwn came back into focus, blocking the overhand strike one half-second ere it crushed his shoulder. Off the block, or rather at the same time, the Bloodhound countered, the shaft of his spike meeting Cai flush upon the cage that housed his heart and lungs. A follow-up kick below the knee to the left shin brought Cai down; a clean straight punch left him unconscious.

Cai heard the charges of Meurig as he drifted away, feeling failure and shame as the light gave way to darkness.

Lancelot and Arthur did not speak further.

Merlin arrived, dragging Cai away that he might attend to him, cursing Maelgwn with ancient pejorative, causing the sky to darken and the thunder to crackle upon the Sea.

Sword and fist cannot defeat the forces of magick and the way of the Otherworldly. Morgaine whipped me; if Merlin is to do as much, or kill me, let me first have my vengeance.

Therefore, Maelgwn made his rush quickly; the other combatants gave way, forming a circle about the two princes.

King and First Knight, to the death.

Meanwhile, the Hosts of Maelgwn were successful. These Britons were undefeated in their generation. In twelve major battles had they decisively bested Saxons, Jutes, Angles, Picts and the pirate raiders of Eire. Moreover, their sigils and chevrons had waved in glorious and proud victory on the field above sixty times after minor skirmishes or raids. But when undefeated faces undefeated, one will of necessity experience a new taste: the bitter bile of defeat.

'Twas Urien and Owain who tasted it. And bitter it was.

The combatants were evenly matched, but

the Hosts prevailed through ferocity and greater speed. Many of Urien's younger, less experienced warriors were overcome by awe and legend as much as spear and shield, the moment being too big for them. They would live to fight again, as Maelgwn's men obeyed the mandate—injuring without killing, disarming without dismembering.

Urien and Owain could feel their numbers waning, their lines compromised. And O, the cursed drums of the Hosts of Maelgwn! *Boom. Rattle. Rattle. Boom.* When the percussion roared so near and so loudly that the dynamic father and son's commands were deafened, so much so that hand signal had to replace holler and bark, they could both feel *and hear* that defeat was upon them. Urien would fight to the death and have nothing of surrender, but the Hosts begged him to cease, imploring him to look yonder to the shore where Rhun was corralled and forcibly loaded upon his ship, along with the greater part of his retinue of one thousand, as if they were barrels of coal or blocks of cheese and no men.

If Maelgwn did here kill King Arthur, the destiny of Cymru would shift to his hands.

But Arthur, the second-best warrior amongst the Britons, ever fought above himself versus Lancelot.

Arthur blocked everything. Everything. Lancelot exhausted himself, the only scratch on Arthur being that which Gwenhwyfar ferch Gwythyr had already mended. Five more attempts—blocked. Now six more—eluded.

At last Lancelot threw down his long weapon and gave his low, guttural command. "Bow!" For he had in mind to kill the man who had killed his love, at short range, with arrows in the stead of steel.

Arthur, finding himself surrounded and his army under the control of the enemy, was in new territory. New territory did not displace old bravery, for the courage of Arthur transcended time and circumstance.

He looked up at his taller foe, dropped Excalibur, and locked eyes. The Bear and the Bloodhound.

But Merlin was there as well, the thunder reminding Maelgwn that other allies had the king. "You will die in the twinkling of an eye, should you loose that arrow."

Maelgwn pretended to ignore the wizard, knowing his warning to be full of merit and no shallow plea. *Then in one twinkling of an eye will I be with Gwen.*

But a screeching, mournful, terrorized cry interrupted all.

All eyes scanned the source and found Caw, begging and commanding the fighting to cease. "The heathen killed a Prince of the Britons! My father is slain. What have we wrought?"

"War is no respecter of persons," said Cedric, attempting to remain stately. "I do not condone what happened, but we *are in league* against the Round Table Fellowship and the enemies of the Bishop of Rome. Acquaint yourselves with killing your own, for this is but the beginning of it." With these words, Cedric motioned and his men left the field at once, without cursing, in graceful marching form, the dead being left where they lay.

Two youthful nobles of the Angles had taken

advantage of the duel—a distraction that gave them cover to apprehend old Geraint. He had fled and tried to fight, making it as far as the manor estate called Llanborth (not far from Penbryn, where most of the fighting had occurred), which was the spot where they slew him.

The Angles, the Saxons, Jutes and Gewessi would immediately spread word near and far that a prince of the Britons had been killed. This would ignite a fire of hope that the Blessed Isles, should she recover from the dragon's flames, were at long last subject to defeat—and conquest.

Caw ap Geraint had killed, by proxy and allegiance, Geraint ap Erbin.

As the shock of looking upon the first noble to fall in the Civil War began to dissipate, more than fifty men from both sides placed themselves between King Arthur and King Maelgwn Gwynedd.

There would be no more fighting this day.

King Arthur and Urien ap Cynfarch Oer retreated, whilst Rhun returned to his homelands in Gwynedd to consider the matter.

The invincible Britons were undefeated no more.

CHAPTER 9
Unlikely Traitors
Derfel Gadarn and Alain Fyrgan

Though seven seeds—sprinkled, buried, and cultivated by many real and perceived hurts across forty years—provided the harvest of the Civil War, and though three woeful blows diminished the Summer Kingdom, leaving in its place a perpetual winter, the choice of side and allegiance for lesser nobles, heirs apparent, youthful heroes not yet famous, novice clergy and a myriad of other wondrous damsels and knights meriting of their own bardic songs was complicated—or else sometimes simple, but always tinted grey.

Arthur as hero. Mordred as villain. Lancelot to tilt the scale and achieve victory depending upon which of his fractured personas was in charge that morning.

Would that it was this simple.

The truth was that heroes were amongst the ranks of Mordred's men too.

Of note was Derfel ap Hoel Mawr. The ladies doted upon the lad, but seventeen, as if he were Lancelot, and men envied his spear as if he were

Galahad. His mind was as Taliesin's, humor as Meurig's, disposition as the Hawk of May's. The bards were already making these and other flattering comparisons, though Derfel had never met any of these men.

And yet he found himself amongst the ranks of Caw, of Llew ap Cynfarch...and Mordred.

Derfel's aunt was Gwen Teirbron, and her son was Cadfan, the Bishop of Llyn and thorn of Morgaine of the Faeries—the same who had established a chapel on Ynys Enlli.

Cadfan was his kinsman.

Cadfan and Derfel had been schooled in Glamorgan under Illtud.

Cadfan hated Illtud.

Derfel hated Illtud.

Illtud, as with all Elders cleaving unto the primitive Church of the Britons, was loyal to Arthur.

Thus Derfel, having no personal angst against the Pendragon, lent his spear to Mordred, breaking his father's heart.

Derfel also was secretly a druid, wanting to be closer, and closer still, to Cadfan as the Catholic Priest possessed the sarcophagus of Mary, and, before the comet suspended his efforts, had relentlessly sought the other Treasures of Britain.

How many hundreds of men or more cast their lot for intimate, personal and like reasons on both sides!

Alain Fyrgan was another such. An unknown offense by Illtud swayed Derfel. The impossibility of promotion moved Alain, brother of Hoel (and Arthur's very own kinsman through the line of Alain's mother, Anowed). Alain was the unwanted, unintentional last son of Budic II. Though a just and kind man and fair ruler, Budic had been so advanced in age when Alain was born that the boy had suffered neglect, lack of promotion, and frequent fosterage. That Alain could attain a place amongst the fabled and magical Breton nobles, or a famous name amongst the tribes, was beyond his grasp; that he might be made a Round Table Companion retired to the realm of the impossible. He would lead a troop and advance no further.

Thus the simple, fleeting thought that Alain could displace his older brothers and sisters, and succeed Hoel should he perish, caused Alain to take his men and leave Brittany, marching under the banner of Mordred.

Alain was elsewise an honest, upright and neighborly man; a kind fellow to his neighbors and of devout faith. Jealousy and lack of promotion was his motive and no other.

Thus Merlin would often observe that *the Sons of Adam's loyalty is limited by their opportunity.*

***

April
AD 537

An ornate stone coffin was borne to the Mansion Llanborth, where Prince Geraint was interred and celebrated. A chapel was erected to establish a place of pilgrimage for the saints to visit and give respect unto the first Cymreig noble slain by the Long Knife in over twenty years.

Arthur returned home to Caerleon, his resolve

tested by defeat. What he found awaiting him suspended character lessons and sent the great man into a spiral of unmitigated sorrow and loss.

Wanting him to fix his talents upon the invasion at Penbryn, none had informed the Iron Bear of the passing of his mother, the beloved Queen Onbrawst.

Arthur had still been at sea when the process of time demanded that they bury her. But the celebration of life, and mourning of loss, continued. Meurig and Illtud had established a choir singing her favorite hymns at all hours, serving cakes and hot wine to the trail of visitors, who did not cease to come visit the beloved Lady.

Equitable respect was given for Queen Gwenhwyfar I. Though she had been out of the public life for two decades, the whole of Glamorgan and Gwent adored her, suffering the king to be happy with his *second Gwen* but never displacing their loyalty to the original Fair Damsel.

King Arthur was regal before all, graceful and strong. Privately, he wept much. Dread and concern filled him towards the senior sovereign in his home — his father, King Meurig. He was six decades and six, and only fourteen years older than Arthur. Moreover, the line of Silure kings had a propensity for living to an advanced age, sometimes into the hundredth year. Nevertheless, the son feared the passing of his remaining parent might not be many seasons hence.

His care and worry for the older Pendragon preoccupied Arthur's every thought for the space of three days, causing him to lose much sleep and retreat daily to the fortress of Lodge Hill, which all knew was *Arthur's sanctuary.*

The fourth morning, bundled to brace the cold air, which was a bitter, whipping and constant reminder of a spring that would not come, Merlin and Bedwyr joined him.

"When two are truly in love—and I speak not of the diluted and common use of the designation, but rather *really in love*—it is said that when one passes, the other, having no purpose and void of his or her very bone and flesh, soon passes as well, though outwardly healthy."

"Yes." Merlin blew his pipe, a long, polished bone pipe that billowed perfect rings of smoke, adding to the intentional drama of any druid, shaman or aged counselor (old Dyfrig the bishop smoked from an identical device, showing that grey-bearded contemplative men puffing away were no respecters of the gods). "It is said so."

"I will be here when you are too old to walk, boy!" Meurig had crept upon the company, covered in six pelts and a thick brown fur hood; yet his smile snuck through. Meurig saw how Bedwyr, Arthur's best friend, and Merlin, Arthur's wizard, worried for Arthur as he worried for his father. And they worried for Meurig too. Greatly moved by their love, the afflicted chose to be the one giving, instead of receiving, comfort. "Mother is gone, son. But I have reason to live." Meurig withdrew his hood. "Your brothers are a disastrous lot, ever praying and preaching and giving alms. They can't possibly function without me!" Each of the three heroes allowed themselves a teary smile, seeing how Meurig kept his humor in so dark a time. "And your sisters—where to start!" he continued.

Full laughter ensued.

"Arthur, son…" Now King Meurig was gentle, but grave.

The son could not give response to the father, his throat choked for sorrow, love and endearment. Meurig patted the head of his boy, then knuckled the scalp as mates do. Well past the median of life, but yet with only blonde, red, and brown and not one grey rebel amongst the waves of hair.

"I have YOU to be around for. I retired my sword and trusted our kingdom, and the very hope of the survival of Cymru, to you. You were far too young: a mere lad tasked to be as a god, a savior. The burden alone, however, we never allowed you to bear. Neither now shall we let you bear it." Meurig positioned himself slowly in his layers so that he could address the group. "Mourn for Onbrawst ferch Gwrgan Mawr, and for noble Queen Gwenhwyfar. Cry hard. Weep long. Remember them in bards' songs and tavern tales, and numb thyselves with much strong drink. But worry not for old Meurig. I promise that my love's spirit will carry me, and that she will sleep in the Lord until we are again together. At that moment 'twill be as if no time has passed at all."

***

The cold leverage of starvation, meanwhile, was driving many of the Catholics amongst the tribes and clans to make their pledges to Llew and Caw.

Blankets and food in exchange for muscle, sinew and sword. Help from Rome as barter to displace the Church of the Britons and the king who had once claimed neutrality but now openly supported them.

Though Caw mourned the loss of his father, pride has a failing memory, and hate comes ever to displace and supplant reason – *so much so that he illogically blamed Arthur for Geraint's decease and not the Saxons of his own band that had done the deed.*

Orders were whispered that those faithful saints of Rome from Powys, from Deheubarth, from just north of Arthur in the lands of Brychan, extending to the extreme southern horn of the Isles, and even from Glamorgan and Gwent, should at once relocate to Ynys Mons or to any havens ready to host them in the cantrefs of Gwynedd. However, the harvest was so weak and the weather yet so bitter that travel was undesirable on most days, and on some days, perilous. As a result, there was no mass migration of fighting-age Catholic Christians to the North.

Instead, in the same village one home was pledged to the Round Table, ever at song about the glorious victories of the Golden Age, crying new hymns about its imminent return, whilst the next home gave its loyalty to the Bishop of Rome and a new future for Britannia and the world. This was the condition throughout the hundreds, cantrefs, sub-kingdoms, and kingdoms of the Cymry.

Resigned to the fact that armies must be raised, armed, and trained, the Round Table Fellowship experienced the same challenges. When asked how long it would take to properly engage Mordred, Cedric, Caw, Llew, Mark *and Maelgwn*, Merlin gave a blunt answer comprising of but two words: "Three months."

The Pendragon disliked the answer but sought optimism amidst the dreary state. "Good," he said. "I believe it will be warmer then. June. We finish this in June."

And whilst the kingdoms of the Britons continued to divide and dilute their strength, the Jutes, Angles, Gewessi and Saxons trained as one united force in Wessex, and in Lloegyr.

CHAPTER 10
No Song for Mordred

The enemy did not join his 'father', Llew (in Mordred's sorry circumstance, the bastard had neither step-father, nor foster-father, nor father-in-law in the person of Llew ap Cynfarch), in Gwnyedd.

Rather, he celebrated his first victory over the man who had violently murdered his love, his very own soul, sitting about Great-Aunt Marchel's cauldron, brooding noiselessly. Barefoot and wearing only trousers, she had covered him in the nine sacred herbs of the druids, which are:

Henbane,
Mistletoe,
Vervain,
Clover,
Wolfbane,
Primrose,
Mint,
Mugwort,
And, last, Anemone.

A lather of ivy salve spread the old crone about the warrior's torso, greasing his chest, back, arms and neck. Next, she placed idols to the four winds and to all directions save the North, which was left null to represent the place of the Christian God, who was as repugnant darkness to the witch. Red candles were spread across the cold, blackened stone floor, forming the shape of a seven-sided star about the Cauldron, and about the Whelp.

She sought to conjure ellyllon, which are elves.

She sought to conjure the Coblynau (who were but a foot high to a man, but full of mischief and malignant designs).

She sought to call the Gwyllon, which are female demons of the night.

And many of the other Tylwyth Teg she invoked besides.

Whilst Mordred remained as a statue, sulking in his sulk, void of expression or response, the intermittent undulation of his chest the sole marker that he was yet living, one of the Fair Folk did give answer to Marchell's ritualistic beckoning.

"What would thou?"

She could hear him; Mordred could not.

"Bravery for the Son of Pendragon. Bravery like unto the gods!"

"Batwings and potions, salves and herbs. Will these not be enough for the Bastard to carry the day against the Iron Bear?" The tone was unkind. The very King of the Fae emerged from the shadows, now in open starlight, a great red tower directly opposite Mordred within the heptagram.

He looked upon the Traitor at length. Had the boundary of Mordred's mischief been harassment, theft, political intrigue and the occasional assassination—a thorn and a prick upon the Sons of Adam who ever boasted their dominance upon the sacred places of the Otherworldly, primal occupants of the Blessed Isles—then would have the Tylwyth Chief done well. *Instead love had found this imp, and love doth undo all, and maketh the imp the very Devil.* A celestial tear navigated the cheek of a creature supposed to be void of humanity.

"I made his mother, and caused her to be selected to make him. And I cursed his mother's mother." Then he roared, as a ravenous lion, "ONBRAWST! I AM SORRY!" knowing that his screams could not rouse the departed Lady. *Neither did the scream of repentance rouse Mordred, for the herbs had placed him fully in a trance, trapping him as a hare caught in the snare, lodged between two worlds.*

"Morgause." He addressed her in her *name of romance*, as already uttered in nighttime fables to scare naughty children over on the Continent. "You believe that by defeating Arthur and controlling this weasel you will purchase the continuation of your kind. But you believe amiss. The One who controls the ones who control the ones who control him reveres no god, neither anything that calls itself God. As a prostitute is used and discarded into the byways, else slain in the alley when shameful loins sober, so too will he be used. And the Wicked Thing that would replace these Britons, these pesky, horrible Celts, will be the destruction and merciless judgment of us all."

The old witch harkened, speaking not.

"I am manifest to arrest your works. The Fae

will not aid you beyond what you've already lured into this chamber. But neither shall I send them away." He began to depart; then, turning, inquired, "Who was it that asked you to summon the Dormarch? For this notion came not forth of your own design."

"The Bloodhound Prince, Lancelot himself, requested these."

"Lancelot?"

"Aye."

Phantom snarls. Faint howls and growls from afar increased. No longer ghostly, real and present claws scraped, stepping out of the shadow; the drip and plop of drool soiled the floor. Soon a company of mystical and dreadful canines were present.

"He bade me fetch them from the Underworld, saying, 'Let Arthur know what it is to be hunted by dogs, dismembered by hounds.'"

Giving no reply, the King of the Tylwyth Teg left Morgause and Mordred to their devices.

***

I am meant never to rule.

Son of a witch, seed of incest, fated to be used by the religious and the ambitious.

There is no Song for Mordred. History will make me a profane thing, the sigil of dishonor.

Vortigern, whose treachery first filled Lloegyr's shores, inviting the Long Knife to our very hearths — even he will be forgotten and I remembered. Mordred the Traitor. Judas and Mordred; woe is me, I share infamy with the Son of Perdition himself!

Treachery, loyalty — I care for none of these

designations and assumptions. We are pawns and cattle in the hands of inconsistent, impassioned angels who fancy themselves gods. How does a treacherous worm differ from a loyal one? Or who looks upon the ants below with individual condemnation?

By extension, my father too is a worm!

But woe and dread, how I tremble at THAT worm.

With a false face he hunted my brother Amr as a stag, and privily he slew him! He swept his enemies away as does the broom sweep the hall, and then he reigned.

So long a reign! Emperor Arthur. Invincible. Promenading and strutting about the whole of the Isles in the Sea, hunting Giants and ridding the world of every creeping thing.

But not the monster in his own house.

When you were on the hunt I kissed her, and when adjudicating liberty and prosperity with your knights and bishops, she lived in the crescent of my arms.

You have ten thousand songs, but never once sang Gwenhwyfar to you. I am Mordred, and I have no song save how that Gwenhwyfar of the raven's hair did love me best.

You took my brother, and I took your wife, and would manufacture a good name that I might take your crown – but as month begat year and year begat decade, you would not die!

There is no song for Mordred, but the bards ought to sing a song of patience for the Traitor of Britain. Patient in the field, patient in the barn, patient in the chapel, patient in her ladies' lodgings, patient under the stars and in the brook and stream. Patient, loving her where I could, when I could, until the process of time and the cruelty of circumstance would that I take a second wife.

Gwenhyfach, the little Gwen. Contrasted by name from the beginning to shine less brightly than Gwenhwyfar, the great Gwen! The fair Lady! The favored child of Ogyrfan the Giant! Forgive me, my Love, that I used your sister in my dark imagination, loving her by the name of Gwenhwyfar in my heart, yet my flesh wanting none of her! That I made my bed with another is my sole unpardonable sin, and I seek not acquittal, my heart!

There is no Song for Mordred. And Arthur would do unto me as he did unto Amr, and his Steward with indomitable club did against the skull of the Shimmering One! O, Llacheu and Amr, and Gwydre, my half-brothers, did not your father slay you all that he might long rule contrary to the parameters of nature? Or was Caw in league with the evil forces, as rumors report, saying that some Masked Villain of Italy manipulated all? We are worms; who is it that maneuvers us in our holes in the soil bed? Is not Arthur the master manipulator? Has he not beguiled Gildas ap Caw, recompensing one son for another?

Arthur will kill me thrice, the triple death of our ancestors. Poison will I drink, a thick noose wrapped and knotted that my throat shall close, the water to drown my lungs. And Excalibur the fabled blade will delight in my flesh, slow and skilled to bring sting but not death afore all this. Unless my mother save me!

Mother! I am your first son. The heir. The paramount. Yet you hid me in the safe lines, having me battle wanton sheep in the stead of invading Germans. Did you know I would find my own brother in the place where you hid me? Where your disgrace and shame was hidden? Then it was you that sent me to Caerleon. Your displacement and shamefacedness to look upon me gave me both my loves! Amr and

Gwenhwyfar ferch Ogyrfan – they alone are angels and no worms!

But your I love yous, Morgaine of the Faeries, fall upon ears most deaf when Gwalchmai is placed at the right hand of the king, whilst I am as uncomely garments shoved into the dustiest compartment of the wardrobe chest.

The Hawk of May. He judged and accused correctly – only the participants he identified were half wrong! Oh, irony that his last years were under the shackle of a bad report, only to be killed by that very man who grieved him so. And both were innocent! Round Table undone by my vices! I defeat you, father, regardless of the outcome of this war amongst the tribes.

But you will murder me and parade my head upon a spike, my four parts to herald the corners of Britain. Unless my mother uses her sorcery to hide me!

Mother! Cymru is your first priority, then Arthur and I by equal measure. Choose; tilt the scale! Will you not save me, for he slaughtered your grandchildren and boasted against our entire house? And unlike the one whose bones you guarded, he shows no mercy, extends no door outward. Morgaine and Arthur adore their Mary, but would the Son of Mary butcher children, or set war dogs upon women? Mother! The stack of your kills reaches unto the treetops – will you not add one more to your count, and in so doing save your son?

There is no Song for Mordred, only a lamentation for the fall of nations. And what will rise from our fall?

Mother! Your Lancelot has lent me his spear. Lancelot is the one you would have as my father. He now protects me against the coming day. Will you not join us, and let our Trinity rule and reign for a thousand years? Forsake your foolish oaths, your commitment to skeletons and Jewish prophets of old. They are perished. We live, while yet we live. Mother! Will you not use your powers that we might prevail? Moth –

"No, the Lady of Avalon will not help you. Because…she cannot."

A loud discourse between Morgause and the King of the Tylwyth Teg accompanied by the heavy gait of five devil dogs (whose breathing alone was as cracked, screeching trumpets) had not roused Mordred from his trance. But none of these are the mighty Maelgwn Gwynedd, *the Lancelot* of the Continent, the foster-son of the Lady of the Lake; the Champion of Britain.

Does he walk between the worlds as the Fae? How much did he hear? pondered Mordred.

Much.

"By ancient statutes that harken back to that Age when the old was overcome by the waters from above the heaven, the spirits cannot engage in open combat, cannot sway the outcome of war. Your mother appears to likewise fall under this restriction."

Mordred began to make the inquiry that all made, but Maelgwn dammed up his words ere they flowed: "I do not know *why;* perhaps only the Merlins know, or perhaps none know at all." Maelgwn had not presented himself for to surmise about theology and the mechanics of the End Times.

Each time Maelgwn looked upon the man he had witnessed in active, passionate congress with the one *he had loved first* an evaluation was made: *would Mordred be granted another day to fill his lungs with air? Would the tenuous allegiance continue?*

"Rise," he commanded.

And the Whelp arose.

"Fetch your garments."

The Whelp dressed himself.

"Is your objective to be king or to avenge Gwenhwyfar?" The evaluation began.

Mordred's answer was careful, thoughtful and honest. "Just presently, during this very ritual, I was made to understand that the only way to prolong my days is to slay the king and beg Rome and the influential amongst the tribes to recognize me as ruler." Mordred paused, then delivered the wrinkle in his modified strategy. "But not for the whole of Cymru, as this can never be." Maelgwn seemed interested, honing in on the realism and resignation in the Traitor's words. "Ruler—not of Cymru. Just Gwent. Because of my parentage, and as my uncles are clergy and my aunts wedded to the Houses of Brittany, I can leverage the military support of Brychan, and—with Arthur dead—make claims in the South. But a Pendragon, nay. They will never accept me."

"You will kill to be king, to avoid being killed by a king?" The aggrandizement of the man reminded Maelgwn of himself, especially during those fits where his bubble was intolerable and the most bizarre and abstract behaviors were justified. Maelgwn felt at once great disdain and sympathy for Mordred. *After all, were our hearts not bewitched and held by the same Siren?*

"I will inform Llew and Caw of as much. The sons of Cunnedda shall rise again; I shall rule in the south and *they* shall raise a dragon in the north."

Maelgwn disagreed. "A Pendragon must needs be a Silure! From the earliest divisions of our tribes under Brutus it has been so. They may nominate an Wledig, but a dragon out of the north? Unthinkable. I flew the dragon sigil at Llongborth to protest Arthur, not to promote one of our own to the paramount position."

"All you say is true. But, Lord of Gwynedd, our world is upside down and traditions are suspended as the elderly freeze and the children grapple for an acorn. We are plunged into chaos. A fire serpent has wasted our land; the harvests have twice failed without the Royal Clans demanding Excalibur be returned back to Llyn Fawr. The old bishops have befriended their most ancient rivals in the druids, whilst the Roman Church is political bedfellow with the Dynion Hysbys."

"The vision came to me clearly." Mordred paused, contemplative. "This is the very hour where a man of the north *can ascend* to be head of the dragons."

"What man?" Maelgwn demanded.

The Dormarch gathered round the seven-foot embattled cedar; two sat erect as griffins, eyes flashing red then black, a blue mist swirling about them. The remaining three lay about his feet and cried as pups yearning a pat. The hounds of hell, claiming the Bloodhound as their master.

"You, Maelgwn Gwynedd." The cauldron gave a hiss, bubbles popping. "You will be Pendragon after Arthur."

CHAPTER 11
Gwenhwyfar Taunts Arthur From the Grave

Gwynllyw ap Glywys was a minor chieftain who once had governed a Hundred in the kingdom later known as *Glamorgan*. His domain extended from the port town of Castell Newydd to Afon Twyi.

A ferocious warrior and one of the scores of heroes worthy of songs and books from the Age of Arthur—*the Age of Heroes and Villains*—Gwynllyw adored the family of the Pendragon. Living so close to the courts and manors (and thus soldiers) of the High King, Gwynllyw possessed the deepest gratitude that Meurig, and then later Arthur, never interfered in the daily administration of his humble realm. The respect for local rule and the constant guards against over-reach of the Round Table, which functioned as a kind of central or *federal* principality, besotted Gwynllyw and many local chieftains to the more famous princes and knights that held seats in that lofty and renowned brotherhood.

At the terminal battle of Mynydd Baeden, Gwynllyw and his men had been amongst the disciplined Silures that waited as statues atop the hill, animating in the twinkling of an eye after such extended stationary time at the command of the Iron Bear. He had been a significant contributor in delivering ordered, methodical slaughter upon the Saxons as they made their vain ascent to defeat, their fateful climb to certain and violent death.

After Baeden, and like many other *survivors* of the Saxon Wars, the volume of fatalities and terror changed Gwynllyw. Having no more taste for combat, having had his soul bruised by reason of three hundred grotesque images of entrails and teeth flashing and clicking through his mind every night, never giving place to restful slumber, the warrior chieftain forsook his sword and instead took up candle, bell, incense and Bible.

When not serving in the church at Llandaff, Gwynllyw and a few other soldier-saints personally labored to build a chapel in Castell Newydd. The project was a labor that wrought healing by distracting his mind from the horrors of war. As for his lodging, Gwynllyw founded a hermitage at the place the bards would later call *Bryn Stow*. He much preferred the solitude of life in a humble cell, furnished only with cot and kettle atop a hill fort, to the courts and markets of Caerleon and Caermelyn.

Until he fell in love.

Then Gwynllyw could not be removed from the city, where dwelt Gwladys — who by misfortune was the daughter of the Chief Brychan, who cast his lot with Mordred the Traitor.

Gwladys owned a shop where she and three

damsels under her employ made fine gowns. She was noted near and far for her silks (with which she adorned herself always, whether under angry winds or smiling sun). Such was her skill, and so coveted her wares, that she traded with merchants upon the Continent and with Rome, and even periodically hosted buyers from the Near East who came praying for a glimpse of Arthur and of his famed knights, and to procure the silks of Gwladys.

She was a brilliant, enterprising Cymreig woman full of verve. Pious but not haughty, faithful to the Lord but not given to empty religion, sensual but chaste, Gwladys was very much ingredients of Gwenhwyfar I and Onbrawst, with garnish of Gwenhwyfar II. *And her body was thirty years younger than the dead queen.*

It being yet early in April, the next major offensive in the Civil War was not to be contested for three moons. Knowing that the chiefs, captains and rulers were busy preparing their men, Brychan boldly entered into Caerleon, communicating with angry force to the two lovers that their union would never be.

The Twenty-Six (subtracting Rhun, who painfully considered whether he could war against his father; Rhuvan, deceased; Gwalchmai, deceased; Amwn Ddu, engaged presently on the Continent; Hoel, likewise; and Maelgwn, at variance with the High King, reduced the count to twenty) were indeed busy, refreshing the skills of veteran warriors and training young men of promise. Although having not a minute to spare, King Arthur himself interrupted his work of warfare to support Gwynllyw, whom the king viewed as a founder of Castell Newydd, and a dear friend.

Reports to the king communicated that Brychan and a few of his men had barricaded Gwladys in her store, along with her lover, and that the shouting and threats were intense. Gwynllyw, now every part hermit, carried no sword and was at a disadvantage, being surrounded. Even in the aftermath of the Red Dragon, some buying and selling had resumed (along with desperate bartering) and young children were at play in the streets of Caerleon, warming themselves, hoping to cause their bellies to forget deep and painful hunger.

The situation was dangerous to innocent citizens—and escalating.

Seeing a dual opportunity to at once enjoy an adventure that would allow him to seek the refuge of disguise and to see justice delivered against the imposition of an unwanted guest, Arthur planned to transform himself into a beggar and approach the shop.

As he carefully organized a pile of tattered rags in the king's chamber, Cai, half-musing and half-concerned, inquired, "In the east Cedric has tasted success, and rallies an old foe."

"Yes; the Saxon rises, even now," said Arthur, struggling with a hopelessly holed stocking.

"In Little Britain, Mark and Childibert would crush our friends and our kinsmen, and install a new order in Cornuaille, in Leon, and throughout the Lady's forests in Broceliande."

"Quite true, Steward." Now Arthur's charcoal, which he masterfully applied to his eyes, was giving him fits. "Hasten to hand me that mirror."

Cai did so, with a grimace and eyeservice. "Llew and Caw would end the line of Pendragon, and make us two vassal kingdoms under the diadem of the Bishop of Rome and her Emperor."

"Frightening to consider." Arthur responded passively, his care fully devoted to evaluating which cap to don.

"At home the Roman Church toys with us with her wealth, making bondservants of the faithful."

"Wherever religion is organized it degenerates into corruption, for it too is made up of men." Arthur was now practicing dragging his right leg while hitching his left shoulder higher than its counterpart.

Cai exhaled, watching a man full of honor and dignity feigning the role of a lame drunkard — and worse, loving the role! "Your son raises an army to unseat you."

"Where are the grey horsehairs I use for the beard?" It was now as if Arthur was fully ignoring his longtime protector.

"Lastly, Maelgwn Gwy —" Cai did not finish the name, seeing the Iron Bear's countenance change.

"That was a fine summary, brother." The lame beggar with the unsightly limp was gone, and the sovereign had returned. "You forgot to toss in a few thousand Picts and whomever else assembles as jealous vagabonds longing at last to see us wiped from the face of the earth. We are encompassed by enemies who are guided by the invisible hand of an ancient Order of powerful Devil worshippers. At the same time, we are ablaze by our own sins and failings. The winter falls on our Summer Kingdom."

"Yes!" Cai thought his friend was rousing him with a fiery speech, articulating the dire straits.

Not so.

"And we can neither delay nor hasten what comes, for a sort of *second Mynydd Baeden is approaching, and it will set the course of life on this Island for the next generation as Baeden did for ours.* It is coming. The course is set, and we will not change who we are because of that circumstance!" Arthur was teaching, but some frustration had crept in, magnifying his point. "We fight for truth and justice, and truth and justice say we help our friends! We let *the situation* change us when we massacred the remnant of Mordred's line. Let us learn to never again react so. Rather, let us change the situation, and not suffer the situation to change us. Do you understand?"

The inflection suggested that a question had been asked, but when the king commanded his words in *that tone,* no response was expected, *or tolerated.* In his wisdom, Cai gave a simple, "Yes, my lord." After much pause, the steward then offered light words to reduce the king's ire. "Go with the long black beard; the grey is obviously like unto a costume worn by the bards during the solstice dancing festivals. It wouldn't fool a dullard, let alone clever Brychan. And your gait is wrong — walk like this."

Arthur roared with laughter and joined in the mocking, theatrical limp. "After so many years, Cai has become as Bedwyr and would cure all with merry and lightness of heart!"

The jesting spent, the serious Cai soon returned.

"Now, brother, what is the strategy?"

"Gwynllyw is a hermit, oft wearing rags as these." Arthur was beaming at the opportunity to misdirect and befuddle his foes. "I will walk into the shop under the pretext of being a poor saint, imploring the captors to make peaceful resolution with the forbidden pair. Then, once inside the door, I will turn and reveal."

"You're going to stroll into the heart of a conflict where our friends are pinned in by an enraged father and his *armed men* and then *reveal?*" Cai wasn't sure he wanted to hear the response, but let loose the question anyhow. "Reveal what?"

King Arthur rehearsed the matter before his steward. A leather tube designed to carry a map or scroll was hanging by a strap flopping sloppily around his left shoulder, appearing innocuous. With a swift twist, the top of the canister popped into the air; a pouring motion followed to empty the tube. In the place of scrolls and parchment, Carnwenhau poked its hilt out, as a snake emerging from the hollow of a tree to snatch its prey, and then disappeared into a shadowy sheath once again. *Along with casting a cone of darkness around its wielder, from which to work the blade with great advantage.*

"Armed soldiers, angry father, hermit's rags," Cai repeated himself for impact, "and a magical dagger.... What could go wrong?"

Arthur grinned, slapped Cai about the shoulder, communicating great confidence, and made directly for the markets of Caerleon.

***

Gwladys's silk shop was in an open market, outdoors. The back of the shop was a section of the city gate itself, the front two posts roofed by a thatched canvas. Three archers stood erect and drawn at the sides of the shop, greatly disrupting neighboring merchants (who had all struggled during the distress of the poor harvest and irregular, bitterly cold weather; the loss of even two buyers due to the conflict could represent not eating for the month), whilst Brychan and two men armed with longswords guarded the front entrance.

Gwynllyw and Gwladys were as penned hogs. Curses and yells filled the air, and the hermit posited the sum of his body in front of his damsel, fearing greatly that hot heads might a missile sling.

As rehearsed, and without hesitation, *Arthur the hermit* limped up to the soldiers. "Cymry threatening Cymry at tip of arrow and edge of sword whilst the Saxons daily strengthen and recover their numbers. May Jesus save us—can we even spare one soul?" *That was almost too kingly,* Arthur thought, fighting back laughter that might betray him to quick-tempered Brychan.

"Mind your business, monk," said a solider.

Brychan did not speak to the hermit, his glare and invectives fixed upon his daughter's unauthorized suitor.

Arthur did not need to win a philosophical debate, nor negotiate a release; he only needed to pontificate and plead for a few moments whilst positioning himself between the soldiers and the shop. *They perceive no threat, and surely will not strike me down.* He calculated quickly. The men found him as a gnat, not an opponent. They hollered at him a few more times, a mixture of mocking and frustration.

"We must attend to this matter! Preach elsewhere!" they cried.

Finally, Brychan allowed the hermit to divert his stare. As he formed the order "Remove him," Arthur had already gained three paces on the soldiers and was firmly under the fabric roofing of the shop. He turned to Gwynllyw, and, tearing at a portion of his fabricated beard, smiled at his old friend and ally.

"I will make the day as night in here; as I do, leave comely Gwladys and flee, sir."

"I cannot leave her, lord. She—"

"Her father treasures her as do you. She will be safe with him, and away from this situation. Then you will call a troop of your men out of retirement. We will give chase and recover her."

"But, lord…" A smitten man is void of reason, and protests.

"Trust me."

Gwynllyw remembered well the authority contained in that tone and nodded.

"Remove him. Cast him upon the road, else into the Usk River!" Brychan's agitation was at its zenith.

"Blessed is the peacemaker," said the hermit. "Let me pray with my friends, and then I shall withdraw."

Brychan had inherited a fear of God from his father, and suffered the fool to make his prayers lest Brychan suffer condemnation of the Church. He approved the request, his eyes rolling, and the sighs intensifying. "Make haste."

The hermit unfastened his leather tube; none questioned the act, each supposing some religious instruments were to accompany the prayers.

Carnwenhau, the enchanted dagger of King Arthur (and amongst his favorite armaments), was at once in hand, the disguise torn away, and a tattered but somehow stately Pendragon stood before all.

"You." Brychan ground his teeth together and flared his cheeks to such an extreme that his eyes disappeared in the folds of his face.

"Women possess their free agency in this land, Chieftain. She is of age; you have no just hold over her hand, or her heart." Upon saying these words, Arthur worked the dagger, causing it to cast darkness in a large cone around the ling, Gwynllyw and Gwladys.

"Hypocrite! Foul! False! The foundation itself, decadent and tunneled with rot, of your *Summer Kingdom* is built upon arranged marriages and the use of women as political pawns!"

"Each lady who sacrificed, that peace might endure, had what you would now deny your daughter." Arthur pushed Gwladys from the cone with a gentle force, knowing that a soldier would catch her away. "Choice!"

Seeing his daughter safely removed from Arthur's *mystical cave*, King Brychan signaled the archers, who fired twenty and nine arrows into the shop. Next, the soldiers rushed into the shadow, returning only to report what Brychan already knew.

Arthur and Gwynllyw had vanished, untouched, unharmed, and surely far removed from the markets of Caerleon.

"I respect that you have forsaken this life, but if you pry the damsel from Brychan and make her your own…" The king handed Gwynllyw a silver breastplate, and Cai fastened the red cape of the Silures about his neck, lacing it over the armor. He still bore the ageless frown of protest that the Pendragon had once again put himself in danger.

"Why wearest thou the frown, brother?" Arthur asked. "Were I to have perished back in that storefront, would not Maelgwn and the Northern Princes have laid down arms, called for a conference atop Caer Caradoc, and negotiated peace? It would be rather favorable were I to have gone to the place where the Merlin slept."

Cai did not contemplate the king's philosophical posit, not for one second, making immediate response. "Were Arthur ap Meurig slain, the Northern Princes would strip the mines to barren, and use Cymreig gold to conscript Cedric and a host of other Boars, and cut through the South as the vineyard keeper thrashes the vine. We who lived would bow knee to the Bishop of Rome and, in a generation's time, German would be our native tongue."

Arthur looked soberly at Cai, then onto Gwynllyw, who was reluctantly reacquainting himself with the instruments of war. "I suppose I should be more careful then."

The three men shared the bellowing laughter of fellows, then entertained plans about abducting fair Gwladys.

***

Gwynllyw's popularity in his hundred had not waned. Moreover, hungry men would rather fight than bear the guilts and pains of entropy. It was not difficult to raise a company of three hundred, and to make for Talgarth, where stood the principal court of Brychan Brycheniog.

Unaware were the Silures that Maelgwn Gwynedd had but recently been nearby and left fifteen of his Hosts behind, aiming to add brawn to Brychan's position, which was north of Gwent, and a key passage into the Midlands.

Arthur, Cai, and Bedwyr were supportive but direct with Gwynllyw. This was his operation, led by him and his own clan. The Round Table companions would provide secondary support and watch the action from the hill called Boch Rhiw Cam. Should trouble befall Gwynllyw, they, being positioned to see all, could descend quickly to provide aid from a high-ground location.

The three heroes rode fast ahead of the three hundred, and set up camp, bringing the gwyddbwyll board and much spiced mead (which they would heat upon the kettle) to pass the time. Cai and Bedwyr pitched a small pavilion to shield the trio from the cold, which gave no mercy, and against the freezing rains, which were as so many thousands of tiny razors upon the skin. Warmed by fire and mead, the men slept well.

The following morning Cai and Bedwyr resumed their gwyddbwyll, a contest intense — and emotional, when coupled with the aching head subsequent to mulled mead. Arthur favored the solitude of hiking and communicated that he would ascend to a vantage wherewith to look down on Talgarth and report the matter upon his return.

The idle time proved to be more enemy than Saxon knife to the heartbroken king. One share of his heart mourned for Queen Onbrawst, and the other agonized over the absence of Queen Gwenhwyfar ferch Ogyrfan the Giant. One chamber grieved the warm grief of fondness, a limitless stream of loving memories and fair times. The other chamber grieved the cold grief of unrequited love; of the self-doubt and questioning of one's worth when one loves something, and indeed must be near, that which reviles and dismisses him.

Hot grief.

Cold grief.

Such dichotomy threatened to burst the Iron Bear's spirit asunder. The pressure around and in his chest was great, the emotional and spiritual impacting the physical.

Hot grief.

Cold grief.

The fingertips of his right hand twitched. His left arm presented a dull pain. His tongue dried as a forgotten sponge and then yelled at him, *Swallow me!*

Whilst Bedwyr tossed dice and Cai mused, *Now try it with your right hand...* And whilst Gwynllyw and his equestrian knights progressed to the beacons slowly, preserving wind for a tussle... And whilst love and hope swirled... Arthur swooned.

Gathering himself to one knee and giving his full weight to an old oak tree, the broken king readied himself to perish, literally, of a broken heart.

In that moment the temperate, honorable, loyal man peradventure captured a glimpse of Gwladys, staring up as if she were arguing with the clouds, pleading with them to give way to the sun. Brychan's palace was constructed primarily of wood, trimmed with gold; ornate, the beautiful round manors in the style of the ancients. An external stairway, painted in white and carved throughout with doves and owls and stags, coiled round, winding and winding until it terminated at the sixth story and transitioned into a balcony where this debate between damsel and nature was conducted.

Temperate.
Honorable.
Loyal.
Lustful!

Carnality, and nothing noble, rushed upon the king to stay his heart.

"Gwenhwyfar?" He peered down. He knew she was not Gwenhwyfar, for he had been first witness to her decease, having fed her but four months ago to the war dogs.

Feeling better, though deceiving himself and healing nothing, the stately sovereign adorned a new mask—a typical man.

She is not Gwenhwyfar, and I love her not, but shall not a king lie with whom he pleases? Her comeliness is as a goddess, her disposition as an angel. Why not have her for myself?

"Why not have her for myself?" The second time was audible.

Best friends sense things. Cai and Bedwyr

had shared the spur of concern quite at the same instant and were searching for their fellow.

Hearing those words, and the fleshly thoughts that begat them, caused both men to think their lord bewitched, ill or drunken. Not knowing how to respond, and distracted by shock, Bedwyr was unrestrained. "Because she loves another man, and you another woman—that is WHY!"

Cai followed that with, "You mourn and are not your right self."

"The woman I love sleeps beneath the dirt."

"That is her condition. Whether she draws breath or is dead as that log changes not your condition. Look not on another woman until the woman you love you no longer look upon. Who gave this proverb?" Bedwyr continued to be strict with his best friend.

Arthur fixed his stare upon Gwladys, but gave response. "Merlin did."

"If you must fill your bed with damsels, do so; yet not her," Cai pleaded. "We can ill afford scandal amongst our own tribes. Neither can we suffer ourselves to lose Gwynllyw to Mordred."

Is this what it feels like to be Lancelot? Arthur was rallying, reasoning with himself. *To give in to passion and do as you will? Is his crazed bubble lurking within me? Ought I not to learn the ways of my opponent?* The upright son of Onbrawst and respecter of women combatted the notion, and rejected it—in part.

"Brothers, you are right. My conduct is wrong. I feel faint and not well; forgive me."

"Nothing to forgive." Bedwyr supported the king at his elbows. "May this tussle conclude speedily that we might see you to your bed, resting and restoring yourself for the real clash that lies ahead."

Partial rejection.

"I do desire to be in my bedchamber, Bedwyr," the king stole one last, sustained gape at Gwladys, "and I will heal my heart with my loins and enjoy some women." Arthur smiled, but his companions were unsure, continuing to be startled by his uncharacteristic antics. "Not that woman, but *some* women," he reiterated, terminating the conversation.

Soon the capable soldiers of Gwynllyw's Hundred arrived at the base of Boch Rhiw Cam, ready to breach the wooden spires that surrounded Talgarth. Their smitten leader's disposition was regret and resolve.

Regret that he had to engage in arms of any kind after twenty years of peace.

Resolve that a tyrannical father, petty and power-mad, would no longer divide the lovers.

The three Round Table Companions could still see Gwladys. Her arms waved frantically, her motions easily confused from afar.

Excitement?
Instruction?
Fear?

Waving and pointing. Pointing and waving.

A deep, elongated and vibratory beat drummed. And then a rattle.

More waving. Desperate waving.

The drumming intensified; familiar horns gave instruction spoken in music.

"Ravens!" Bedwyr cried.

"And not just so—rather, the Hosts of Maelgwn! The lady's arms are begging retreat!"

Cai started screaming for Gwynllyw to withdraw, searching for his steed in a hurried, upset fog of mind.

"They cannot hear us from up here." Arthur's was face ashen, filled with colorless shame. "I climbed too high. Gwenhwyfar haunted me from the grave, and I pulled us from the range where we might do good for our kinsmen."

Cai had found his steed and his fellows' besides, and they made haste.

It was so; Gwladys was doing all to wave off her betrothed abductor.

The Hosts of Maelgwn were but fifteen. *Fifteen professional killers who had seen real and ongoing combat for the sum of their youth. These were hard men; these were amongst those who had won the Saxon Wars for Cymru.* Each was aged above fifty, but fought with the vigor of a young warrior.

Though none were tall as cedars, as their master, each member of his Hosts were *as him.* The style, the movements, the invincibility. It was uncanny and rumored unnatural that there were so many emulations of the Bloodhound Prince. *And he had hundreds more in addition to these.*

But these were sufficient for the battle at hand.

As Maelgwn had moved on from the location, he was not present to give strong instruction and reminder of cautious and careful blows — of mercy and quarter. Without their lord to bid them behave, these Northmen slew the Silures with strokes and slashes empowered by the anger and rage reserved for the Long Knife, not for their own Cymry.

Fifteen killed two hundred. One hundred remained when Cai, Bedwyr and the sandy-haired, blue-eyed, fabled king at last arrived.

Gwynllyw bore a hurt upon his left arm, and his bloody cough revealed broken ribs. He did not judge the Round Table Fellows for the tardiness, thinking them to have been in the rear lines, else in the chaos of the fight, all along.

Arthur gave some confession, concealing more than he revealed. "The spirit in those hills detained us; forgive me, brother. In the space of one hour, with your life you shall be."

"Nothing to forgive, Emperor. Gratitude and thanksgiving that you rescued us from that villain, and have provided us hope that we may marry. I owe you all, O just and pure king, along with the renowned Cai and the indomitable Bedwyr!"

"Can you ride, old warrior?"

"I can, lord," he responded. "Only not well." The greying warrior-monk was anguished, bleeding and broken.

"Cadog is one of your own," Arthur offered an encouraging smile, "*and he is one of my own.*" He motioned to the Round Table knight. "Conduct him some yards hence, and encompass him with nine swords, that he might witness the remains of the day. We will deliver this damsel!" Excalibur was unsheathed, the ring and song of the Sword of Power overcoming the battle drums of Maelgwn.

Three corralled fifteen, allowing the remaining one-third of Gwynllyw's soldiers to breach the spires and extract the princess with great ease. King Brychan retreated with his guard, opting to renew swords another day.

"Hearken!" Arthur hollered. "They will counter,

neither slashing nor swinging first. And their diagonal they will not break. See to it that you do the same. Be their mirror! Be their mirror!"

Bedwyr continued to master fighting in an inverse, left-handed stance. Illtud, who was a master of leverage and the relational impacts of weights and measures and force, had designed a sword that the Round Table Knight could wield with one hand, never needing to add the supportive weight and strength of the other. The distribution of weight achieved gave the approximate force and reach of a longsword, only with the dexterity of a dagger.

Assuming that deformity would equate to an easy kill, hubris consumed one of the Hosts, who abandoned his teaching and rushed upon Bedwyr.

The Raven's head rolled, spinning thrice and lighting at the feet of his fellows.

Arthur's three opponents were more calculated, precise, and difficult to overcome. The heat of battle had distracted the Iron Bear's broken heart; he felt recovered, healthy and strong. Whether false or temporary, the recovery served him well, for his opponents *were as mirrors. And the opponent in the mirror can neither be dodged, nor struck, tackled, nor run through.*

Excalibur clipped the heel of one, causing him to withdraw *(and Arthur was glad that a soul was spared, desperately hoping that this elite soldier would one day make his charges under the wavy red dragon banner once more)*, but the other two fought on.

Brute force wins some battles, and skill wins more. Strategy with skill translates into almost certain victory. However, when the scales are even—brute force equal, skill equivalent, strategy identical—'tis one attribute that determines the victor.

Wind of lung.

For lovers and fighters, he who lasts longest wins. Many skilled lovers are laughed out the bedchamber one minute after they enter. Likewise, many who grapple possess knowledge of forty arm-locks and fifty holds to subdue a man, yet are winded in one minute and find themselves panting—and pinned.

King Arthur was fifty and four, and fatigue should have made his steel heavy and his movements slow. Rather, his verve only burgeoned as the conflict was prolonged. The Merlin had imparted to him secret methods on how to keep his heart (that muscle of flesh and not the spirit of the man) rate to differ little whether resting or running. He had learned this secret forty years ago, and it had enabled him to win countless protracted matches in games of skill, versus giants and hags, and when locked in real combat upon the field of battle.

The Hosts of Maelgwn did run long, but Arthur longer. Where Excalibur, and its wielder, was concerned, one tired error, no matter how minute, could mean death. And for the mighty men of Gwynedd, two more needless souls were added to the heap: a growing stack of bodies charged to the account of Arthur's offenses and Maelgwn's loins.

Having finished them, Excalibur paired with Cai's club to fell the remnant.

Victory.

But the wages were great.

"There remains no ambiguity. The Chieftain Brychan is as the gatekeeper between the North and South; and he is wholly devoted to Mordred, to Rome." Arthur sorrowed as he panned over the Ravens, lying dead or gurgling the last gasps and rattles of death all about the spires and gates of Talgarth. A heavenly fortress and manor carved in wood, a dwelling of repose, hunting, merriment; a place to cease from vocation and appreciate the romantic beacons. *Blood stains cannot be removed from woodwork, nor the soil cleansed when watered with native blood; the Blessed Isles herself cries out that the Titans Arthur and Lancelot soon end their madness.*

"This will not soon end," Arthur stated plainly. "Neither can we suffer the enemy to establish himself so close to Caerleon. The hilltop ring guards should have easily noticed the swell of military activity here," he complained.

"Too many experienced watchman perished by the fiery mouth of the cosmic dragon," Bedwyr responded.

"I know," Arthur conceded, and sighed. "We must train new watchmen rapidly. Moreover, we cannot suffer this war to be fought here. Our numbers are depleted, our people morose. It must not be so. We will give pursuit, the terminal battle of this war to be contested in the North."

***

Arthur, Bedwyr and Cai returned with doubled obsession to the matter of raising, training and preparing their army.

Gwynllyw and Gwladys married immediately, conceiving a son. So thankful were they that Cadog had shielded and sheltered them (for he had conducted them safely to Gwynllyw's modest cell, and then remained, toiling with his own tools, hands and sweat to transform the dwelling into an abode befitting a dazzling and enterprising woman like Gwladys) that they called the newborn Cadwg, meaning *'battle glory'*, a variant of the original Round Table Knight's own name. Cadoc was greatly honored, finding joy in that babes in every cantref were called Arthur, but few were christened with his namesake.

CHAPTER 12
Finalizing the Lists
Urien Denied Again

May
AD 537

Some bards, using numerology and a smidge of theatre to teach and preserve the histories of the Cymry, cite but three souls escaping the Battle of Camlan (that fateful and dread pitch where Arthur and Mordred engaged at last) with their souls; others sing of seven; yet others twenty-four and two (matching in count the original Round Table Fellowship), that the death of one Administration hailed the beginning of the new.

Not discarding pedagogy for the cause of precision, 'tis true that the survivors, both among the faithful Britons and among the deceivers who found pleasure in opportunity and sophistry, giving their swords to the pleasure of Mordred the Traitor, were scant. However, many champions and heroes of the Age were not part of the census, counting as neither dead nor living, for they abstained from the battle itself.

The men and women of the fading generation,

Arthur's generation, who had defended the sovereignty of Cymru, had paid a wage that wrought a life of despair, night-terrors, fits, incontinence, shakes and insanity. Their fractured condition had been caused primarily by engaging in gory and vile combat when in the flower and formation of youth—fourteen being the age by custom and necessity.

For this Civil War, Arthur refused to repeat the requirement and, to the credit of those confederated against him, so did his foes. Only warriors above twenty and five battled at Camlan.

Peredur and Gwrgi, the youthful Grail questers, were withheld, lacking years. Likewise Trystan.

Whereas some were too young, the Senior Monarch, Meurig, was persuaded to abstain from Camlan, with much protest, on account of having *too many* years. He had returned his sword to Llyn Fawr after suffering the injury that had brought fear (whether of superstition or substance) to the Royal Clans that the harvest, on account of his pierced loins, might fail. The wonderful commander had carried himself with a limp for the past forty years, but in all other measures of a man he had fully recovered. None would protest his assumption of a temporary office as King of Glamorgan should Arthur fall at Camlan. For this cause he would remain in Caerleon. *However, by those ancient decrees, he could never again serve as the Pendragon or High King of the Blessed Isles.*

Gildas the Scribe was ordered to remain at Neath, charged to continue penning his histories and registers. Gildas adored Arthur as a father, but he likewise adored his father by blood, with whom Arthur would soon war. Therefore Gildas was thankful to remain neutral, burying his head in scrolls and parchments far from the crooked river, rocky hills and waterfalls that fed the field of Maes-Camlan.

Mark remained on the Continent and would not be counted amongst the participants at Camlan. Not so his foes Hoel and Gwythyr, but Amwn Ddu, who is the *Black Knight* in the epic poetry of the Cymry, was strategically held from the field.

Arthur's older brothers were monks and no warriors, and monks they remained (though Frioc was privily developing ambition as he witnessed the chaos and calamity of the rulers, thinking, as many do, *I could govern for the better than these*) and many other Saints—and Sinners clothed in the vestments of Saints—did not perish at Camlan, *as they lacked the courage to be at Maes-Camlan in the first place.*

The noble Rhun ap Maelgwn Gwynedd agonized for two moons, eating little and sleeping less. Llongborth had given him a first-person witness to what would come to pass: fathers slaying sons, brothers slaying brothers, Cymry in league with Picts, Saxons improving in both technique and presentation. His witness was sufficient. He did not consult his father, neither druid nor bishop, and in the end, grieved with trepidation and uncertainty, he sent a message to King Arthur, informing him that he would lend two-thirds of his men—who, by individual election and full persuasion of mind, chose to continue with the Silures—but that he and the remaining one-third (including the sons of Rhun) would remain in the north, ensuring that a strong vein in the lines and branches of the Royal House of Cunedda would continue, though Maelgwn might fall.

Arthur accepted the Raven's offer and sent blessings to his ally Rhun; bidding him Godspeed, beseeching him to rest from his distress, not begrudging his choice.

***

Arthur summoned Urien and his son Owain, inviting them to join the Pendragon for cider and custard pastries in the library—a favorite refuge for thought, reflection, strategy and solace for the king. Rebuilding the Round Table was not a priority when the army lacked armor and the people lacked supplies for basic daily living. Also, the king favored the spot because his wizard had returned to him here.

And Merlin did now join him, as did Meurig and Bishop Dyfrig.

Urien, coy, wise, grizzled, instantly knew the ambition of the summons when he saw the inner circle of Arthur's inner circle puffing upon their pipes, thickly filling the library with the smoke of meddling in the lives of other men.

"No." Urien objected ere his hand lifted from the iron ring fastened on the door.

"There now, my friend." The Iron Bear made efforts of consolation. "Drink here with us; elsewise let us ride to Lodge Hill."

"No." Not yelling, but directionally louder.

"Please, brothers, sit." Arthur cocked his head

to the right, blue eyes welling with empathy, but honed with resolve.

"No!" This one a yell. A few old tomes creaked in response.

Owain, usually of hot temperament and reactive disposition, seeing that Urien was surrounded by Elders who would not be swayed, sought to cool his father. "Please, Da—"

"No! No! No!" It was followed by a steam of inarticulate cursing in tongues and diction older than the Merlin himself.

Presently the same rose.

"You are younger than Arthur; your lands are in the North. Should your brother Llew and the Traitor prevail, your father will surely negotiate a peaceful ongoing alliance with you." Rings of smoke sailed across the book-filled room, as a sailing vessel glides towards the setting sun. "Whether the Council of Nine scheme and conspire to beguile these shores, or whether the Saxons seek to expand by sword, or by fornication as they do now in Lloegyr, a remnant of what once was must remain, lest the future shadow hide the past in a blanket of dark lies and revision."

"The son of Meurig ap Tewdrig, the Emperor and Lord, Arthur, savior of the Britons, will take the head of Cynfarch Oer—whom you designate as *my father*—and Llew will follow him down into Hell!"

"May it be as you say." Arthur's voice broken. "Nevertheless, you and Owain, along with one third of your own..." the king was a friend first, and struggled to finish the edict, "...will not join us when June arrives and the Knights of Old drive north to face the menace of the Ages."

Urien was of stocky build but at the same time of great height, being a full head taller than Arthur. He had auburn and yellow hair, which was wild and curly upon his brow, but neatly tied into a dozen leather and jewel-decorated braids that fell about his shoulders. His beard was profound, and likewise braided. He was the type of knight that seemed to live in his armor, to sleep in his armor, and to take hold of every moment as if it were a dragon to slay, well pleased to one day die in his armor.

A hard man. A man of war. A man of order, of faith and of loyalty.

Owain had only witnessed his father weep once. And now the tears returned, for the same cause.

"I missed Mynydd Baeden, deployed on some vain quest to find this misplaced druid." Urien was frustration incarnate. "And now he prances back into our camp with the frolic and twirl of the water-sprites and I am made to miss the Siege of Mordred."

Merlin was not offended, knowing that Urien had given the whole of his life, another warrior hatched at fourteen, to the cause of unity, freedom and defense of Cymru. Urien did not relent, continuing to lash out at the wizard, even as his moustache became comically matted by tears and the issue of nose that accompanies crying.

"And where were you, Merlin? Give my quest, which was not voluntary, meaning—for surely your quest, which was at your whim, must have been to save Arthur himself!" Urien chose an extreme, not expecting the candor of response.

"It was to save Arthur himself. And I have not yet saved him, nor delivered him out of harm. For this cause have I returned."

Merlin's enigmatic words quieted the room.

Arthur wept. Urien wept. The three Elders made efforts at stoicism.

"When my chapter in the Songs hath ended, Urien will still be slaying Saxons, I promise." Arthur's words.

After a great pause and a nervous adjusting of his cape, a fidget with beard and brow, and the alleviation of his tears, Urien fixed his moustache, allowed his shoulders to slump, and calmed himself.

"What will you do if Owain and our Ravens arrive in a wave of thirty thousand? Will you turn your arrows from Mordred and loose them upon us? Will you refuse our aid? Or surrender?" The questions were a half-portion of jest.

"If it keeps you alive, and hope for the Summer Kingdom alive, then I will send Merlin to Brittany presently, and command you to go find him." The Bear of Glamorgan smiled. "But he is old, so sit with me and enjoy cider, giving him the lead by a week or two."

The heroes of Mynydd Baeden managed to turn tears into laughter, and mourning into fellowship. Two more of the original twenty-four and two would part the Fellowship, by design and by tactic.

Urien left his youngest son, Pasgen, to receive fosterage in his ancestral lands of Gwyr, which is in the cantref of Eginawc, in the realm of Deheubarth. Owain and his father and a large retinue parted company with their Round Table

Companions, returning to the Old North; Llew and Caw dared not bring ambush or injury during their journey.

CHAPTER 13
The Summer Kingdom was False, and You Knew

The Lords of the Old North had promoted Mordred's idea many times afore. That Maelgwn should be High King was not a new notion. That which was new was that Maelgwn gave the concept place for consideration.

Maelgwn had witnessed, being side by side with the Pendragon during the unfolding, unraveling events, Arthur's *look* when they had caught Mordred and Gwen II in adultery— performing *the very act of adultery.* Arthur had not ceased being Arthur when he had fed the queen to his mastiffs; rather, in Maelgwn's opinion, his lifelong friend, and Sovereign, had been lost instantly, signified by *that look.*

Was that the look I wore all those years ago when bewitched in Avalon's sacred orchard? Does madness enter in an instant and immediately signify its birth with the expression of that look?

From age sixteen to the very moment of *the look,* Maelgwn had acquiesced to the following:

Arthur was more honorable—*until now.*
Arthur was more stable—*no longer.*

Arthur was less blemished by scandal, a ruler beyond reproach—*reproach and defame aplenty now loomed over the head of the Silure.*

Arthur was a man of reason, never under the spell of passion or impulse—*save when he hurled her from the tower to the hounds below.*

Arthur could better unite and galvanize the Tribes—*Rome versus our ancient relic of a church, the druids gnashing and gnawing upon the Dynion Hysbys, every tribe and household at variance under the reign of the son of Meurig.*

Arthur had better command of the customs and law—*I have twenty and four bards to help me with this, even if Taliesin has forsaken me.*

Arthur was the Prophesied One. It was his destiny. *Prophecies fail, portents oft interpreted by what the Seer wants instead of what the Seer sees.*

Maybe it is to time to think on Lancelot and Head of the Dragons.

The estranged Champion of the Round Table thought hard on these things, looking at Arthur in a new light, forgetting his own darkness.

Two of his other seven other-selves manifested to remind him.

Did King Arthur slay his uncle for three minutes betwixt the legs of his wife?

Did the Son Pendragon exhaust the flesh of youthful boys, brimming with life and virility, and then slay them that their protests or political leverage in the scandal might be buried in the Deep, silenced by the dirt?

Did the rightful High King betray a tribe of Picts, PICTS THAT ADORED AND WORSHIPPED US, that he might lie with the queen?

The Merlin gave you one charge, one command, one

duty. Proclaim it in somber recollection. Proclaim it!

The splinter of Lancelot taunted Maelgwn in this regard for the space of fifteen minutes.

Proclaim it!

"He charged me protect Galahad my son above all else. For in Galahad were all the wrongs of both Arthur and Lancelot made right. The north and the south united, and Camelot secure for a hundred generations."

And did you meet your charges?

"No."

No! Instead you distracted yourself with women, and jealousy, and self-aggrandizing madness! The Madness of Maelgwn shattered this kingdom, not the failings of the just and great king, or the manipulations of the Church, or the conspiracy of the satanic elite. You, High King of Cymru? You were to guard Galahad! Instead he chased after relics and lost his life to empty superstition! Taliesin said well, 'You are the ruin of Cymru'!

"Maelgwn—"

Interrupted by one of his bards, the Bloodhound Prince reassembled, decided that he did not deserve to rule, undecided whether he *wanted* to reign.

"I asked for solace." A dreadful, low voice.

"Forgive me, but urgency demands I disquiet you."

Maelgwn grimaced and nodded, for truly there remains no privacy during a time of war. He motioned for the bard to report.

"Warriors from Glamorgan overcame Talgarth, causing Brychan to flee. Many of your elect have fallen. The stronghold in the South—lost."

"We were discreet in that stationing. Surely

word of our trespass so near Arthur will have come to the king's ears." Maelgwn assumed Arthur and his Fellows were ever occupied with training his inexperienced army, aghast that an offensive, small battle had been fought so soon after Llongborth.

"Cai was there," the bard stated. "Bedwyr too."

"Cai would not leave his lord's side. He is a protector and no commander," Maelgwn responded, shrugging his marble shoulders, his hands opening flat and elevating to the heavens, then clenching as an eagle snatches its kill upon the brook. "Arthur was with them!"

"Aye," answered the bard. "The bards say that he fought as a youth upon the field, that Excalibur twirled and whistled; that he was as a god with lightning bending and bowing to the will of his hands."

The jealous version of Lancelot manifested, capturing control of the host. "And what will the bards say when I slay the Lightning Bearer?"

Filled with fear, the bard responded, "That the Grandson of Cunedda has at last restored the diadem that has belonged here from the days of Brutus, long usurped by the dark tribes in the South."

The flattery allowed the replaceable bard to keep his head, and Maelgwn hastened the training of those opposed to Arthur, hoping desperately that the cold would abate, or at least give pause; that those declared against the Pendragon, dispersed over the whole of the Island, might have opportunity to leave their homes and voyage north where the efficiency of preparation, and of census, might be a thousandfold more efficient.

That Arthur had anticipated the placement of a garrison in Talgarth, and exterminated it, gave Maelgwn great cause for alarm. No further operations would be launched in the midlands, and certainly not in the south. Rather, he would prepare a defensive strategy, knowing in his bowels that the king was readying to face those confederated against him far away from Caermelyn and Caerleon; the Civil War would be conducted in the northern realms of Cymru.

***

Mid-May
AD 537

Queen Onbrawst and King Meurig had taught their oldest son, both by the behavior they modeled and by direct instruction, that physical romance—kissing, holding hands, and intimacy—must be connected with love, lest an empty carnality develop in a man or a woman.

Though bewitched from his youth by the dark-haired Gwenhwyfar II, Arthur for the greater part lived these values, having had very few lovers in his fifty and four years.

Seeing the damsel whom he had perceived as the sole and exclusive love of his life willingly and hotly ravaged as an animal (enthralled by, and returning to the ravaging to, her true love) tormented the king. His knee ailed. He fought a slight cough that would not surrender his lungs, and his handsome face showed more than a few new wrinkles (though his appearance was that of a man in his early thirties, his sadness begat a false perception of aging, and the ugliness thereof).

Convinced full that he would now never enjoy what his parents possessed, a season in Arthur's life began where he chose to be as the world and dabble in fornication. After returning from the incident with Gwladys, he slept with three women in three days.

The polite, gentle, and *loving* (though absent of *love*) man remained, for he was kind, careful and engaging with each, building them with warm words and doting compliments.

After each occurrence, at the very moment the lass would robe and depart his chamber, an emptiness seven times worse after the act than before would overtake the king, causing him to make haste in dressing, hiding himself in his formal armor. He would then rush to the shrine of his first wife, Gwenhwyfar ferch Cywryd, *Gwenhwyfar the Red*.

Her place of rest was the chapel called after Saint Julian, a martyr slain in Gwent in Roman times. The malaise of freezing and unpredictable winds had not allowed a full reconstruction, but her stone sarcophagus was complete. It had been hewn with devotion, adoration, and regality, and expressed an artistic humility that was a perfect and lasting representation of the person whose body made permanent abode therein.

But Gwenhwyfar's spirit was not there. A stateswoman of faith in Christ and unwavering patriotism, a splendid Sovereign, and a better mother. She had been wholly devoted to her children. Then the Saxon Wars had broken her spirit, the act of surviving her own sons murdering her whilst she lived; a human shell hung upon a ghost haunting a nunnery.

Mordred had taken nothing that was not already gone and, in her final days, her last acts of wisdom, grace and reconciliation had imparted strength and a familiar comfort to Arthur, preparing him to once again do what he must, and what none else could. *To murder another son.*

And so Arthur would warm his flesh with a damsel by night, and seek consolation and support from his deceased wife by day, kneeling before her grave, lost in deep contemplation. He donned the one-piece helm, fashioned in the Corinthian style (for the Britons come from that kind of stock, being Trojans) where the eyes and nose were fully encased, and the cheekbones as well, leaving but the lower lip and throat exposed. Arthur's helmet was silver, enameled with a blue as midnight, which matched the tunic and leather beneath his heavy armor. His cape was the crimson that all Royal Clans the world over seem to favor. He presented himself to the queen polished and shined. The image of the Blessed Mother, debossed upon a small oblong shield, was fastened to the left shoulder, the Iron Bear sigil about his neck served as meeting point for the ties of his cape; the Sword of Power was thrust deep, more than halfway up its shaft, into the clay floor at the base of her shrine.

"One more time, O wife of my youth, great friend, proper and true queen, one more time I will do what I must, though it render me without issue."

Arthur felt a great shadow behind him, cast by a dark faerie. Having no need to rise and validate with his eyes what his bosom already felt, a whisper vibrated up through the sides of his helmet: "Sister."

Gwyar, in this moment fused fully with *the Morrigan*, was raging with anger older than the Lakes, indignation deeper than the Bottomless Pit, a righteous fury that rattled and shook, an incensed, caged demon jerking and tugging violently at the bars that gate Hell.

Disregarding the greeting, the Sorceress Morgaine cut to the quick: "Nay, you will not."

A broken, disjointed exchange of phrases and unilateral comments ensued—the kind that lacked order or sequence. The way that siblings long to resolve disputes but run round the issues instead of addressing them directly: in this manner did they speak. He remained kneeling, behind the midnight blue *mask*, and she stood behind him; whether in this moment she was three and a half feet or thirty stories tall (or at once, both), Arthur could not discern.

"My sons are Gareth, Gaheris, Ogyrfan, Gwalchmai and Mordred. Four of the five in preference choose you, their uncle, King Arthur of Caerleon, over their father Llew. Gwalchmai is fallen to Lancelot. Would you see the rest follow him to an early grave?"

"Women know things," Arthur said.

"I sought you out, hoping against hope that you would show Mordred mercy. In the place of mercy, you slaughtered an entire house of my cousins by marriage, of friends of our youth there employed. You slaughtered my grandchildren!" Thunder crackled.

"You knew." Arthur had no fear of the Sorceress Morgaine.

"Why did you not order me to Lodge Hill, that we might congress before actions so rash, so murderous, so *UnArthur?*"

"Twenty years of peace through the Isles, but not in my own home! Twenty years a fool!" Arthur's voice was animated, rising and falling, but he was as a statue. "The sacred rite was to prove I was fit to rule, yet my seed begets only treachery and perversion."

"Gwalchmai gave his life—for you. He is gone. Galahad is gone, Llacheu and Amr too. Would you have every fighting-aged man under forty a corpse? Would you have the old Four Chords rule well beyond our season, governing over a pile of younger bones?"

"But three chords remain, for your rival Gwenhwyfar's blood feeds the soils of Cymru." This time, he responded to the fragmented statement.

"My rival!" This missile found its mark.

Arthur could feel a shift in the wind, his armor conducting heat to his flesh; soon he was a fount of perspiration trapped in a metal box. Yet anger continued to override fear. Fixed in a contemplative bow upon one knee, supporting his weight upon the hilt of Excalibur, he remained.

"You loved Lancelot, and she loved"— Arthur measured his words—"another." More measuring. "She sat upon a throne, having my ear and my attention, whilst you mastered herbs and fought with priests over enchanted relics. Lo, I declare, she was your rival."

"She was a whore and the ruin of Britain!"

"And you knew!"

"I love you!" Stone fell from stone, the power of her words making the chapel ruin *more ruined*. Then she shrank; the sweaty king, feeling her defeat and her suffering, rose and turned.

Little Gwyar ferch Onbrawst and Meurig the healer, protector, mother and patriot, stood before the king. He fully armed, she in two pieces of brown leather (a top and trousers) fastened by a heavy knotted rope—the attire one wears, be they man or woman, when a hard ride of great distance is required.

Sister.
Advisor.
Companion.
Sacred lover.
Friend.

The angry Bear slowly removed his helmet, and the two Silures looked long at each other, recollecting and reenacting much history and countless deeds in the looking glass of the other's eyes.

"I love you too, Gwyar, more than any person who liveth."

"Any save your half-alive, half-apparition wizard." She smirked.

"Yes; second-most, then." Arthur patted his brow. "What exactly *is he?*"

"I only know that he and I meddle and manipulate and do our best to support you, Arthur. You are the hope of Cymru. And of mankind. We succeed, and we err. I did know."

Though the dispositions had cooled, the confirmation was as white-hot coals upon Arthur's head. He stayed his tongue, and did not respond in anger; the burning truth cracked as an egg, running in every direction down his face, then onto his chest and at last running off onto the floor below.

"I concealed the matter, and it almost destroyed me, bringing more shame than our *incident* in the cave. Putting the Harlot to the knife discreetly would have destroyed you, so happy and in love, the Summer Kingdom thriving. My own son, OUR own son, I could not slay, leaving me only to tell you, or for mercy's sake let us have our season in the sun."

"Mercy and secrets. Let's examine what mercy and secrets have over these many years wrought," Arthur began. "The wages of mercy upon Cedric is the imminent end of the Lloegyr from the face of the earth, and the rise of Saxons born not in the Nordic Wilds but a day's ride to the east of this very spot!" Arthur watched a few rays of sun, resilient and unwavering, brave their way through broken glass and charred wood, lighting beautifully upon the stone box that housed the queen. "For mercy's sake, Mark menaces the Continent. Dispossessed of land and cattle but not slain, that *mercy* has grown an army, here a little, there a little, that could shift power to the Franks and, worse, drive our cousins into the Sea. And his hooks in Cornwall could trouble our borders besides, should we survive the Civil War and be so fortunate as to draw breath and have heartbeat to entertain troubles." A few more rays touched upon Gwyar's raven hair and illuminated specks of gold in her large eyes. "Secrets taught Lancelot that he was above the Laws and Customs of the Tribes, and gave license to his madness. Mercy and secrets would I have none — only immediate justice and transparency. This is what I have sworn, and this is what I beseeched and begged of my companions, including you, sister."

Gwyar reached up, straining to reach her brother's shoulder-shield. At last she was able to trace a few lines around the image's outline. "Some secrets are good, brother. Did we protect the Mother of the Lord so long in vain?"

"Well, no—" Arthur began to frame a response.

"And mercy is its own reward, as saith both the Christian God and the benevolent goddesses of old. Foreswear neither mercy, nor the selective wisdom as to when it is meet to conceal a thing, Lord Arthur, for these are the hard prerogatives of princes; and you are the best of princes."

"Did my half-dead wizard script these things for you, sister?" Arthur smiled, his hand tracing the outline atop Gwyar's tiny fingers. "She was wholly dedicated to mercy, and we love the Blessed Lady."

"We very much love her, in spite of the priests' blasphemy and abuse and spite-filled treatment. And her walk and every moment was wholly given to mercy, grace, and truth. I find these things not in the Church that claims her, nor in the Creator God whose *Jewish King Arthur* she bore, but—"

"The second Merlin, Taliesin, has shared with me much about the distant and silent God and the purpose of His Son. Should we again have an hour of peace upon these lands, I would share his *secrets* with you."

"Mercy and secrets." She smiled, seeing the conversation come full circle.

"Aye, and cider." Regrettably, Arthur discontinued as brother and assumed his office for the next part of their discourse. "Gwyar," he began, "even were there no scandal associated with Mordred's birth, Gwalchmai's accusations, or Lancelot's guilt—and even if my offenses and missteps with the Champion of the Britons had never been—this war *would have come.* There is a force behind the Saxon Tribes, a force greater than and indeed controlling Rome, a force that our local diverse sects and colleges bow to as some enlightened guild when, of a truth, they are of darkest evil. Because Rome is as a toy on a string to this *force,* even now giving blankets and coal and victuals to the faithful in our own villages, using the leverage of feigned help in a crisis to control the masses, this war was inevitable.

"And the South must win. The Roman Church would rid the Isles of your gods and goddesses by assimilation—"

"And your bishops would banish us by statute!" she protested.

"Let us not take up again Vivien and Dyfrig's debate at this time. For the survival of us all, the Round Table Fellowship must both wage this war, and prevail."

"I will not let you kill him." Gwyar was resolute. "He is our son."

"If he falls into the controlling hands of the Council and their masked master, what then?"

"We Ladies" (here she referred to herself as

the Lady of Avalon and Vivien, the Lady of the Lake) "are good at hiding things."

"He is neither horn nor scabbard, treasure box nor chalice, but a man of flesh and bones. We must prevail, no matter the personal cost."

"I will not suffer you to slay our son!"

"Will you strike me down, as reports say of Maelgwn?"

Morgaine of the Faeries was unable to strike down Arthur Pendragon.

On the merits and mysteries of God's plan for the Ages, the otherworldly thing could not harm *the real king* (for Arthur was not a ruler promoted by the will of Man, but rather was set to fulfill some part of the Great Conversation, and the Consummation of All Things). Therefore, he could strike her down and not rather the reverse, though she be far exceeding in power. Knowing some measure of these things, her answer concealed much.

"I tried to prevent this Civil War, but did not slay him; neither will I bring my brother, whom I love, to be undone." A pleasant response, chased by eyes set aflame for the warning that followed: "Now this is the final time I give plea, prayer and warning. I will not suffer you to kill Mordred; and from the pitch of war, refrain to place Gareth, Gaheris and Ogryfan!"

"Round Table Knights all! They will join the company, lead men and add more songs of praise and heroism to their names, bringing the confederacy of traitors to bow and beg—and, by the might of the Sword of Power, be scattered to the four corners of the world never again to make war upon these exhausted Isles!"

"Brother, I will call the Dragon. His breath will I direct to envelop and shelter my sons, creating a protection of confusion, that neither lance nor arrow shall find them. ALL of my sons. And the mist shall encompass and hide you as well." Morgaine was determined to this, intervening against the peculiar rules and laws that bound her kind to doctrines of non-interference. She would find a way, though the heavens fall.

"Have not the People presently had their fill of dragons?" Arthur demanded. "You will at once protect both Mordred, who fights with Rome, and the remnant of your sons, who stand with me?"

"I will not suffer my sons to perish."

"Your aims approach treachery, sister." Arthur freed Excalibur from the floor. It gave a metallic hiss, sparking as he freed it from the clay and stone. Sibling squabbling resumed. "In your *mercy and secrecy,* you knew these dark days would come. Whether it was a good thing to delay them, or a grievous sin in delaying this hour, we cannot say. I hate that you allowed me to live a lie! But I know you sought only to protect me, and give our tribes an age of peace and prosperity. My anger kindles, but the Merlin's lessons ever remind me, and us, to press on towards the mark ahead, not looking back at decisions for good or ill that brought us here." King Arthur then ordered Morgaine of the Faeries away. "In a fortnight we assemble and ride north to finish this. If you yet respect your Sovereign, exile thyself to Avalon and there remain until the dead have been buried and the lost mourned. Then return to Caermelyn and reconcile with me. Then let us yet embrace in ongoing and grievous mourning, and after this mourn more. When the sorrow is spent, we will draw breath yet and, seeing that the sun yet rises over the valleys and the birds sing and swoop over the lakes and brooks, we will heal this land."

"Into exile I go, obeying the Emperor of the Britons." Morgaine was not shaken by Arthur's attempts to see her physically removed from the scene. "Thunder and lightning, rains and MIST I can cast from anywhere, most especially from the Sacred Isle."

Siblings change subjects when subjects become painful. Rather than continue a circular, unwinnable dispute, Arthur succumbed to jest, that one last fair memory be created for the two heroes.

"Sister, what have you done with Cai? I can no more lift my face from the wash basin except a hand-towel be at the ready by the intrusive brute." Arthur laughed. "You didn't slay the king's Steward, did you?"

Gwyar allowed a smile to escape. "Herbs. The potion I gave him has given your childhood protector the best sleep he's had in forty years!" The smile gave way to a mutual laugh, then a strong embrace of merriment.

Arthur would do what he must. Morgaine of the Faeries the same. The faerie withdrew from the king, who immediately made for his helmet *mask*, returning to quiet contemplation at the side of Queen Gwenhwyfar.

CHAPTER 14
My Heart Turns to Camelot as the Floor Around Me Burns

Mid-May
AD 537

Gwenhwyfar applied a soft knock to the door; though it was barely a rustle, her parents knew the sound.

Gwythyr rolled to his side that he might face Alienor, who feigned sleep. Tickling her ribs and tugging an ear, he began to rouse her, then made her fully awake with a wet, childish kiss. "Your turn, my Swan."

"Gwythyr!" she protested. "'Tis your turn, and she is her father's child."

"You only disown her when it is the middle of the night. 'Tis YOUR turn, and by the by, she is the very image of her mother."

Slight knock. Rustle. More ironic mousey sounds came forth from the Lioness of Lyonesse at their bedchamber door.

"I am daughter to both! Hearken and let me in, I pray."

"She can command thousands with the wink

of an eye, can cause wells to dry at the snapping of a finger, yet she whines and whimpers outside our door," Gwythur goaded the girl.

"I cannot sleep!" she exclaimed, still a mouse.

"She'll not relent," Alienor mused.

"She'll be out there until cock crows." Gwythyr made jesting protest.

"Da!" The Mouse-Lion heard the ongoing mocking.

Gwythyr protested about the hour, as parents do, and dressed, at last presenting himself at the door.

Before he could fully greet the princess she burst in and jumped upon the bed, then took her father's original spot, lying next to her mother.

"I supposed I could sit upon the footstool." Gwythyr sighed, and then laughed.

"Respite escapes me. My mind is disquieted. My head races in circles, running as children round the Maypole, not ceasing or easing. Is it true? Will I really lodge in Gwent two nights hence?"

"Aye, daughter, but brace yourself, for the golden city is in ruins and the people despair much," said Gwythyr.

"Turrets and towers, founts and theatres, minstrels and markets. These things do not render a city great. Rather, it is the liberty they stand with, such unrelenting resolve that ignites the flame of freedom within the bosom of every man and draws us to adore them. And that fire was kindled in our own lifetime in the south-east of Cymru, in that place we call Camelot. It is no trivial thing to be alive during a dispensation of heroes and legends. In my eyes, I know I will see it as it was. I will weep with honor for what it gave me, gave us, and rejoice with a forward-looking, longing hope that its best days may return."

"Even while the sun yet hides in his chamber she is stately." Gwythyr was the proudest of fathers.

***

Both parents deeply appreciated the maturity and optimism displayed by the heiress of Brittany, especially in light of the dire turn of events causing the Royal Clans to make haste from the Continent and *repatriate* to Cymru.

Hoel the Good and Gwythyr were losing ground in the protracted battles against Childibert the Merovingian and Mark ap Merichion. Lacking the reinforcement of the three hundred the Round Table Companions had provided was material; both morale and momentum was being lost as they abruptly returned to the Isles.

Moreover, the absence of Derfel upon the field was devastating. The *new Lancelot was in the company of the old*, instead of fighting invaders under the banner of his father. Where battles are concerned, one person can sway the tide, one hero make the difference. *True leadership and success are infectious, as often said the Merlin.*

These two factors were principal in the decision for Hoel, the greater portion of his sons and daughters, and Gwythyr and his whole house, along with other chieftains, bishops and thirty troops, which is nine thousand men, to abandon the sister-cities of Brittany and return to their ancestral homelands in Britain.

Gwythyr faced the truth that Mark would soon defile his very own bed, the women and soldiers soon to soil the baths and pools. There was little concern that the Merovingians or Mark's commanders would burn the villages, or in any way damage the castles, chapels, founts or dykes. Their aim was to conquer and occupy, not raze. Provided that they controlled their Germanic conscripts, the kingdom would be intact when Hoel and Gwythyr returned to restore their land and, one day, place the diadem on the deserving crown of Gwenhwyfar, the Lady of Lyonesse.

As for the residue of the Bretons, Amwn the Black Knight (Arthur's renowned brother-in-law by his sister, Anna) would lead an exile into the magical forests of Broceliande. Though the otherworldly beings who occupied the wood were given to mischief, they had an affinity for the Bretons, as the Bretons were Cymreig. The vastness of Broceliande could conceal thousands; provided their circles and groves were not disturbed, the Fae would be content to host. Sufficient soldiers were left behind to protect against the sweeps and manhunts Mark would surely conduct, but Hoel wagered he would be too busy erecting his new kingdom to be overly bothered with scattered and defeated refugees hiding in huts and tree-houses.

Amwn would serve as Protector of Brittany, keeping as many of the citizens alive as possible until Hoel (and peradventure, Arthur, Cai and Bedwyr themselves) should come again, and liberate them.

***

"Your restlessness comes not by reason of our defeat nor our hastened departure, does it, daughter?" Alienor asked.

"My heart commits treason," Gwenhwyfar responded. "Mother, where I should cry out over our world, which collapses into chaos, I can think ever and only about—"

"Your heart is no traitor. The barn could be on fire whilst you fed the horses and you wouldn't even smell the hay burning, nor feel your boots cooking, when under the consumption of this condition."

"I am the Lady of Lyonesse; no passion consumes me." Gwen made a vain effort at resistance of the open and plain truth.

"Were that 'twas only passion, for passions ebb and withdraw as the moon-tides." A mother's wisdom. "Just verbalize it. Let it out loudly; it may give you rest." A mother's instruction.

"Say it." Now Gwythyr goaded his daughter, making tea for the trio with clanks and clamors of protest and the disquieting of his rest. "Say it"—he served the princess the first cup—"and then"—he handed his beloved wife the second—"get thee back to thine own bed!"

"Well, then." Gwenhwyfar slurped the tea as a child, assuming the immaturity of her accusers. The family roared in laughter. They knew they faced a short but treacherous sail in the morning, a dangerous journey to a land where few had sufficient food for their own families. The worry about feeding nine thousand more would cause unease, and potential strife. Yet the family embraced, and mused, and were merry in the moment, knowing their lives would change forever not many hours hence.

"Well, then." A final gulp emptied the cup. Gwenhwyfar rose from the bed, straightened her gown, and ordered her hair, acting as if she was readying to make a prepared speech to an assembly of elders or bishops.

She paused. Gwythyr of Leon had repossessed his spot in the bed and he and his wife sat against the headboard, leaning forward in anticipation, squeezing their pillows.

"I love him!" Gwenhwyfar declared. "I love him to distraction. The sea boils and the sky falls, and I think only on him. I love him such that it frightens me that I may lose myself."

"Who is the boy?"

Alienor smote her husband with one pillow, then two. "Don't embarrass our girl further, causing her tongue to identify what the whole of our little kingdom knows."

"Arthur," said Gwenhwyfar. When she proclaimed the Bear's name, she felt as if the sun arose anew in her heart, and dark times gave way to the light. "Arthur." And the sun rose again. "I love King Arthur of Camelot, and I shall love only he, forever."

"And we love you." Gwythyr stood and embraced his daughter. "Only corral your love, and let patience guard your precious vessel. For he must first win a war versus an opponent that outmatches him. Should he overcome, and be the victor, only then can he be of equal disposition to love you. And love you he must, else avoid him—though we love him—you must." He spoke not of Mordred, nor Lancelot. A father's wisdom.

***

"See them flee unto the Sea, the beginning of the extermination of the Walles on the Continent." Simon Magus was amused by his rhyme—a sinister self-aggrandizing cackle, amplified by thin black steel. "Son of Merovee, govern well here," admonished The Mask. "And mark thou Mark." More wordplay, more cackling. "After all, he is as crazed in the brain and mad as his father ever was."

Childibert beamed, seeing cowardly Frankish warriors clip at the heels and upon the backs of the last of the Bretons, frantically shoving off on their long platform boats. Some were maimed by chained whips, while others absorbed arrows flung chaotically and maniacally straight up in a blind arc; the invaders made sport, casting lots on how many would fall into huddled groups of women and children. Mercifully, the winds carried most missiles into the sea. But injuries and losses were many, such that foamy blood remained long after the final boat exceeded the sight of the devilish onlookers.

"And now, the Council of Nine likewise departs. Be not tyrannical, but rather kind, that you might earn the people's affection ere you close the fist of dominion over them. That celebratory slaying below," Magus spoke of the brutish behavior by the victorious Franks, "is uncomely. I adore the kills, but be smarter about such things." Every instruction Magus gave the king had the underpins of weighted threats, *for I favor Arthur as our puppet. Be a good second choice, for second choices are come by easily.*

***

Word by messenger was first given to Iddawg of the *exodus* of the Bretons. The lad had settled into the unspoken office of Emissary to the High King. His bloodlust spent, his lies consuming him, his face was either ashen or green at all times. The cataclysm of the comet had created diverse illnesses and maladies, allowing Iddawg a cover for his guilt.

Arthur and Cai were visiting with the Pendragon's uncle, Caradog Freichfras, calling another from the Saxon Wars out of the repose of retirement to once more take up the lance and defend Cymru. Caradog would lead a more permanent sacking of Talgarth, ensuring that Brychan could not recover and rear-flank the Silure-led armies. This was a final and necessary step before the armies rode north, and the interpretation was easy to understand; old Caradog would take the Beacons, and the larger army would move north, meeting the Ravens and their confederacy of Saxons, Picts, and the vagabonds of Mark somewhere above Powys but below Gwynedd.

Iddawg the Pale-Faced Liar, knowing the Iron Bear was absent, trembled as he approached the Merlin, who had vanquished seven ciders whilst sitting at tea with Illtud, for the peculiar Christian druid did ever glare into the boy's soul, and fill him with fright.

"Cornuaille, Vantes, and Leon have fallen, but perhaps their temporary defeat will gain a long-term victory by reason of numbers or arms." Illtud chose optimism, greatly vexed over his kinsmen, presently sailing to a war-torn land filled with sorrow and confusion.

Merlin engaged in the conversation, but his eyes never left the messenger. "I do not disagree," he said, contemplatively.

"You are the greatest war tactician since Caradoc ap Bran, old friend." Illtud sought to edify Merlin, who bore criticism spoken and unspoken due to the perception that his counsel to punish the House of Mordred and shock the north into a cessation of war-making designs had not only failed, but thrice-fold worsened the matter.

The wizard remained as an eagle upon Iddawg.

"Thank you, Illtud. However, my devices and schemes are better than Caradoc's, for I escaped my prison." The men laughed as historical enthusiasts do when none else in the room comprehend the reference.

"Your heretical faith yet concerns me. But I am your friend, your kinsman. Your strategy will be successful this time; faint not, Merlin." As intelligence is weighted, only Taliesin and Merlin were at the level of peer with Saint Illtud. And the respect of a peer was oft given by the schoolmaster.

Merlin saw the bottom of another scrumpy. Then a ninth. Flicking the sediments of the heavenly sup where they had splattered here and there on his beard, the bard rose. Standing, he towered, and towering, he emanated an authority such as a god toys with men as clay chess pieces upon the earth.

"The thing about my last strategy failing," he opened, causing Iddawg to stumble backwards and catch himself upon the stool where the Merlin had but presently sat, "is that it didn't."

My impish lies born of want that Arthur whip the Whelp are found out! The Merlin is no man, but like unto the legends about the seven, nay, ten-foot-tall elves that torture men for ten eternities in their hollow hills and their caverns beneath the lakes. I am undone!

"You look as if Death himself hath come for you, boy." Merlin knelt slowly and Iddawg recoiled, knowing judgment was nigh. Merlin clutched the boy by the nape of his neck, authoritatively, but having no outward malice, and pulled him close. To his own drinking horn. "Sip on this—slowly, not rapidly like the master cider imbiber before you."

"How many legendary names and titles must be given the Merlin?" Illtud jested jealously.

"Well, we have a few for you, bishop." Merlin smiled. "The lad is ill. I pray you give us leave, my friend. Leave me to sit awhile with Iddawg and see to his recovery."

"Of course, I think tea and prayer in the stead of your hard drink will best bring the color back into him—but go to it. I will seek out Cai and Bedwyr, that we prepare to receive Hoel, and we will renew discourse of your schemes and strategy tomorrow." Illtud retired from the company, speculating that Bedwyr might be training in the valleys of Cwmbran, quite near to the Caerleon and the place of their discourse.

As Illtud was out of earshot, Merlin assumed a far different tone. "Why wait until tomorrow? Iddawg the Emissary, let us speak now of my strategy. The one they say failed. But we know the Merlin's strategies never fail, don't we, boy?"

CHAPTER 15
Whos Afraid of Morgaine Le Fay?
Cadfans Change of Heart

As men struggled to forage and hunt, and the ladies had scant success in merchandising or bartering in the village markets, Bishop Cadfan continued his schemes as agent for the Satanic Cult he served. Having previously made use of Mark's soldiers to vandalize and pillage his own parishioner's churches, he then turned to the very people he tortured, taking advantage of their calamity by offering blankets, munitions and food. In return he required that they acquiesce to one simple favor.

The continued deification of Mary, and diminishing of the local goddesses.

Traversing the north, he engaged village elders. If a bishop would allow Cadfan to change the name of their chapel, calling it after Mary to replace Michael, or Paul, or some great Cymreig saint or warrior, the town would eat; else, Cadfan would coldly and expeditiously pack his wagons and leave. Desperate for warmth and food, many churches became *Saint Mary's* in the five short months after the Red Dragon and before the final hours of the Civil War.

The enterprise of rebranding parishes, coupled with his ongoing taunts and hunts to wrest the remaining relics from the Lady of Avalon, rendered the bishop of Enlli exhausted. The travel was arduous and the weather ever in tumult. His foot would never heal, a constant reminder of the wages of treachery against the Iron Bear of Britain.

As the first days of June dawned, Cadfan found himself presently returned from a visit and *conversion* of another Saint Mary's, reposing in Ynys Mon at *the chapel* where resided the coffin where once had slept the Mother of the Lord. Even villains can be overwhelmed; even criminals can come to places of hard reflection when conscience confronts their crimes.

Cadfan made his home in a hermit's cell located to the east of the chapel. He hastened to his bed, his body at full rest whilst his mind would give him none.

Morgaine of the Faeries. For how many long years have you hidden the relics from me? Thy womb is closed, thy childbearing years long past. You could have put Llew away, found love, married anew for happiness instead of political obligation, enjoyed your old sons, and made new babies besides. Instead the prime of your days you have loaned to a God you know not, for a quest you never obliged, for the mother of a Jewish man your kind curse! Why? Why rather not let my Master align with you to charge the talismans and, using them, to rule the world?

Because Pagan and Christian alike know unprecedented evil, and any person who regards his neighbor would die ere he or she let powerful things fall into the hands of maniacs and devils. That is why!

Cadfan shot up in the bed, fevered, the debate between his mind and his spirit spending him. His mouth as cotton, he swallowed and gulped at a bedside pitcher of water, hoping to rehydrate his deserty throat. Then sleep, or sleepless sleep, came again.

Morgaine of the Faeries. Rival. Enchantress. More character resides in one stray strand of your raven's hair than in the sum of my entire constitution. Why do I hate you for what Illtud has done? Why hate I any man? Am I not a Breton? Am I not Cymreig? Has my preference for the doctrines of Rome truly driven me to serve those who would enslave, nay, destroy my kin? What would it be to win? To rule over a field of bones and command councils of headstones? Morgaine is right to hide the Treasures of Britain from me – more so from the Council of Nine. Conviction fell upon his bosom, a weighted lightning bolt from heaven. Again he woke, ill, violently nauseous. Guilt brings forth pungent vomit.

Oak branches quickened and gave scratchy knock upon the chalky wall, rebuking him with a hair-raising scrape and chilling screech. The owls that own the night joined in; a chorus of clamor and judgment. A few hours ere the sun rose he slipped back into slumber. And the convictions continued.

King Arthur. The reason we have liberty to debate and disagree. He only sanctioned Rome when Rome maneuvered to deny him the freedom and power she coveted for herself. He moved against the Dynion Hysbys on the careful, thoughtful authority of several witnesses who implicated them in a plot to murder his friend and overthrow his government. That is not tyranny — rather, justice!

King Hoel Dda. Uncle. Never an unkind word. You provided gold and provision when I and eleven besides departed the Continent to receive schooling at Llaniltud Fawr. What happened there under the ill tides of Illtud was not your doing, neither were you aware of it. Did not Maelgwn Gwynedd have like passions? He wars against you, Uncle, and joins with a perverse, split man. And now you and thousands from our clans are displaced. You bring your bowmen and your swords, and your mystical fighting arts against the North — because the North is against the good.

Groans, tossing and turning.

And Derfel, the new Lancelot. Only minus the madness. You have joined me against reason. Loyalty over evaluation. O, the misplaced vigor of youth! I have led you into the snare. In what manner of world will you fulfill your years? If under Arthur, as a free man. If under Magus, a pawn or spear made of flesh meant to be discarded after the using.

Magus! At this, Bishop Cadfan was fully awake. His pierced foot continued to complain, and a fever coursed through him. He made tea. But it did not stay down.

Magus, you have seduced me. You are not the Church of Rome. The Church of Rome is beauty and charity and tradition. You are no successor to Peter, nor Clement, nor the Church Fathers. You are the anti-Pope, and the forerunner to the Anti-Christ. Why have I allowed you to seduce me? I fight for the wrong side no more —

When a man would return to God, that is when the Devil knocks on the door.

Rap. Scratch. Tap.

These were not the tree branches that tortured Cadfan throughout his sickly night. Heavier sounds, the product of hands. *Metallic, gloved hands.*

Rap. Scratch. Tap.

Injured, exhausted, nauseous, and combatting a sweaty fever, Cadfan opened the door to his cell, drawing one deep, contested and troubled breath, then exhaling. He looked up at the dark powers that had come to visit him at the holy chapel of the Blessed Lady in Ynys Mon.

***

Anger is like hot coals, which are enflamed by a light breeze or soft blowing, yet are extinguished by heavy winds.

So it is with leaders, parents, or men and women in authority. The day-to-day, tactical things enrage them. Incompetence, insubordination, minor errors. These are the light breezes that unleash the wrath of the mighty; even those of level heads and soft dispositions. Mothers spare not the rod when the daughter's room is disheveled, or the crockeries still stained. Yet those same mothers hold their daughters in the embrace of grace and consolation when an unwanted pregnancy occurs, offering herbs and solutions in the place of screaming and punishment.

Merlin was a hot coal. A white-hot coal.

The Summer Kingdom had been at the tip of the blade when Iddawg was charged with giving Mordred the Traitor Arthur's offer of *a way out.*

When Iddawg betrayed the king's message, instead provoking Mordred to a desperate and violent answer, the blade penetrated, and the Summer Kingdom began in earnest to bleed, nigh unto death.

The lad's foolish act, his desire—having never seen the death in war—to see renowned heroes ride once more, vanquishing Giants and monsters and villains, would have been likewise committed by any of a dozen boys in a like position. This was a generation that listened to bardic poetry, and viewed bardic theatre, hearing and seeing the glory of battle, embellished and polished by professional minstrels and storytellers; never hearing the cries of mothers burying their sons, nor seeing bone and lung exposed in the field, nor breathing in the stench of black blood—a smell that lives in the nostrils decades after the fighting has ceased.

Merlin's anger was numbing. *How many souls will perish, how many lives be ruined over youthful lusts? How many will die, directly on account of this young man's lies?*

Merlin's anger was just, and capital. The boy had directly misrepresented the king's decree, made a shamble of the strategy—*my strategy!*—and proceeded to tell six score lies to cover the first. He was deserving of death. An immediate, painful death, that he might know in his final moments what so many thousands would soon know on account of him.

Grace.

Mercy.

These are stronger than anger, and love heavier than wrath. This is why a loving mother or father barks and hollers at little infractions but is soft and results-oriented where major sins occur, seeking solutions and not punishment for its own sake.

Mercy is the withholding of what the guilty deserve.

Grace is the giving of unmerited favor, the active gifting of what is not deserved.

God showed mercy in withholding His righteous judgment against a rebellious, evil world.

God showed grace in gifting salvation to every man, providing that they simply trust Him.

Taliesin had preached these things to the Merlin afore. And, when the wizard's anger burned hot, these truths were the heavy winds that cooled him.

Do we rank sins? No. Whether the mark is missed by the space of a thumb or by ten yards, the arrow still missed, and missed equally. None of us are good. None of us differs from the other. We all need mercy; we all should extend grace.

Arthur favored Iddawg. Merlin noted a paternal glance, the glow of a mentor from the Sovereign towards his messenger.

How many fighting-aged men will survive this Civil War? How many able men to serve their wives and children, and provide their muscle and skill to working the land? What profit is it to give one more Cymry warrior to the Isle? She is full of blood, and cries against it.

Merlin did not depose Iddawg. Iddawg knew that Merlin knew, and Merlin knew that Iddawg knew it.

"Far from the borders of Cymru, deep in the

vast Wood of Caledonia, in the land of the Picts, resides a hermit called Laolkien. Go to him and there remain in exile." Merlin began his decree, Iddawg's head bowed submissively: the dog slumping beneath the banquet table, having been caught purloining meats from the children. "Arthur has beseeched those of us closest to him that transparency and truth, even disastrous, calamitous truth, reign, and that secrecy and scheming be put out of this land." The druid's tone intensified as he struggled not to smite the lad. "Therefore I will inform him of your gross lies." Grace and Mercy struggled back. "But I will delay for five days, giving you space; peradventure you may survive the roads, the raiders, the soldiers anxious to gain an early kill, and the Picts besides. Arthur may visit upon you triple portion of what befell his first wife, our rightful Queen Gwenhwyfar I." Grace and Mercy prevailed. "But I will beg of him to forgive you. In exile you will remain, pledging to only return if Arthur himself calls you back into service."

"And if he never calls?"

"Then your sentence will be a prison without walls. You will spend your days, and die, in that forest."

Iddawg wanted to bawl. To cry thanksgivings that he could keep his head, to blither a thousand remorseful words. He wanted to confess with his mouth, that it might lather his soul. But the Merlin permitted no such opportunity. The emissary of the king swore oath to accept the condition of the exile and departed the Round Table Fellowship to do penance with the Wild Man of the Woods, be it for a month…or a lifetime.

***

"Perfect timing, I perceive." The slithery Italian voice, once a seductive flavor, now tasted as gall in Cadfan's ears.

"The Continent has been converted. Childibert and Mark rule, the descendants of the Silures have fallen." The bishop robbed Magus of a glorious introduction. "And now you are here to see the Paramount King slain—"

"Aye, and risen again." The response was in Latin, and not Cymraeg. Motioning Cadfan to walk with him, Magus and the rest of the Nine made procession to the chapel. Being directed to see Mary's coffin, and having seen it, he gave the Breton Bishop many accolades. "And the Cup, or the Ark of the Covenant? What of these?"

"The daughter of Meurig possesses, hides and enchants these lands that none can acquire them, lord. Her skill exceeds my skill, her magick greater than our shamans, her wit—"

"Your praise of her drips with respect, teems with affection." Magus's words changed from accolade to scorn.

Broken, bruised, exhausted, surely to die and then burn in some Christian concept of Hell for ransoming his soul to the Horned God, the dispirited priest was resigned to the fact that his hour of reckoning had come. *This cult will kill me anyhow; why lie?* "Affection, no. Respect, yes. She has outmaneuvered me for years! And now as I reflect, here at the consummation of your great work, she showed me mercy. A multitude of mercies."

Simon noted that the possessive pronoun

had changed from *'our'* to *'your great work'*, and that his agent Cadfan had now become a meek, feverish risk. "Mercy?" Having been in *every situation*, the Masked Man remained calm, now evaluating every communication, mood and emotion. "How?"

"By not killing me, which she could have done with no further effort than a man squashes the roach. She probably preferred not to clean the squelch from her boot and thus let me alone."

"I appreciate your use of metaphor, Walles, and I concur. You *are* a crawling thing and no man, fearing a witch no taller than a schoolyard girl!"

"Is your dilution and delusion and deceit effectual with your Council, and your members scattered in orders and sects abroad?" Cadfan the Bold emerged again, despite ill-health. "You know who Morgaine is, and I am certain your person, or at minimum your meddlings, had somewhat to do with the circumstances surrounding Mordred's birth and thus her selection for those cursed spring rites!"

"The bug has a big brain." Simon taunted his impetuous accomplice. "Is it your desire to leave our illumined brotherhood, Walles?" The Nine had compassed Cadfan. He noted that they uniformly advanced a step. Somewhere and somehow, candles had been lit within the sanctuary.

The bishop was barely robed, having neither sword nor dagger. Prey pacing in a snare, he speculated that his end was nigh. "I do!" Repentance reigned within the sorrowed Breton.

"Merlin left our order." Latin words,

whispered in threatening overtures. "Strangled. Poisoned. Drowned. And before this beaten, bashed, gashed and bruised. The triple death awaits renowned criminals, as your own ancient customs."

"The Merlin lives," was Cadfan's retort.

The Nine advanced. Eight grey robes; each unnaturally tall, the hoods perversely long, concealing faces. Eight shadow ghouls, and one superior, clad from head to toe in crimson red.

"Should it surprise any that the child of the damned would not die as men do? Are you a Fae, that you too would roam the earth until the end of days as a wandering star?"

Cadfan ignored the question, knowing full well that he was but a man. A pathetic man. Instead he attempted redirection.

"I respect Morgaine. Yes, she has killed, she has erred, she has blasphemed the Church, she has brought shipwreck and calamity. I've seen her suffer failure and setback. And yet…" The more he reflected, the more he respected the king's sister. "She has a purpose."

"Tell me of the lass's purpose." The voice was more serpentine than of man, a hiss filled with words.

"Your great work is to build a kingdom, or conversely to delay a kingdom," Cadfan began.

"Immanentize or delay. You have grown in your understanding." The hiss was now garnished with parental pride.

"Her great work was to build, and sustain, a kingdom. The Summer Kingdom. In the Summer Kingdom the function of those who rule is to protect God-given rights and elsewise leave people alone! In this regard, the Summer Kingdom favored liberty over security, freedom over utopia, and privacy over Statism! The Summer Kingdom, filled with diverse beliefs and faiths of every sort; arguing, laughing, studying and above all, protecting one another's right TO EXIST!" Cadfan captured a glimpse of a shadow cast in the anteroom of the Church. He gave it little regard, pushing forward with what was sure to be his final sermon. "So obsessed became I with the imposition of my denomination that I never understood what Arthur, Dyfrig, Bedwini, Merlin, Vivien, and Lancelot labored to give us. Just in this very moment, I understand Camelot!"

"Your golden age is no more, Walles."

"Twenty years!" Cadfan immediately countered. "Fallen, sinful, corrupt man made it work for twenty years. This will inspire a thousand generations — and because of it, you will not win, should the Most High God tarry in sending His Son to avenge the Saints."

The red mask turned so slowly and with such theatre that time seemed to still. "Corded rope." A short command given to one of his Adepts in Latin.

"You fear the Summer Kingdom." The bishop continued to verbally assail Satan's Princes. "And Morgaine of the Faeries, second only to Arthur, is the champion and the heroine of the entire Matter of Britain. YOU FEAR HER!"

Another shift and flicker of a shadow.

Cadfan was right. Simon Magus did dread the ancient thing that indwelt Gwyar ferch Meurig. Her function was to resurrect Arthur as a false god. The unintended issue of the first rehearsal of the deed had brought forth an abomination: a monster for the god-king Arthur to slay. But she was unpredictable, too powerful, and filled with her own convictions and those unionized with her host. The Elven King, that ancient rascal who had ruled the Isles in the Sea ere Brutus colonized the shores, had owed different debts to the Morrigan, to the Council of Nine, and to Arddu himself. His charge had been to give Onbrawst a changeling, not put the Morrigan *in Gwyar*, keeping the best parts of both babe and goddess in one house of flesh.

This very ritual was intended for Judas Iscariot and Arthur. A fusion. Differing from possession in nature and essence. Morgaine the Changeling was to be taught this art by the king of the Tylwyth Teg. Instead he did unto the Nine in the person of Morgaine what they would do by Arthur. She needed no training, her powers greater than her Faerie Father – perhaps greater than the Father of Lies himself.

Morgaine could raise up Arthur as the Anti-Christ, fulfilling her designed purpose. Or she could avenge herself and slaughter the Nine. Her only limitation in using her craft was to determine the outcome of a battle. Should the God of gods break His own decrees, or make an exception in permitting her to do this, her powers might be without limit. She has fifty and six years in this incarnation, and yet has not fully actualized, not accessed all that she is.

Simon Magus believed that he could manipulate Morgaine to complete the rite. He trusted in his god, who was Satan, to aid him in doing the same. But the priest had exposed his sarcastic minimalizing. He DID fear Morgaine of the Faeries.

Suddenly, originating from a lower trajectory and another room, a voice attended the shadow Cadfan had glimpsed. And this voice *had no fear;* it was jovial in nature.

"Arthur, Dyfrig, Bedwini, Merlin, Vivien, and Lancelot? You forgot one!" The uneven thump of a walking stick. Instantly, the Bard Taliesin stood between Cadfan and Simon Magus.

Each of the eight soulless, faceless hoods turned in concert, beholding what had been a hunchbacked toadstool before, now boldly in the center of their demonic, candlelit and dramatic circle. A small dog protecting a lame stag from a pack of wolves.

Simon, the Ninth of the Adepts, marveled, a curious grin behind his red mask. His eyes were patient, and searching to understand the reason for the visit, which was seemingly as spontaneous as his own.

Taliesin all but ignored the Nine; leaning his walking stick upon Cadfan's hip, the bard took each of the bishop's hands, looked him over thrice, and fixed upon the pierced foot.

"You are not well, old friend. Allow the druids to mend your foot, and chase away your fever with our herbs."

Cadfan's shame was as if Taliesin, in his extreme kindness, had slowly ladled hot coals upon his head. "What judgment from above hath brought you here, showing tender kindness to your enemy?"

"My enemy is no man, for our foes are not carnal; rather, the spiritual forces behind men are with whom I war. *'For we wrestle not against flesh and blood…'*" The famous bard looked away from Cadfan, and at last acknowledged the presence of the Council, identifying them through the Scripture quote: "'...*But against principalities, against powers, against the rulers of the darkness of this world, against spiritual wickedness in high places,*' as says the Apostle Paul in his letter to the Ephesians." Taliesin resumed his focus on the friend of his youth, again ignoring the wolves. "Arthur gave me to Urien, who will join the campaign, and it was upon my heart to come and see how you do, seeing that you also are in the north."

Cadfan could not help but interject with a humorous inquiry. "Did not Maelgwn Gwynedd first give you to Arthur, and now you are passed around again?"

Taliesin ever appreciated a good jab, even if he was the object of it. He chuckled.

"You are discarded more than an old leather house slipper." Another jab.

Another chuckle. "I am not put to the circuit of many princes because I am a bad bard, old friend; rather because I am the best bard."

"Oh, Taliesin." Cadfan exhaled once, and his merriment turned to mourning. "What I have done to our kingdom, to the venerated offices of our Royal Clans, and to the king's own sister is treasonous, and worthy of death. My sins are unforgiveable."

Simon's interests in the next words were keen; he lifted his mask, though in a manner that the others did not see, that he could absorb every word.

"If even one sin cannot be forgiven, then did Christ die in vain. But the Good News exceeds this. For all men have already been forgiven their sins. Christ became your sin five hundred and thirty-seven years ago. The transgression of every man was put to His account. Simply trust this truth, and His righteousness will be imputed to your account, by grace."

"How can this be? 'Tis not what Religion teaches."

"The bonds of Religion were created by these fellows," Taliesin said.

The hooded Adepts closed the distance, offended inside their robes. Their masked leader paused them.

"If you stole a garment from the market and I, being full of mercy, arrested you not, but rather begged the shopkeeper apply the charge to my account, and being full of grace, paid the debt with my own gold, what then would your balance be?"

"But I have done wicked things."

"Your balance, Cadfan, please." Taliesin softly insisted that the Catholic priest see the logic and wondrous light of grace.

"My balance with the shopkeeper from whom I purloined would be at nil. The debt paid in full," he conceded.

"So it is that Christ paid the debt for every man. What if the thief were never baptized?" Taliesin tested.

"Debt still zero."

"And never crossed the archway of a church building?"

"Debt forgiven still, the being in church having no relevance on what was paid in the sinner's stead." Cadfan answered true.

"God is already reconciled to you, Cadfan. Be thou reconciled to Him. And give your sword and your good foot to King Arthur Pendragon, who is surely the man of God."

"So." Magus hoped the Chief Bard of the Britons understood Latin. "You are the lad from Glamorgan who stole the world's finest wizard from me." He could discern that Taliesin did well understand him. "Are you not yourself the son of that famous witch Ceridwen? What is this marvel, that so many sorcerers and shamans turn to Christ in these bewildered Isles?"

"Our sect of the druids has ever waited for the Most High God to remove the scales and confusion, and reveal Himself to us. This He did by the preaching of the Apostle Paul."

Simon hated this name, the word a flaming arrow in his ears. The chief of sinners turned saint, spewing grace, begetting more sinners-turned-saints. It was repugnant and foul in the ears of Magus that he shared a room with a *real believer. For many were religious but most were lost, unwitting dupes and pawns of his master.*

"This Catholic bishop to whom you may or may not have brought the light of salvation today. I will miss him; he was a good agent and did much to bring about the end of days. I have but one question of him, then we will send him to meet God—yours or mine."

Cadfan remained bold, having no fear of death, full of deep contemplation and coursing with conviction over Taliesin's tidings. "Ask it, then haply I receive what is just recompense for my deeds in the flesh, knowing now where my soul goest."

"Does…" Simon paused, switching from Latin to Cymraeg. "Does Morgaine of the Faeries still have the cup? Is it now returned to its secret place within Yns Enlli?"

"That is two questions," Taliesin mused.

The conclusion was clear. The Council of Nine were wasting their time engaged in the current enterprise. The Bishop of Rome himself was at sea, making his way to address the confederacy and denounce Arthur, rousing the troops before the battle drums banged. Alan Fyrgan the Traitor's troops were positioned to defend against the first wave, and camped in the forests between Powys and Gwynedd, awaiting instructions on where to march. Cedric had assembled his men; likewise were the Picts standing ready. All was in order, and but two tasks remained for the Puppet-Master.

Have audience with the Whelp.

Find the Cup and use it to control Morgaine.

Sinister and knowing the Scriptures, commanding every word from Genesis to Revelation (for the Council must needs first know every Scripture in its proper context, that they might pervert and misuse it), he goaded the Christian Bard. "Taliesin, son of Ceridwen, Grail Guardian of old, protector of the Mysteries and the relics. Pray you, give me the next verse, a continuation of the first you preached afore."

"Certain to oblige." Taliesin was bold. *"'Wherefore take unto you the whole armour of God, that ye may be able to withstand in the evil day, and having done all, to stand.'"*

"I see no armor, neither shield, nor sword—and yet the evil day is upon you! Kill them." He motioned.

"The verses are spiritual, not physical.

Destroy our flesh; Cadfan *has* withstood you, and the day. But..." Taliesin straightened his crooked back, beamed with a confidence that illuminated the room, took up his stick, still resting upon Cadfan, and tapped it thrice upon the floor.

Tap. A smile.

Tap. A wink.

"But what?" The accent was especially thick when readying to clutch at the prey.

"But I physically want to be here to see Arthur restored, Maelgwn restored, and you defeated. Therefore —"

"As I said: no armor, neither shield, nor sword." The order having already been given, eight swords with black blades were drawn, and already in flight.

"Therefore I brought the Tylwyth Teg with me. Though a Christian of Christians, I'm still a Briton, and we are a peculiar people."

Tap. A swift look to the chapel doors.

A blue, luminous, plasmatic *shield* surrounded Cadfan and the bard. Every sword shattered upon the enchanted shell, breaking into a thousand pieces, the steel becoming as sand.

The king of the Tylwyth Teg gazed long upon the coffin of Mary. "An elect Lady, of purest heart and bravest disposition. I remember you well, Mary. I see why men would have you as their goddess, though you would turn in your place of rest, protesting and railing against the same." Returning his attention to the mortal recipients of his assistance, the shield changed form, becoming a whirlwind or animated faerie ring, cycling up, down and round about the two.

Three and thirty-three thousand pixies swarmed the eight as so many little bees, each encased in their own bright star. Having no recourse but to wave frenzied hands and kick against the air, the Nine fled the church, cursing and crying, the Fair Folk giving chase.

Of the otherworldly rescuers, only the great Elf remained. "Retreat."

"The Lord Arddu has written a book wherein are described punishments as have never been imagined since the foundation of the Earth. The Creator God is a Being most boring, to think that a Lake of Fire is the most dreadful way to perpetually punish a man or an angel. My god has much darker designs than this! And *YOUR NAME* tops his ledger, being reserved for the most creative of these!"

"Better to fear the Creator than the creature." The Fae, who would typically have vanished in an impish fashion at this moment, remained to watch Magus depart, chasing after his retinue.

Knowing that the two men were secure, he approached Taliesin, giving dire warning. "Morgaine will do all to see that Mordred and her remaining sons besides come to no harm in the battle to come."

"It is my understanding that she cannot intervene, Lord of the Wood and Stream," Taliesin responded, showing careful respect of the Otherworldly Being conversing with him.

"Pray you are correct, Grail Guardian. I fear she has found a way. Even now Avalon is surrounded by a mist such as never before. She has pushed the Holy Isle into the realm of shadow with her fog and would wield the dragon's breath to shield her own."

"Can she be stopped?" Taliesin asked.

"None knows the resolve of the Sorceress Morgaine as I do," Cadfan quickly interjected. "No, she cannot. Once set about a task, the Lady will not be deterred, save perhaps by her brother."

"Then I will abandon my commissioning to Urien and to Arthur return."

"No, Taliesin, see to the battle lord of the North as bidden by *our king*. Let me do this thing, I beg you."

Though all men are forgiven, the repentant are still driven to do good deeds. Not for the purpose of being saved but, contrariwise, because they *are saved*, and thankful. Taliesin understood the importance of this quest, vain as it might turn out. Cadfan would warn Arthur of the Morgaine's mists. Meanwhile, Taliesin would pursue an additional scheme.

"Lord of the Wood and Stream, ere you leave again as you listeth, will you not walk with me, that we might speculate together?"

"I like you, bard, and will hear your scheme. Let your druids come and heal this *new man*, and into yonder circle behind the church, over there where the treeline changes, *we* will go. And there to hear your scheme and after release you, elsewise keep you in our court for five hundred years."

Praying they were but mischievous words of no weight, Taliesin the brave laughed with the Faerie King, and did go with him…

CHAPTER 16
Unarmed and Disappointed

June
AD 537

Where the Llyn Peninsula diminished into the sea resided a small village that the bards would later call *Aberdaron*. Waist-high grass of every green and moss-covered rocks garnished cliffs that framed a steep, natural border round the land's end. The drop from where homes resided and villagers dwelt, where the waters crashed upon the rocks, created the illusion that this region was as a magical realm, 'floating upon the sea'. Five walking minutes south of Aberdaron, a hidden harbor hid beneath the rocky overhang. The rather difficult but brief descent brought the traveler, so oft a pilgrim from Rome, else a druid or saint making their final sojourn, to a cove with smooth, flat rocks that appeared as a natural stone floor. The inlet, Porth Meudwy, seemed to be designed by God Himself for small vessels, which fitted perfectly here, and shoved off from the mainland.

To Avalon.

West on Llyn Pennisula, now further west but

bending down the horn of the mainland, turn south, proceed to Aberdaron.

From Aberdaron, south to Porth Meudwy.

Board a barge or hired vessel at Porth Meudwy. By ancient decree only two sets of sons from two families were learned in navigating the *impossible waters.* These alone, or the boatmen of the Lady of Avalon herself, could bear a soul unto Avalon. Should the sons' sons refuse to sail (for they could read the weather, seeing beneath the currents what the untrained eye doth not see), then one could hire their own coracle and engage the trepid currents themselves — else swim. Many hundreds and scores of hundreds had done the same, and perished.

Avalon.

Ynys Enlli.

The place of healing. Of groves with apples that defied nature, growing under impossible conditions wrought of tempest and wind and climate. The resilient trees. Hew them down and leave one sprig or root and they returned, stronger than before. Better than before.

Avalon.

Ynys Enlli.

The little island of mysteries that harkened back to the antediluvian dispensations. Of all the islands that had broken away from the mother, and the mainland, this atoll, with one small mount that cast a shadow over the plain, hid the forests and concealed the founts, was coveted above all. The Romans coveted tin and the Hebrews lusted for gold; the Picts sought iron and the Saxons possessed an insatiable hunger for lands. Yet the sum of these material goods were as a farthing compared to the quest of all men to but touch the soil of Avalon. And now she was within the grasp of Simon Magus and the Council of Nine.

But Avalon was missing.

***

Two metal fingers and a steel thumb pinched two Roman coins, each debossed with the face of an emperor from old.

It was not that the boatman refused. It was that he was paralyzed, bewildered, frozen, and consumed with worry that his right senses had departed his mind.

A wall of fog rose nine hundred feet towards the heavens, and spanned three days' ride by horse, both east and west. The mist seemed *alive*, dancing and pulsating. *And disappearing.* At once it would dominate the landscape of the peninsula, an awe and a fright to the villagers (and these men and women, being neighbors to Avalon, saw supernatural and spiritual oddities each and every day), most of whom thought the fiery comet, or its kin, had returned to take up the work of removing the Cymry from the world of men; a moment later, clear skies.

Though the fog made the expert sailor a blind guide, it was the moments of clarity that caused him to refuse to launch.

Avalon disappeared.

The wall of fog would return, sometimes ascending from the deep, other times descending from the sky above—and whirlwinds and spins and cyclone shapes besides.

Avalon reappeared.

Returned, brimming with life and mirth. From Porth Meudwy an onlooker could see a dozen different kind of birds at play, flying in majestic dance patterns around the shore, then hastening to fly towards and over the zenith of the mountain, dissolving beyond the vanishing point of the horizon.

Avalon disappeared.

"A Sorcerer yonder experiments," the masked devil commented in Latin, still extending payment.

The seaman spoke only Cymraeg, but no matter; he emphatically refused employ.

There was a substance to the mist. It was heavy. Some of it broke from the rest and crawled to the mainland. When this happened, Magus could no longer see his own hand, let alone the obstinate fellow before him.

"None can sail in this, neither fight." He was angry, but wore no anger. Addressing his cult, he conceded: "We will not find the Grail on the Isle of Apples today, because we will not find the Isle of Apples. We must leave Morgaine of the Faeries to her own devices. Peradventure she will lead Arthur to this very place and facilitate our work, unknowingly. Whether this come to pass or no, let us to the House of Llew ap Cynfarch Oer, that privily we might have audience with the Son of the Pendragon."

***

Bishop Cadfan prostrated himself before King Arthur's Court in the Round Table Hall, a broken and barely functional remainder standing in the shadowy ruins of the castle fortress Caermelyn above, that once shining city upon the hill that the poets on the Continent referred to as *Camelot*. The city of freedom and the pulse of liberty that beats within the bosom of every man.

Merlin's great invention had been cleared away, the old wizard defiantly declaring daily that he would personally see it repaired to past glory. Instead, the Round Table Fellowship sat upon their ornate chairs, which were as thrones, in a great circle without the table.

With mourning and humiliation, Cadfan detailed his treachery; from the early days at the feet of Meirchion the Mad, whose progeny Mark the Cruel terrorized the Continent, to the plot to deify Mary, right through to the present unwelcomed visit by the Council of Nine during his moment of repentance and conversion. He shared all—all that he knew. Cadfan had not been in Simon's inner circle but had been of import nonetheless, perhaps two rungs outward from the same. Because of this, his gathered intelligence obtained, of the plans and aims of Maelgwn, Mordred, Caw, Llew, Cedric, Mark, Childibert and the diverse Pictist and tribes of Eire, was of tremendous value to the Silures.

If the information was valid and not another act of conspiracy, lies and diversion.

"Merlin?" Arthur needed no expounding, having a living *truth-discerner* at his side.

The druid peered into the soul of Cadfan. A few whispers were exchanged, and two to three questions asked. The assembled knights and chieftains were silent, drawing a collective breath, unable to hear the Merlin, desperate to hear the outcome. The verdict was swift.

"Forgive him," Merlin declared. The exhale of the gathered was collective; a few jeers, but more showed grace than judgment, happy to see that rifts *could mend.* This was important for the morality of Arthur's core leaders, and would surely diffuse as an affirmative waterfall, splashing upon a hesitant, angry, and hungry army.

King Arthur, famed the world over for balancing mercy with justice, might well forgive Cadfan, embracing him with a brotherly hug, seeing his wife and children succored, and showing him love as one loves his neighbor. He might then put him to death in a swift, civil and dignified way (the butchery and malice showed Gwen II being an aberration in the reign of Arthur). Conversely, he might prescribe restorative justice, including restitution or works meet for repentance.

Neither was the king a dictator. Cadfan's offenses were against the Sovereignty of Cymru, against the whole of the kingdom itself. Were it a matter of a local crime, or some regional intrigue, Arthur would exercise no jurisdiction, only giving his opinions and protests *as a man*, in every way equal to his kinsmen.

Where a matter did fall under the powers loaned the Round Table by the Tribes, Arthur carefully consulted his twelve, and Lancelot his twelve, until consensus was reached. In this way, power was checked, and cool heads designed to prevail.

Lancelot's chair as Champion of the Britons was vacant. Be it by reason of death, mission, exile or ambience, the twenty-four was no longer whole. Nevertheless, Arthur conferred with the remnant of the Round Table Fellowship. This he did, as ever, in the open of the day, before all. *Let no act of the Government be done in secret*, had taught Merlin, Meurig and a score of Silure chiefs for generations before Arthur had carried the precept forth, becoming a beacon of republican government in a tyrannical world.

And so the remorseful bishop stood at the base of the judgment seat, happy to die, having had his moment to declare his resurrected loyalty for Cymru. This council proved to be far exceeding in kindness, in humor, in war embrace, and in grace to that Council of Nine, the leader of which that he had but recently called Master.

After a short discourse, Bedwyr whispered in the king's ear, then said aloud, vociferously, "Our course with this rogue is as a clear as the surface of Llyn y Fan Fach, which is as a glass mirror!"

A man of great conviction and repentance can *say* he would rather die clean than live dirty, until the actual pronunciation of death is given. Cadfan, no less sorrowful, did fear the forthcoming words.

Bedwyr paused.

The pause continued.

No chair creaked, no boot shuffled. Silence encompassed the hall, and even the birds held their beaks. Bedwyr glared at Cadfan.

After some time, Arthur gave the Good Knight a look that communicated, *This is becoming uncomfortable for all, even me, and I'm High King!*

Bedwyr's fixed stare was unrelenting.

At last he rose, bidding by motion that each Round Table Knight draw his sword. This they did, each pointing his long weapon at the confessor.

Gwenhwyfar ferch Gwythyr was amongst the viewers, cleaving to her parents, watching the high drama unfold.

Seventeen swords formed a circle of death round the bishop. *And one of those the Sword of Power!* Excalibur's hum of victory was the only sound to be discerned, seemingly in the whole of the cosmos.

Bedwyr peered down his blade. *And then winked at Cadfan.*

The man could not swallow for fear, neither form spittle in his mouth, but he did manage a bewildered cock of the head.

"The surface of Llyn y Fan Fach is a mirror. What does a looking glass do but expose the ugliness therein? A mirror shows us *our true selves.* Who amongst us, in these gray days, does not covet mercy? Who here has not committed some great error, or horrific war crime?" Bedwyr looked as though he suffered great physical pain in holding his cold, brooding expression, for now the entire assembly knew his silent stares were a yarn, his drama aimed to scare Cadfan with the love that simulates an older brother catching the younger stealing biscuits — often accompanied by judgmental lectures, soon followed by remembrances of when he did the same things. *Brotherly love is frightful, then warm.*

At last Bedwyr broke, the laughter as a rushing damn.

"Let this act here today remind us that, ruins

and rubble or no, this *is yet* the Summer Kingdom!" Each sword was withdrawn, instantaneously sheathed. "Be thou restored, brother!"

Clapping and great laughter ensued, the witnesses seeing mercy motivated by and reminiscent of what they had fought to earn; what they fought for still.

"One further demand." The High King himself quieted the hall.

"My lord?"

"How far will they suffer us to advance? Where does Maelgwn make his stand?"

"My kinsmen Alain Fyrgan is positioned in the village near the chapel of Tydecho. There he will make a great name for himself abroad, delaying your passage whilst the Saxons surround you from the slopes above––"

Having been fostered nearby, having wrestled the Giant Itto not far from there, having supped with his Champion countless times not one hour north of the place, Arthur was thoroughly familiar with the favorite territory of Maelgwn Gwynedd. "Camlan," he interrupted, having his answer. "Lancelot would have a second Mynydd Baeden, save in his country, this time, instead of mine."

"He means to stall you in the wood, force you through the meadow, corral you on the farmland, then draw you to a low-ground position, causing a forced ascent up Craig Y Gamell," Cadfan continued in full cooperation, having truly changed allegiance.

The Bear of Glamorgan approached and then embraced the one whom he had pierced. "We will dress your foot; I apologize for wounding you." Herein was the greatness of the king on full display. Cadfan had in every measure shouldered much of the accountability for the ruin of Britain. And here *Arthur apologized to him!*

"I know the fighting dance of Vivien, having grown up in Brittany," Cadfan responded. "Let's not waste nursing but one wound." A pleading look. "Permit me to take the field with the Round Table Knights, and under the Pendragon banners run into a glorious death!"

"Rather, limp," Bedwyr offered. The assembled roared. The bishop blushed, feeling accepted and whole.

"A one-legged patriot is preferred to a two-legged fool. Join us," determined the king.

Some clamor and side-discussions erupted. Meanwhile, Gwenhwyfar negotiated the crowds, hoping to be near the king and announce her arrival in Cymru. Arthur had been at all hours training and planning. Hoel and Gwythyr notwithstanding, he had not greeted the flood of Bretons who were suddenly under his command, and newly his neighbors.

But she was unable to get close enough to make eye contact with him.

The High King once more settled the crowds and ordered the circle. "Rest well this night, and the next. For the hour comes when we attack our foes, and our brothers. But prior to this…" Arthur looked again to Cadfan, a consolatory gaze, for the news would be hard. "The battle of Camlan starts today. Today." A hush fell. Fear. Anticipation. Confidence. Despair. "Cadog, Cai, Gareth, Bedwyr and I will be as thieves in the night and go ahead of the armies. We and nineteen bowmen will go ahead of the army. We will remove Alain's guards and watchmen, who will surely be stationed on the road that connects Powys to Gwynedd and terminates above Caergof.

"Giving neither signal nor warning, we will harass, discomfit and terrorize Alain where he waits. There is not a forest in Cymru that the Sons of Adam do not share with spirits and Fae and creeping things. Fright will destabilize their constitution, then arrows will fill their encampment as so many angry wasps, causing them to feel that, just as one is put to flight, three more replace it, more wrathful than the first. In this manner, twenty-four will slay nine hundred"—for three troops were now under Alain's lead—"and the woodland become a feast for the birds. Dead men cannot stall our advance, save to trip upon their corpses, and their design would fail."

Hearing this, Cadfan understood that there would be no place for surrender, for the tactic demanded stealth, and not engagement in an open field. The reality of war now pressed him: *Alain Fyrgan ap Hoel the Good will surely die, not many days hence.*

"I will go as well." Being more *physically persistent* than the Lady of Lyonesse, Hoel (who was also a Round Table Knight) pushed his way to the center of the ring and stood next to Arthur, and before Cadfan. "It is not for you alone to bear the burden of battling your offspring."

Arthur could not refuse his demand, for he knew it had a double intention. Hoel would see his son for the final time and, if possible, save him. The Pendragon would not deny him this, and offered, "Should they abscond the scene and depart in a direction contrary from Mordred, we will not give chase. May the terror of the first few that fall warn the remainder, their lifeless eyes and cold bosoms beckoning them to abandon the vanity of their cause."

"And if they refuse to turn from their allegiance to madness, let the earth and the Underworld welcome them." Hoel had seen his gilded little kingdom fall, and would avenge it — even against his kinsmen, or his son.

Some discourse continued, the crowd dissipated, and Gwen found a valley of shoulders through which to sneak, pop up, and present herself to the king.

Her gown was dark blue, her jewels and plaits the same, for she knew that Arthur adored this hue, and would wear no other color if convenience permitted or if fashion did not forbid it. Usually her hair was kept not overly adorned but practical and modest, falling about her shoulders, else bound in simple ties. Here it was prepared to shimmer and shine, two maidens and three hours a protested testimony to the preparation time. This Gwenhwyfar's eyes were blue, matching those of the one she loved so dearly. Ever regal but never pretentious, the Lady of Lyonesse felt outside of her own skin, uncomfortable. In fancy apparel with painted lips and crimsoned cheeks that favored her high cheekbones and revealed a slight, adorable pointedness to her little nose, she did illuminate the shadowy hall. A splendor to be desired by any man, she was in one part Vivien's beauty and in another Morgaine's strength; at the same time she was not comparable by attribute or likeness to any, being wholly unique.

What mercy! What wisdom! Her inner voice complimented the one she pretended was already hers. A proud smile. *Lo, there he is – what shall I say?*

She was close enough now to grasp his hand, or to throw herself upon him with a passionate kiss. *Temperance; self-control.* Her mind chastised her heart.

The king did see her. He began to mouth a greeting, but his line of vision caught the tallest of Britons racing from left to right, and then behind him. Arthur turned at the torso so that his feet still faced the lady but his shoulders and head were in another direction. "Merlin!" he hollered.

The wizard stopped to talk, hearkening unto the beckoning of his lord.

"Where is Iddawg? Bring him hither, that I might dispatch formal message to Gildas ere I depart with the men." A natural, unassuming, normal request.

No secrets. Cover no sin, and disguise no error, for these things manifest and undo us. Merlin swallowed but once, then came out with it: "Iddawg has found himself in the snare of youth. Let us away, and we will discuss expediently."

Arthur adjusted his position. He did look upon Gwen, and gave a friendly, yet disinterested and distracted nod, his every thought upon hastening to give Gildas final instructions before leaving, desperate not to delay his men. Altering his plans, he directed Cai: "Send three of our swiftest to Neath, and fetch me Gildas, that they may hasten to catch us, for we must talk as we ride."

Cai set about this charge.

And Gwenhwyfar set about hers.

She would not shed tear in public, nor make a spectacle of her emotions. Rather, she did sprint as a Greek competing in their games. Banishing her ladies (who were as sisters and no servants), she peeled her gown off and loosed her hair violently. Tears finally fell at the same time her locks lit on her shoulders.

I am a fool and a child! The man loves me not!

***

"Must you personally lead this advanced expedition? Surely we have thousands of stealthy young men who could make quick work of watchers, messengers and guards," Merlin protested, he, Meurig and Dyfrig joining Arthur for cider ere he departed for Gwynedd.

"I was fostered there; I know the area as I know Glamorgan and Gwent," he responded. "Besides, no one can disguise himself and navigate the secret roads and pathways like Arthur Pendragon." A comforting, confident smile to calm the older men.

"With this I cannot disagree." Meurig continued to glow as a proud 'new father', though well past the median of a man's years.

Arthur and Merlin articulated the battle schema several times, and when this was finished, Dyfrig posed an important, thoughtful question.

"You have reported well your aims and where

we are strong. It seems the veterans of the Saxon Wars are revitalized and the new soldiers ready to share in old glories, adding their own songs to Bardic melodies and tavern lies." Dyfrig paused, waiting for the payment of laughter, and he was well compensated. "But tell me," he continued, "where do we have risk? Where are we weak?"

"Armor and smiths." Arthur did not hesitate. This issue concerned him the most. "The Red Dragon melted much and made ash of much more, and the generational skill of smithing and forging has been greatly damaged. The demand for arms and weaponry simply exceeds the supply." He was frustrated. "We are all uniformed in matching sigils, that we might discern friend from foe. But underneath some have leather, some have mail, some heavy armor, others a few salvaged sets of our specialty silver skin." Arthur shook his head, disgusted at the lack of equipment and uniformity. "Where armor fails there is space for error or thrusting amiss. We must be perfect. And this is our greatest risk."

CHAPTER 17
Embrace Your Abomination

June 19
AD 537

Creating a circumstance where Simon Magus could have private audience with Mordred was proving very difficult. Although Cedric had complete knowledge of the Council's aims, having received vast sums of gold and supplies for campaigns in times past, Arthur's other enemies were in league against the king on their own accord—and for their own motives.

Mordred would see in Arthur's death his true love avenged, and elsewise lived life day by day, his sole objective keeping his lungs filled with breath and his head attached to its neck; he took advantage where he could over the *cattle that is mankind* along the way.

His proposal to support Maelgwn as High King (thus avoiding ongoing strife amongst the confederacy's own ranks) in exchange for protecting his ascent to the rule of his ancestral lands of Glamorgan and Gwent was well received. The northern Catholics would have their strongman in the brooding and unpredictable

Maelgwn, who would likely be more hermit and less king, and they would have their puppet in the south. Should an assassin from Caerleon or Deheubarth, ashamed to have an abominable bastard ruling over him, put herb to drink or arrow to back some random early morn, it would be of no matter. Caw and Llew, having stabilized the kingdoms, would simply insert another of their own.

Mordred knew as much, but was content to tread forward where his lot had currently fallen. He had *a Cai-type figure* in Eda, a steward and protector who never left his side. And insomuch as a monster with no apathy can enter into friendship, he was fond of Eda, though he was no Amr. In Mordred's twisted morality, affection was a fixed sum, allowing him but one brother, and excusing his crimes and hatred for all others in the aftermath of his loss. Mordred had *loved* but two in his forty years, and Arthur had murdered them both.

And soon the Pendragon would come for him as well.

If the bards were not prejudiced and blind, they would record that all that Mordred did was in defense of himself against the tyrant Arthur. But Mordred will have no Songs.

As the sun rose two days before the solstice, 'twas this Eda pounding upon the door, beseeching Mordred to rise and dress.

Following curses, degradations and loud rants, curly locks as an unkempt curtain over one eye in the crevice at last appeared. "Eda! What?" the crevice barked.

"The Father summons you, lord Mordred."

"My father assumes that because he shares this rooftop with me he can call me at his whim, and command me as a slave!" The door closed, with a tantrum and belligerent words. "No wonder my brothers opted to live near Mother!"

Though Cai guarded brilliance and Eda protected a fool, they each shared the same attribute true to all stewards: patience.

"Not *your father*" — *and Llew is not your real father besides* — "rather THE Father. The Bishop of Rome."

Now the door opened.

"What hath the Religion of Rome to do with me?" Mordred wondered.

"Pope Silverius will address the gathered armies at noon on the solstice, blessing our campaign and condemning Arthur the Tyrant, and Illtud his false Prophet."

Realizing it would be of great political advantage to have the favor of the Potentate, Mordred would suffer his prayers, or sprinklings or bells and candles, entertaining his superstitions with a smile.

"With your own eyes see that it is true, and no assassin guised in vestments, Eda."

"This I have done, lord."

"Wait, then; I will dress. Then you will conduct me to him," said Mordred, offering no apology or courtesy after his rudeness against the mountain of muscle that shielded him.

Although the Round Table Fellowship had deprived Llew's grandfather, Meirchion the Mad, of land — especially in Corneu and the southeast of Cymru — his issue, who were of the ancient House of Coel, were allowed to maintain many of their holdings in the Old North. This had been done to safeguard the dignity of Urien and his siblings, but had had the unintentional result of leaving a wolf in the pen. Once again, past mercies caused present disadvantage, for the northerners in league against Arthur enjoyed vast lands and large, well-defended fortresses in the *betwixt and between* lands above Gwynedd but below Alba.

It was in one of these, a walled, wooden fortress that housed two hundred residences (not including guards, stable-hands, smiths, those working the kitchens or governing the lead conduits, and networks for managing excrement and waste), where the chiefs and princes who were against Arthur lodged—save Maelgwn, who slept peacefully in a small hamlet called Dinas Maddwy, near to his farm at Maes-Y-Camlan.

The Saxon, Pict and Cymreig royals, including Mordred, were surrounded at all times by bowmen from above and mounted cavalry below. Maelgwn was guarded round about by the Dormarch: the hounds of hell Morgause had summonsed that he might avenge Gwenhwyfar II, giving Arthur an ironic death. Drest of the Picts, Cedric the Saxon and his Gewesse raiders, Llew and Hueil ap Caw, reposed in comfort, though it were daytime, using women and meat to feed their fear, knowing the battle was nigh.

Maelgwn, meanwhile, was tormented by *all seven of himself*, refusing to permit visitor, counselor, or strategist. None knew exactly what Lancelot would do, only that somehow he *and the Witch Morgaine* would decide the fate of Cymru.

It was during this opportune morning hour, and not during the cover of night, with distracted kings and Maelgwn riding through another fit of division, that the *two Popes* entered the fortress, and within the fortress, a small chapel in one of the nine palace courtyards. The Bishop of Rome was expected, along with his retinue, from Rome. None found it queer that he was a day early, and none questioned that one of his Cardinals was maimed, or the victim of some deformity, and lived behind a mask.

When Mordred was washed and shaven, and clad in simple black attire, he joined Eda in the courtyard. "Something feels amiss. You are certain that no ambush awaits?"

"It is the presence of the Pope himself that causes this unease. It is his office. His person. His celebrity. How many thousands of the faithful sleep the sleep of death, never having opportunity to wash his feet, or give oil for his hair?" Eda embodied all that was wrong with religionists: obsessed with theatre and ritual and stations of men, yet a rogue and a defiling cheater in his own private conduct. The type that believes the tithe or saying of loud prayers to capture onlooking eyes is license for misconduct and evil.

The illusion of religion had no impact on the Whelp. "You worship this man?"

"Nay." Eda was quick to deny idolatry, as are all idolaters. "You are nervous on account of his fame. I can think of no equivalent in our land… it would be like walking into a chapel and being spoken to by—" Eda snared himself, making an overtly embarrassing analogy.

"King Arthur." Mordred glared, flipping the latch, his stare never leaving his verbally disloyal steward as he wantonly entered the chapel.

***

In the chapel were twelve rows of paired pews, a processional pathway betwixt, facing a great pulpit and communal altar, which was situated in true-north within the fellowship hall.

Above the pulpit a large crucifix was fastened with gargantuan cords to two rafters that rose and then bent to vault the ceiling. To look at the ceiling from the floor gave the parishioner, whose hereditary blood was still coursing with heathen traditions, the appearance and appeal of a grove; no detail of Catholic assimilation was spared.

The figure that was supposed to be the Son of God was of Catholic invention; pitiful, puny and pierced, fair-skinned, with hair like unto the Merovingian Kings who claimed him. The real Jesus had been as an ox, being a carpenter by trade; he had been olive-skinned like his kinsmen in the Near East, and had worn his hair and beard kept and well-groomed, fitting with his culture and the times. He had also been beaten beyond recognition, his lungs and organs exposed to the open air on account of Roman scourging. This Catholic "art" was insultingly contrary to the Biblical record.

Moreover, the real Jesus had not long remained on the Cross. It had been His shame to be there, but His passion to do the work of reconciliation for all mankind. Once done for all, He had ascended into the heavenly places and had no place in the sculptures made by blasphemous men perpetuating myths and imagery about the Savior being in a state of ongoing weakness — mocking Him.

Mordred fancied the blasphemy. But this particular cruciform he fancied threefold, and marveled. For the Cross, which was in height three times an average man, was upside down. Real blood, perhaps of some goat or child, streamed from the statue's eyes and wounded side, drizzling steadily upon the altar below.

There, kneeling, was a man, clearly a cleric, all in white. He wore a cap that gave the appearance of a fish's head and his cloak, also white with golden trimmings, was as a rolled carpet; a train of fabric with no end.

The Pope.
Kneeling beneath an inverted, Satanic Cross.

But he kneeled not before the altar or the dark relic; rather a second man. This one stood and faced the pews, as if he were preaching to an invisible congregation, his hands stretched out to further mock the Christian God.

His garb was black as night, and no flesh was revealed. *And he was masked.* This mask was made of lacquered porcelain, and the shaping was subtle but sure: he wore a face like unto a goat or hooved thing. Its expression was locked in permanent, freakish grin.

The black Pope.
The anti-Pope.
The False Prophet from the Book of Revelation.

Mordred was too immoral to fear what he ought to fear. Were this a ruse, five bowmen could have risen from behind the pews or baptismal font and filled him with a just death. He neither searched out the room nor performed basic measures to understand its composition; rather, with awed gawk, approached the two *Fathers*.

***

"Did you really slay this many Giants?"

"I take no pride in it. Something brought them from their slumber, causing them to think on nothing else but filling the countryside with perpetual violence." Arthur had been fond of many of the otherworldly beings that had met their demise by Excalibur or Rhon, wielded by the king's own hand.

Gildas, twenty years and one, continued to see Arthur as the god-king who had saved him from the Masked Devil as a lad. He faithfully did what the Pendragon bade; preparing histories, lists of kings, wedding registers; copying noteworthy land grants and church documents; collating the chronicles of the Cymru. These works were not songs, nor epic poetry — rather facts with minimal narrative and bereft of opinion or perspective.

Gildas ap Caw was objective, of temperate constitution, and possessed the memory of a bard coupled with the research skills of a schoolmaster.

The young man traveled with the small group of Round Table Heroes and their elite bowmen, who were preparing to pick a fight with nine hundred idle men, likely enjoying ale and harp presently, trusting in their soon-to-be-dead watchmen for warnings that would never come.

"I want you to record the battle census, and

then to hasten and leave." A potentially final task issued by the king. "Though we adorn you as an emissary and accompany you with the white flag"—a custom started by the Roman Empire; from ancient times those waving such were not to be harmed, even by barbarous foes, the Saxons notwithstanding—"I cannot promise that the Saxons, or malefactors under Mark's employ, will not attack you, nor that Mordred will not murder you in order to hurt me."

"I understand the risk, my lord," Gildas said.

"Confer with your father; gather counts from Llew and from your brothers. The Pictish chieftains share our ancient codes and will not harm you. But tarry not amongst them. Count Cedric and Mark's lines from the ridge, then hasten away."

"Is Mark the Cruel amongst them?"

"Nay. He and Childibert close their fists around Brittany at present." Arthur closed his as he described theirs. "Derfel will lead his men, but we pray that upon seeing Cadfan turned, he will drop his spear, and abandon his post."

"It is rumored that Derfel is comparable in skill to Galahad."

"Yes. If he engages, many Silures will fall to his spear. He should be a Round Table Knight and, I hope, one day will be."

The king and his scribe enjoyed further conversation, then long silence, for the time was at hand that they must part ways. Gildas and a small company would travel the old road, built by Britons but claimed by Romans, in the light of day. Arthur required Gildas to dress as a Raven, and two bearers were constant with white banners; one on foot and one on horse. The Iron Bear did not need Gildas's count, for the army already had a sense of its opposition's forces. Rather, he wanted Gildas to record an accurate history, for truth's sake and no other motive.

Gildas would document the numbers and the notables and then leave. Unfortunately, the victor of the battle would be dictating the outcome of Camlan to the lad. The scene would be too dangerous for a man of letters with no sword. Arthur hoped that whomever sang the songs of Camlan would set aside embellishments and give Gildas a factual account. Too many foes had threatened to remove the Caermelyn's light from the world, and the Pendragon greatly feared that the histories would be altered or redrawn.

With proper timing and some good fortune, Gildas would have visited with his father, Arthur's great rival Caw, gathered his counts, conducted interviews and then hastened to the safety of Urien, who was ready to receive him, before news of the slaughter or surrender of Alain Fyrgan reached the Caw's ears. Elsewise, his son would be in grave danger, being accused of distracting the northern armies, giving them cause to arrest or kill the brilliant young man—hurting the nation in doing so.

***

"So." The Goat relieved his hands from their crucified pose, folding his arms. "The Divine Child Mab stands before us, looking ferocious and virile. Truly blessed is the line of Meurig."

The use of flattery as a means of control is

typically successful, but some great chasm was present in Mordred, preventing him from being flattered or uplifted. Magus searched the spirit of the troubled man and beseeched the spirits that he might know more of his innerman. An audible answer was given. A highpitched whisper that was from no place, and yet everywhere at once, the demon giving but one word: *"Fear."*

"Fear?" The Goat acted offended. "What should the son of a god fear?"

The secret and evil workings of the Church displayed in the open of the day did not frighten him, nor the dichotomy of the white and black popes peering at him, nor the spirits that made the chapel their comfortable home. Of a truth, nothing frightened the firstborn son of Arthur other than…Arthur.

Mordred made a brief attempt at changing the subject, endeavoring to absorb and make sense of the situation, and company, in which he found himself. "Are you the reason for all this death?" (The question arched back to the Saxon Wars, and before, for the Blessed Isles in the Sea were ever under covetous invasion.)

The Goat used *simple Latin, and spoke slowly, that each word was an hour.* "No. This is." An overly-long, gloved finger approached, and then poked, Mordred's bosom. "Man is the cause of death." The pace of speech increased. "Our college has simply had four thousand and five hundred years to develop a science, and art, of *helping you.*"

Mordred found himself in the presence of pure evil. And he favored it.

The Goat again demanded, "What do you fear, divine child?"

The Black Pope possessed an instant power over Mordred, as if Satan himself *wore the masked man as a mask.* The Whelp drooped his head, an adolescent boy receiving repeated scolding from an irritable parent.

"King Arthur," he confessed. "Spells, meditations, medications, incantations, mind sciences and more. I have done all to arrest my dread of my father. Yet I cannot."

"Only hate and arrogance conquers fear, and you are the sum of both. You are his shame, the dung on his unspotted cloak." Magus clutched Mordred by the hair, not violently, but authoritatively. "Is this what you think you are?"

Mordred was paralyzed. Hard truths fell from his numb mouth. "Yes."

"Does not the Scripture," for the Devil loves the Bible, and takes greatest pleasure in twisting and perverting or misusing its meaning, "teach 'AS MAN THINKETH, SO IS HE'?"

"I don't know this part of their book."

"No matter." Magus was now in Mordred's mind; molding it, reshaping it. "Men think you are an abomination. Good! Which of the great gods was not born of pure stock?" Simon the Teacher lectured. "Did Horus recluse himself in a cave; does Zeus hurl thunder shamefacedly? And of Tammuz son of Nimrod, our first pattern of the World Ruler—did he not take his own mother to wife, and beget demigods?"

"Even the Dynion Hysbys, the druids and pagans of every sort, recognize and reject such unnatural issue, and I AM unnatural issue."

"They are cattle, knowing not their own gods, or the Mysteries thereof." As Mordred viewed all men as livestock, the reference found its mark. "Boast in your uncleanliness, as did Caligula before you; rage against normalcy and the shackles of what conscience calls *right and good.* If it feels good, it *is* right and good. You are the son of the god-king Arthur and his sister, who is the Ancient of Days, even the goddess Morrigan. None save Lilith is more senior of her kind. The primal witch is IN YOU!"

For the very first time, ever, Mordred's drowning fear of Arthur began to assuage.

"And god-kings die that—"

"They may be reborn again in their sons," Mordred responded. "The Roman Church—She will never accept me."

"Has She not already pledged support for you in this Civil War? Her highest officer is before you."

"But the priests, the people—"

"Corrupt the priests with gold and feed the people, and they will cleave their own feet, and eat them." Simon loosed the Traitor's hair, freeing both hands for his dramatic preaching. "Those who fear the old gods will follow you, Son of Pendragon, provided the crops yield and the harvest is bountiful. We control the church. Leave fear of him in this *House of God* when you leave, for 'perfect hate casteth out all fear'; win this war and then DO AS YOU WILL! THIS SHALL BE THE WHOLE OF THE LAW IN YOUR NEW DARK CAMELOT!"

His mind melted, folded, hammered, then folded again by the Master Mind Smith, Mordred departed quickly, resolved that he would win the war and remarkably, not only survive decades of fornicating with the High King's wife, but *become High King*.

Eda could see and feel that Mordred was changed from the congress with Evil. He ordered his golden armor refashioned and took up a new weapon; a battle spike with rounded, fin-like blades along the front edge, which was both a hand-guard and additional killing option. Mordred's was longer than that of the Champion of Britain, being as a modified two-ended spear in appearance.

***

"We have elevated his confidence. He will engage Arthur upon the field rather than run as the field mouse."

"Still, Arthur will not be bested by this empty, pathetic man," the White Pope offered.

"Of course I agree, son," Simon Magus was well pleased with his work, "but his rage and hate may wound the king, or his courage might give Arthur a second of pause, allowing for a stroke to sneak through. We but need the Whelp to wound the Bear ere he meets his sure end."

Confident that the Popes would make calamity and chaos of Britain, and that one of their Anti-Christs would from the chaos rise, Magus gave Silverius final instructions on how he might address the armies, soon fully gathered, at Camlan at sunrise on the summer solstice.

CAMLAN ACT I

CHAPTER 18
Alain's Cowardly Retreat and the First Day of the Dark Ages

Dusk
June 20
AD 537

Alain Fyrgan ap Hoel Dda commanded three troops, which is nine hundred souls, in the Battle of Camlan. A deserter from Arthur's kinsmen and renowned Breton ally, the chiefs of the Old North had offered the ambitious prince glory: the first wave of defense against the Silures, whose thousands of men would have to funnel through the winding valley and the thick, thorny wood, making their many numbers as though they were few. Alain would devote souls to the strategy of *delay*, empowering Cedric, with his Saxon, Gewessee and Lloegrian forces, to flank Arthur as his armies slowly emerged and fanned out in the fields and meadows of Camlan.

If he survived, Alain would be given the diadem over a small subdivision of Brittany, under the headship of Mark and Childibert, who would carve the country as if a pheasant.

Knowing that the attack would be soon, either this week or the next — for the whole of the Island now noised about how Arthur would pursue Mordred and Lancelot up north — Alain was alert; but, trusting in his watchers and guards, who were stationed at beacons or on mounds and roads within a day's ride, he reposed and slept, though it were still day.

***

Snap — two pops — crackle.
It is but stags upon dried twigs.
Three more snaps, and close snaps.
Stags are not so large, nor deliberate in their gait. 'Tis men!
'Tis not men.
Screech and shadow, shadow and screech. Screeeech!
The brown owls; nothing more.
Owls cry not in the day!
Ohmmmm. Snap. Screech. Whistle. Ohmmm. Now distant. Now near.
That hum, as the chant of priests. Illtud's choirs, I say!
Worry not the men! All forests protest! We are nine hundred. Disquiet not the spirits!
Spirits! Thou sayest true! Spirits!
Silence.

Alain Fyrgan was disquieted. Fully awake, scrambling for his armor, yet slick as a buttered hen, unable to dress himself.

Snap — three pops — shuffle.
Wailings. Wailings. In Cymraeg, wailings. Haunting wailings!

Spirits!
Spirits, else men!

"Can a spirit drop a dead man from up there?" A young solider pointed to the treetops where was perched a knight in light black armor, a kill impaled on three branches that had been modified with skill and haste to serve as a large fork. *The kill a warrior, one of Alain's own. One of the watchmen!*

The knight, who was Gareth, son of Morgaine of the Faeries, negotiated his kill off the fork and flung him below, the body splashing at the feet of Alain.

This occurred at the southern-most entrance of the Wood. Screams were heard in chorus from the north, the east, and the west as well. As quickly as he had appeared, Gareth was gone, leaving Alain's troops alone with their terror. Disorder erupted; infighting and clamor.

Then the arrows were loosed.

The Elves had given to the Cymry special knowledge of archery in the days of King Brutus of Troy. They immediately regretted that they had imparted this gift, for the men turned it against their hosts. This skill had been passed down from father to son, father to son (and daughters besides, who equaled men, and were often more accurate, having better dexterity of finger and thumb).

And those charged to chastise Alain were the most elect. These archers loosed two arrows every second; in ten seconds' time, twenty lay dead around Alain, who was unharmed. The missiles launched from every direction; many warriors ran upon a shaft in flight, the dart entering the face, bits of shaft and steel exiting the back of the head.

The Cymreig bowmen killed what they aimed to kill, and who they targeted not was safe as a newborn babe in his mother's arms.

Alain was as that newborn babe.

Shriek. Howl! Drums.
It is men AND ghosts. We are undone. Run!
Silence, save the sound of breathing, and running.

As the warriors scattered and fled, the arrows resumed. This time so many were loosed simultaneously, and then consecutively, that no sound separated them. *Whisp – whisp – whisp – whisp.*

The newborn babe shat himself, soiling his trousers and vomiting the whole content of his stomach at the same time. Frozen in terror as crimson pools rose to his ankles. Excrement, vomit and blood bathed the coward, who was no man of war.

The arrows stopped.

Dusk was but moments from giving way to full darkness. A hooded knight emerged, holding a lit torch in one hand and a shimmering blade in another. The last bit of sun touched on the hilt, and Alain knew of the script and markings, for every child born the world over had been told stories ere bed of the sword and the Boy King.

The light of the torch revealed the sandy hair beneath the hood.

"Aaa—" dry heaves—"Arrtth—"

The King of the Britons never withdrew his hood. He turned Excalibur a few times, that the glory of the blade might reflect light upon the disgraced visage of Alain.

It is not as the bards describe, and the poets do lie! I cannot move. And breath I have not; will he cleave me in twain, that I will die in my own shit?

King Arthur barely addressed Alain, speaking only to the ground, for the misguided fool did not deserve the address of the noble sovereign.

"I would not have your father, *my friend,* see his offspring as this. Take thee a blanket and run—*now*." Arthur gave direction, pointing with Excalibur in the way where Alain would have safe passage from the scene.

Thus did Alain Fyrgan lift no arms against Arthur, instead emptying his bowels and making hasty flight from the Battle of Camlan.

And the Round Table Fellowship earned a victory in the first offensive of the woeful war.

CAMLAN ACT II

CHAPTER 19
The Ridge of the Saxons and the Fall of Cedric

As Hoel Dda, Gareth, Cadog, Arthur, and Cai guided their small company of archers to victory, a second wave, also few in number, had already been dispatched. These were led by old Gwynllyw, and Merlin was amongst them. Their task was imperative, but the performance thereof wretched.

To put every watchman, guard, messenger and any fighting-aged boy or girl that could relay report from the south into the midlands and up north into the enemy's ears to the sword. No exceptions.

Perfect stealth was not the objective, nor could it be. The movement of so many thousand souls by trains of wagons or by flat, hulking riverboats, and the galloping pound of hoof on Cymreig and Roman roads, could not be achieved covertly. Rather, the objective was to delay, even if but for half a day, the warning of *when* the armies would arrive. In this regard, by the time the scattered souls were tortured in the forest by the bowmen, or any other word came, the news would be confused, delayed, amiss and too late.

Having complete knowledge of every hilltop, watchtower, and inn along the routes, the Silures executed an assassination operation. They met with great success, each kill breaking the heart of the knight who delivered the terminal strokes. The second wave equaled the triumph of the first, and Merlin arrived before sunrise, meeting with Arthur in the forest. He was readying for the next maneuver, wishing the match was gwyddbwyll and the stakes pints and boasting rights, and not the very soul of the Blessed Isles in the Sea.

***

Before Sunrise
June 21
AD 537

Caw wept uncontrollably, holding his son, who had now grown a full head taller than his father, with such intense emotion that none could look upon the embrace, lest the whole company sob.

"Your histories are *our history,* regardless of outcome. Arthur, though I loathe him, did well to choose my son, Gildas the Brilliant, to be chief of scribes in our time. Finish your counts and your interviews. You are safe. But then, as he commanded you, hasten to Rheged, where Urien will offer you protection and lodging." Bitter words given by Caw, but reason favored Arthur's aims for the lad.

Caw reckoned that, after at last ending the legend of lies that was the Round Table Fellowship, the northern princes would have to then deal with Urien and Owain, perhaps adding to the chapters in the Civil War. Or perhaps negotiating terms, preventing further loss of life.

Regardless of outcome, Urien favored Gildas (as did all Christian-oriented men, who promoted him and Dewi as the next generation of young Saints, philosophers, historians and wisemen to see the Church forward — should the Britons not annihilate themselves in this foolish, vain strife) and would bring him no harm, nor imprison him as hostage or make political intrigue of the situation.

The long embrace having ended, Gildas labored to finalize his census, which he collated and added to his Register of Neath. Knowing, lest some miracle prevent what was surely at hand, the losses would be immeasurable, the Scribe prepared the document in the past tense and affirmed what he had seen, having been with both sides, signing it with own hand:

'Recorded and attested before God and Man on the Summer Solstice morn, five hundred and thirty seven years from the Lord.

'As sands of the sea, so are the occupants, both of Britannia and sundry strangers from abroad, gathered to wage this Civil War, principally between the North, by ancient and accepted borders and boundaries, and the South, by ancient and accepted borders and boundaries, at Maes-Y-Camlan, which is in the land of Maelgwn Gwynedd.

'Let those who would pilgrimage to honor their dead, or to rescue their effects, be informed of the sure location of bones; in the shadow of Craig Y Gamell; above the village of Mallwyd;

by the chapel of Saint Tydecho; along the crook and wind of the Afon Dyfi; there look; there dig.

'Of the total number of souls, approximately three hundred and thirty-three troops, or one hundred thousand.

'And of the one hundred thousand, forty thousand lent their spear to Arthur, but twice thirty thousand gave their shields to Mordred and Maelgwn.

'And of the forty thousand that lent their spear to Arthur, half of these were of the tribe Silure. Rhun ap Maelgwn gave to Arthur two thirds of his own from Gwynedd, which was six thousand, and likewise Urien ap Cynfarch Oer did allot two thirds, also summing six thousand.

'Thus twelve thousand Ravens joined to the Round Table Fellowship, fighting their kin at Camlan, the remainder being eight thousand Bretons, who left one thousand of those exiled to rebuild Caerleon.

'God be witness and hearken ye the world over that not one Saxon, Angle, Jute or barbarian of Germania did with Arthur ally; neither would he conscript, employ or sup with them.

'But not so the Ravens, who have forgotten the Night of Long Knives, and abandoned reason.

'Of the sixty thousand conspired against the High King, half of these, or thrice ten thousand, were Ravens, excluding the elite hosts of Lancelot, who numbered five hundred, the remnant of the twenty-four times twenty-four being reserved to preserve their kingdom should the Bloodhound Prince fall.

'Cedric's numbers were about thirty troops, or nine thousand Saxons.

'King Brychan gathered about three thousand from the South, and the Midlands.

'Alain turned from Hoel, causing nine hundred Bretons to fight for the North.

'King Drest brought down diverse painted Picts from every part of Alba, having ferocity and great numbers, their census being one thousand times ten.

'The residue, numbering about six thousand and six hundred, hailed from Eire, else were confederates of Mark ap Meirchion.'

***

Simon Magus had departed, narrowly escaping the sweep performed by Gwynllyw and Merlin. The Black Pope, having ensured the White Pope was thoroughly rehearsed, would return again to Porth Madwy, examining again the accessibility of Avalon.

***

Maes-Y-Camlan was an open farmstead, a natural pitch, as if designed by God or the Devil to be repurposed as a battlefield. Flat enough here for mounted cavalry to safely execute their patterns, hills and short mounds there to make quick ditches and embankments for foot soldiers and archers to gain high-ground positions. The farm spread up, then terminated on the lower slopes of, the Craig Y Gamell. The mountain was one thousand three hundred eighty and nine feet tall and was the gateway to Dinas Maddwy. And Dinas Maddwy was the gateway to controlling the northern kingdoms of Cymru.

Craig Y Gamell gave the appearance of the thighs and womb of a great goddess. There were two distinct slopes divided by a deep gulch, which was hewn straight and clean, then widened and fanned towards the navel of the mount; the zenith of the mount was curvy but flat. To be an eagle soaring above Craig Y Gamell would be to look at the mother of Cymru come into her fullness — about to be delivered of a new future for Cymru, be it for good or ill.

The northern armies filled the mountainsides, looking as ants upon a log, except for the Saxons, whose camp was five miles east in a place the bards would later call Nant-y-Saeson, *the place of the Saxon.* But King Cedric and ten of his battle lords were present with the chieftains, lords, bards, scribes and renowned men assembled atop the westernmost slope of Craig Y Gamell. Drest the Pict, Caw, Huell, Llew, Mordred and many more were present, warming themselves with hands clasped around pewter mugs of scalding tea, waiting for the Pope to manifest and address the assembly.

Maelgwn was not amongst them. Rather he was a mounted statue residing alone on the eastern slope, at a slightly higher elevation than his tenuous allies. And they dared not trouble him, giving him space, knowing his blade would spill much blood, praying that it would be that of their enemy.

A red carpet, sewn with ornate designs of Ostrigoth, Visigoth and Italian origin, was carefully rolled out, then held to the rough surface by four large cherubic statues, made of onyx stone or gold, alternating in arrangement. A procession of priests and trumpeters with long brass cornets followed and at last Silverius, the Bishop of Rome, showed himself to the throngs of knights.

A servant of his own company (for the Cymru had neither slave nor servant, the lowliest of occupations treated with honor, respect, and compensation) placed a pillow at Silverius's feet. Although his vestments were simple, consistent with the fashions of the Church in Rome, he exuded arrogance, hubris, and dominion.

Kneeling slowly, his knees upon the pillow, he ritually rested upon both elbows, bending the whole of his upper torso, almost prostrate on the carpet, his position as a submissive dog. But this was a pretense; an empty rite. He slowly kissed the ground outside the boundary of the red carpet, quickly rising to his supreme posture thereafter.

Meanwhile, another procession had ascended the hill. The shock and fear of so many thousand soldiers froze them, for they had named their sons after him, and now here he was, riding with his wizard and his steward, three men against sixty thousand.

"When *his eminence* kisses the ground prostrate then erects himself again, that is his ritualistic announcement that the dirt now belongs to the Roman Church, and to HIM, its governor!"

A few veteran Saxon warriors, who were there with Cedric for the Papal Blessing, shuddered, having heard before this authoritative, hammering tone. In their ears he was more fearsome than Odin, more thunderous than Thor! *It was King Arthur himself, and lo, Excalibur!*

"You foolish brothers in the north. How many more times will we suffer you of Ynys Mon and Gwynedd, and the Old North, to invite the invader to our shores, and concede him our lands without even unsheathing his sword?" Arthur seethed. "What we just witnessed was an INVASION of Cymru."

"A rather aggressive opening statement for negotiations that precede the fight." Caw took the lead in addressing the confederacy's mighty foe. Meanwhile, young Gildas, snared by the curiosity of the procession from Rome, delayed his departure and was a hundred yards off, watching and listening to all.

Silverius was dumbfounded. Popes are not accustomed to disruption or reproof, even by princes. He ignored, or rather supplanted, Caw's attempt to engage discourse, and started to sermonize the masses.

"Yes, I have claimed Britannia for the Universal Church. But hearken unto me, and reason, brethren. Were not the powers to bind and loosen given unto Peter and succession—unto me? God would govern the earth and, as the Church are the People, the Government is therefore the People."

Arthur gave thunderous, interruptive laughter.

Merlin followed with the same. "Nay. Peter spake of a time when the Lord Himself would rule through the Twelve Apostles, through the Twelve Tribes, through Seventy Elders, over the Nations. I see not Jesus here, and you would twist what was written to Hebrews and make it your own—"

"Now is not the time for theological analysis, old friend." Arthur nudged the tall Briton in the side, his helm elevating just so due to his smile. "You sound like Dyfrig and Illtud, bantering about words during a time of war!"

Merlin blushed. "Never ought I to sound like them!" The Round Table Companions jested as if they were back in the library, and not in the center of the enemy's lair.

Before Silverius could recover control of the discourse, Arthur continued, and his rage returned. "The Government are NOT the People, and the People are NOT the Government. This is the trick of tyrants as old as fallen man himself—allowing you," Excalibur pointed at the Bishop of Rome; several mounted knights shifted, hollered protest, or drew their weapons, "to do whatever dark and manipulative deed you will, all in the name of the People. The Government is loaned power by the People, not the inverse. For the most part, the People ought to have the Government as I do; which is what best qualifies me to govern, as I desire ever and only to LEAVE THE PEOPLE ALONE!"

"Provided that they are Cymru." The Pope altered his game, seeking to make of Arthur a respecter of persons. "But God has made all men and women the same, each possessing of equal rights. Behold this assembly, Lord Arthur. Look how those of many nations now gather as one. This is the future of Britannia; that the Saxon, the Pict, the tribes of Eire, and the Britons might share these Isles. A brotherhood of Man under the Fatherhood of God. Your ways are dying, and before you is the New World Order."

"The utopian ramblings of a tyrant," came Arthur's retort. "When has the Saxon embraced nobility, or the Pict not traded a man's hide for a satchel of corn, or a horn of mead? You would put all men under one tent that you can crush him, not that you might make him free. God hath appointed the bounds of our habitation; let all men live free, WHERE He has appointed them."

The helm of the king then tilted towards the sky and turned east, his booming voice hurled in the direction of the other slope. "I offer the contest of Champions, a final plea that lives be saved. My sister did rework thy comely face, and the white hair suits you, Handsome. Come now; let us stand together and resolve our strife, Lancelot."

Whichever of the splinters sailing the shattered vessel that was Maelgwn Gwynedd, this one was not moved by the Silure's goading challenge. He moved not. *But Mordred moved.*

Newly filled with satanically inspired assurance, the Traitor had taken up again the golden armor, underlined with black mail and cloak; he sprinted towards Arthur, then halted with the skid of raging bull, sizing up his kill ere the strike.

"Remove that," said Arthur.

"Remove yours," replied Mordred.

Arthur did. And Mordred did.

Mirrored, identical eyes, the only part or attribute passed from the loins of Arthur to the demonic shell that now confronted him.

You would have made me the cuckold, and taken my queen, and my throne.

You murdered my true love. She NEVER loved you. She loved me, or that brute atop that ridge at times, but never YOU.

You will be removed from the Earth.

YOU will be removed from the Earth.

The enemies never spake these things, and said nothing.

"A challenge of Champions to settle this war, only it will be Eda, and not Mordred." Llew voiced acceptance of the terms, and the other nobles agreed.

"Eda, Mordred, then Lancelot, followed by whomever else you would add to the list." Arthur continued to beg a fight. "However, there is one condition before we circle and celebrate peace ere the Sun reaches the height of his circuit."

"Present your terms," said Llew.

The Pendragon asked Merlin to speak.

"There will be no State Religion in these Isles," he began, "regardless of outcome; all Cymru will renounce the intrusion and invasion of this synagogue of Satan and the law of Caermelyn will be restored: namely that men worship whatever God they will, only that they don't kill their neighbors for it, or force him to do the same."

"We will not renounce the Church at Rome, nor the Holy Father. The primitive Church of the Britons once held some truth, but apostasy hath mined through her soul as a canker. Rome is the future, and is of no threat to the sovereignty of Cymru." Caw was resolved.

"They are kind unto the old gods," offered the Saxon king, Cedric.

Arthur calmly put his helmet on again and motioned the banner carriers to wave the flags, indicating the departure of chieftains or emissaries before the battle ensues. All civilized men honor such pre-war negotiations, and often suing for peace or mercy is successful.

Gwladys, the enterprising merchant, had fashioned a new ensign for Cymru. Working from the red dragon sigil flown by Arthur, by Meurig, and before them Tewdrig, and before him the Pendragons of old, she had added a thick stripe of green below, and white above.

"Have we not had enough of dragons?" Huell ap Caw, the cattle thief, raider and thorn of the Midlands and of the South, insulted and mocked: "Dragons of flesh, dragons dressed as Silure kings, and dragons from the sky; HAVE WE NOT HAD ENOUGH OF DRAGONS?"

"Ignorant and debased, you do shame your father, who is at least an honorable foe." Merlin's defense of the flag was swift. "The white is heaven above and the green the earth below. The dragon is no longer a symbol of the power of the king or supremacy of the warlord. Neither a veneration of worshiping a wise serpent."

"What then?" Huell was not interested, shrugging his shoulders dismissively.

"The dragon is a symbol of what we have overcome. What we will ALWAYS overcome. Though heaven fall and the earth perish, the Cymru will survive. Though we falter and fail, though we stumble and fall…. We will get… back…up!" Merlin's words were rousing, and some of the northmen cheered.

Arthur noted the time invested in the theatre and returned his attention to Cedric.

"Today, we conclude Baedan. Twenty years

you've waited, and today you will make your stand against me." Arthur motioned to the Saxon's sheathed long-weapon. "Is it exercised and ready?"

"So Camlan starts today?" Cedric asked, a mixture of trembling and eagerness to at last slay the Pendragon that had defeated his people for an entire generation.

"Our troops will be in crimson silks and matching plume." Arthur made a full circle, communicating to all that might be able to hear, repeating himself two or three times. "The dead may not be removed during the battle; royals shall not be mutilated or defamed, neither their torques or rings purloined." These courtesies were basic, and all agreed.

"When do we commence?" Cedric pressed again.

Arthur waited a few more minutes, letting the intensity boil.

"King Cedric," the authority of God's voice again was selected, "is your steed swift?"

"Aye, Pendragon."

"Five miles. How fast could he bear you five miles…east of here?"

"Twenty minutes to negotiate these slopes, and half an hour at most for the rest."

"Oh, he is faster than the Great Stag." Mocking words in *that tone of authority*, confusing all. Arthur turned and bade Merlin farewell; the wizard fearing none of the sixty thousand, he would go to Lancelot. "Give me one and a half hours, for I am aged, and my mare's knees trouble him, as do mine."

"Granted! In ninety minutes Camlan begins!"

"Begins?" Arthur calmly put Excalibur to sheath and turned his steed, and the small party began to retreat, the new Pendragon flags waving proudly, tossed to and fro by the morning mountain breezes. At just the right time, he turned, but did not stop. "Begins? In ninety minutes most of your men will be dead—for the battle began two hours ago."

"Trickery and ruse!" someone screamed.

"We are distracted, ambushed!" cried another.

The soldiers were not wrong. Arthur and Merlin had had but one objective with their bold entry into the heart of darkness: delay and distract.

Eda raised a spear and would loose it at the king, but Cedric beseeched him to lower the missile. "The Silures presently hack and chop at my men, my sons. I beseech you, let me have first chance. I beseech you!"

Mordred's *Cai* reluctantly withdrew, and Arthur's horse, contrary to his report, had perfect knees and was swift as the wind. The small retinue rapidly disappeared down into the farmland, then the thicket, and then were as small black dots on the trails below.

Gildas could not help but wonder, *Was I, too, a pawn? Bait tangled ere the trap wire yanked?* For the first time in his life, the young master had a pang of doubt about Arthur Pendragon. A pang that remained as he traveled further north to Rheged.

***

In addition to crafting brilliant new flags, Gwladys and her hired help had fitted the warriors with forty thousand red silks, and forty thousand red plumes. The production had been on a grand scale, her organizational gifts unsurpassed. Gwenhwyfar ferch Gwythyr had happily given hours of her own labor to the task, busying her hands that they might distract her disappointed, aching heart.

Each silk was fastened to the breastplate, creating uniformity and allowing for identification during the tempest of battle.

Gwladys's lovely chest pieces and plumes were where the uniformity ended. The shortage of armor, and the smiths to fashion it, had not been fully overcome by the Round Table Companions. Because of this, the quality, form and nature of leather, fabric, wooden or metal protection under the silks varied, creating risk.

Bedwyr. If there never had been an Arthur, a Galahad, a Gwalchmai or a Lancelot, he would have been known as the greatest knight that ever lived. In an age with a surplus of heroes, his Song was not sung frequently, nor loudly enough. It was the subtle, discreet things that separated him from the rest. His indomitable humor, his overcoming disabling wounds, and his empathy for others — these were the characteristics overlooked by damsels at tea, or minstrels in the tavern. These were also the characteristics that would cause all men everywhere, and for all ages, to measure what was good and just and right by the Cymry and their Round Table Fellows. And Bedwyr was the best of these.

As the Silures enjoyed their final rest for water and final adjustments, less than an hour's ride from Nant-Y-Saeson, Bedwyr noted a young warrior of similar proportion struggling with defective latches and cracked rivets. Bedwyr gifted the lad *his silver skin*. The countenance of the downtrodden, frightened boy immediately shifted, confident that he was surely invincible, wearing the actual armor designed by the Lady of the Lake and worn by a Round Table Knight!

The battle began at sunrise, at about the time when the Pope's procession began. The South, outnumbering the Saxon forces, and exceeding them in skill, tore through them as a starving dog tossed pheasant carcasses after a great banquet.

The Bretons rained arrows; the Britons swept through with mounted troops. The Saxons were on the defensive from the onset, and never recovered.

Merlin ordered that songs of victory referencing Baedan and the Twelve Battles be sung in Latin and in Cymreig. Drums drowned out screams, and horns muted death rattles.

It took the Cymry longer to move and stack bodies so that they might continue the slaughter than to perform the killing itself. Veterans were taken back to the days of invincibility, and new troops gained the confidence that comes only by earning the first kill. Then the first five kills. Then twenty.

Hoel and Cadog noticed *an absence*.

And that absence was Bedwyr.

No timely jests. No glorious speeches. No magical, infectious motivation.

Ogyrfan son of Gwyar was the first to find him, slumped behind the debris of a broken supply cart.

Within the first thirty seconds of the battle, Bedwyr had felt a latch give way on the armor he had traded with the young warrior. Having but one hand, he had had to choose between *fiddle and fix or hack and whack.* Seeing his strait, a Saxon made a sloppy but somehow fortuitous swing with a double-headed battle-ax. The weapon was so sharp that Bedwyr did not feel the blow connect, nor did he suffer pain. Thinking he had either avoided the ax or absorbed the majority of the wound on the lower half of his chest plate, Bedwyr recoiled, reset his stance, and slew the Saxon with no difficulty. Then he collapsed.

King Cedric arrived, already filled with dread, seeing nigh the defeat of his divisive confederacy against the High King. The High King, meanwhile, had arrived moments earlier, and tasted the Golden Age again, fighting as a much younger man. Unlike tyrants and politicians who send others to die for their gain, the son of Meurig led his troops, ever willing to do that which he expected of his men. Even aged rulers of the Royal Clans were like-mannered. When their skills diminished, they would fight less, or battle only behind a ring of guards, but they were there, and not on some hill far away as a coward.

Arthur led by example. He led with his blade, not with his mouth.

And now his blade found Cedric.

Cai's club splattered grey matter on the Saxon king as two of his warlords fell upon his horse's front hooves, dead before they hit the dirt.

"Dismount!" Arthur challenged.

Cedric knew he was going to perish. He could

feel men falling all around him. Even if he did manage to defeat the Pendragon, ten Britons would run him through soon after. There was no escape, no secret route, no help from the shadowy Council of Nine.

He dismounted, hoping to earn victory in his final duel, and then hoping to die a brave death.

Arthur dismounted as well.

Cedric fought a defensive, slow match. He had no desire to rush upon Arthur, for the Cymreig warrior would counter any mistake; and all knew that counter-fighting was Arthur's special area of mastery. Moreover, the longer the match, the longer Cedric would draw breath and live.

Through the process of time, Cedric made minor errors, and suffered minor cuts. Spent, and bleeding from nine wounds, he withdrew, and removed his helmet.

"Will you suffer my sons to live?" he begged.

"You have become the unintentional founder of a nation. West Saxons and Lloegyr seem to be melding, and not many years hence shall be one nation. We do not attack other nations, and concern ourselves only with the defense of Cymru. Provided your sons at home *stay home*, they shall live, and—should this plague and calamity pass—prosper." Arthur offered kind, and true, words of solace, knowing in his heart that no Saxon ever *stays home*.

"Thank you, Pendragon. You are a just sovereign." Cedric engaged with his final reserve. And engaged amiss.

King Arthur ran Excalibur through the armor, through the heart, through the spine, and out of the back of Cedric. Twenty-one years after Mynydd Baedan, the third and last of the Germanic Chiefs was slain.

The rout had no ending and victory for the Round Table Knights was sure, each of them soaked head to toe in Saxon blood, giving shouts of praise and songs of triumph.

Bedwyr composed himself and stood aright, though his injury was grave.

CAMLAN ACT III

CHAPTER 20
Mist
The Misery of Morgaine

Arthur and his fabled companions had finished the Saxons prior to noonday on the twenty-first of June, five hundred and thirty-seven years from the Lord.

Though some of the younger warriors expected a reinforcing wave of Ravens to come, or to have to next deal with the pesky Picts, the more experienced knew that this would not be. So confident were they that the combat was finished for the day that they disarmed, washed in the river Dyfi, and set about erecting a small city of white tents, that they might have comfortable respite ere the next chapter of the Civil War.

The South was winning. Decisively.

The North's original strategy had been *slow them, flank them, make them climb.* However, the South had not been slowed in the woodland area below the farmland, and the force dedicated to flanking them lay in lakes of blood, piles of flesh. Although the scales were more balanced after the annihilation of Cedric, Arthur was still outnumbered by approximately ten thousand men. Therefore, the North would keep their backs to the slopes and their armies facing Maes-Y-Camlan, and simply wait for Arthur to cut back west from Nant-Y-Saeson and conduct the climatic final chapter on Maelgwn's farm itself.

Arthur's armies still had some risk of defeat, for fighting from a low-ground position is disadvantageous, and typically results in a resounding loss. Low-ground wars are only won through protracted, small skirmishes that bait those on the high ground to abandon their advantage, become overly aggressive, and leave a crease in the ranks that can be breached. Once some portion of Arthur's men were on the same level in the slopes, he could push the remainder of the Ravens down into the gulch, and then the farm, and have equitable chance of finishing them.

Moreover, Arthur planned to send scouts to cut supplies and to starve his foes, making the ridgetop a prison. Mordred's men could descend the opposite side of the hill and replenish themselves in Maddwy, thus conceding Craig-Y-Gamell to the Silures, or press down the mound for water, supplies and food, and in so doing, sacrifice position.

The scene was an inverse of Baedan, where Arthur had forced the Saxons to ascend; here he would cause his treacherous kinsmen to descend, else flee north, else starve.

The "waiting" part of war had come. Both sides knew as much, and rested.

***

June 22
AD 537

"Brother, wake with great haste!" Cai was pulling Arthur from his cot with the angst of a child tugging at its parent to rouse and give gifts at a harvest festival. "Get up!"

"I wasn't lying to those rogues about *my knees*," Arthur jested, still in the drift of sleep, not alert enough to be startled. *After all, Cai's job is to over-worry and overthink.*

Cai found a tunic in Arthur's chest, and quickly unfolded linen trousers, almost dressing the king.

"But these don't even match—I will look awful before the men!" Arthur's mood was jovial, energetic, grand. Maelgwn had won the day at Llongborth, but the Pendragon had smashed his foes at Talgarth, in the Wood, and at Nant-Y-Saeson. *I am up two, old friend. Perhaps you will abandon this cause on this day or the next.*

"That's the problem, brother. The men WON'T see you—come!"

Arthur did the bidding of his well-meaning, overbearing foster-brother, giving two more jokes and one more protest, and was mid-sentence when he stepped from his pavilion. He stopped jesting. *Stopped speaking at all.*

A mist had enveloped the camp. The whole of the camp. Forty thousand souls: the fog so thick that none could see his fellow beyond the measure of six inches, unless they were in a tent or cave.

And the mist was enchanted, ethereal. It possessed substance and moisture, hues of yellow and green, flashes of blue.

Fear and confusion reigned. Clamor, debate, indecision, curses and sundry prayers that God or some god would remove the spell noised throughout. Cadfan found Arthur's forearm and identified himself, imploring his lord for audience. Arthur guided Cadfan within the folds of his tent and lit a candle, though it were morning time.

"'Tis Morgaine," the bishop informed him.

Before Arthur could respond, shouts of shock shook the tethers, the ground filled with stamping horses and bewildered knights.

The fog was gone. Though not all.

A swirl, a spinning cone of mist, concealed Gareth, Gaheris, Ogyrfan and, suddenly, King Arthur as well.

Five miles northwest, a mist shrouded Mordred as well.

Cadfan repeated, "'Tis Morgaine."

***

"I cannot control it; woe unto Cymru." The Sorceress's elbows rested upon the fount where she looked upon the results of her webs, and they were woven amiss. When causing pilgrims to lose their way, or priests to be befuddled, the mist was her servant. Where war was involved, it was as a wild brush fire, a hungry, slapdash dog.

Morgaine was undeterred. Thrice clockwise she motioned the green scrying waters; pause. Thrice clockwise once more. But the Vision did not improve. Her sons and brother were at once entombed in the protective cloudy cottons of the mist in one moment, the whole of Gwynedd the next, a mountaintop or gully bottom the following.

Her nine priestesses were grieved for the Lady of Avalon, and sorely worried for her. She neither ate nor slept, and was ever at her magickal workings. One maiden, called Thitis, who was patroness of stringed instruments, carefully laid Morgaine's head upon her lap (the Sorceress gave no protest) and strummed songs of soothing, melodies of mourning, refrains of rest.

"If the Christian God is truly the Most High" — she spoke as Gwyar—"then why will He not favor me for so long protecting the mother of His Son?" She wept. "I honored His Son, killed only His naughty priests…" Tears outlined a brief smile. "Why can He not spare the remainder of mine?"

"Men have bargained and bartered with the gods since the beginning, Mistress." Thitis continued to strum, for music was her method of communication. "I don't think even the gods can ultimately burglarize the free will of Man. And Man is a warring, killing sort."

Gwyar wept.

She was overcome with grief and introspection, grieving for not only the loss of her sons, which was imminent, but the passing of the Summer Kingdom.

"What makes me special, or differing from any other mother?" she judged herself. "The thick, fiery-haired, red-hot-tempered Pictish woman, hunting seals and making pelts in remote north—is her mourning and passion less than mine? In no way. The Jutish mom, whose young, yellow-haired boy is right now toiling in a foreign land, hearing songs and curses in unknown tongues, terrified as the Briton leaf snips his throat. Is her anguish and restlessness of no import whilst I moan over mine? The Raven. O, my sisters from Gwynedd and Ynys Mon! My mothers, my kinswomen! Is not each of their sons worthy of a bard's song? Why is Gwyar superior? Men, and women, ought not to think too highly of themselves. What hath my meddling wrought?" Here she called out to *the other noteworthy meddler.* "Merlin! What hath our meddling wrought?"

"A light of freedom against a darkness unimaginable when you and I are exiled, and Arthur sleeps." A direct, prophetic answer was given. The voice matched the wizard's, but whence it came, the weeping lady knew not.

But, through the blur of swollen eyes, a man did appear. A comely man. Youthful, virile, a heathen through and through, he seemingly stepped out of Britain's pagan past. But this druid was from Gaul, and had been apprenticed in these parts.

"Accolon," Thitis beckoned to the lad to approach and kneel near the fount where they lay, "bring it, that she may recover, for our Mistress is undone."

The young druid wore a giddy crest made of holly and went about without shirt, having only a single gold torque round his left arm as clothing above the waist. Only a simple plaid wrap below; and he was barefoot besides. Having a small dagger, he made five perfect slits in a plump pomegranate and opened it with careful, sensual skill, squeezing two wedges into a wooden goblet; giving Gwyar juice wherewith to drink, and fruit wherewith to eat.

Her attendants had not heard the voice of the wizard, but the words were at once painful and edifying, and the beautiful form before her reminded her that the Isles had heroes yet to come, futures worth defending. If a dark age was coming, she would fight it to the last, and not gently.

Gwyar had fallen. Morgaine of the Faeries rose.

"I like him," she commented to Thitis, with a new voice. The other maidens giggled.

If there was a full and lasting fog, the armies might withdraw. Then she could assassinate individuals over time, sparing her loved ones, mitigating the loss of life. If an isolated, covering spiral of mist was about them, then they might escape, and live. *Broad or acute, only consistent!* Her resolve returned, for better or worse, and the Faerie did her spells cast, and her powers work, harder and harder still.

***

Lancelot and his Hosts camped atop the eastern ridge and remained, for the most part, inert. They hunted and prepared a well-organized camp, complete with a great log table, over which were spread parchments and maps. Merlin spied them out, but did not yet approach.

They watched the mists ebb and flow, come and go, swirl and vanish. None knew quite what to do; Lancelot calmly commanded them to take little food, to be vigilant, and to elsewise do nothing.

***

"Follow the sound of the crooked river, that we reach Camlan—let us at least do that much," commanded Arthur. The distance to be covered should have taken less than three hours, even for so many souls, carts, supplies and horses. Instead: twelve hours.

Darkness had settled over the field of Camlan, and approximately forty thousand soldiers were there. Cheerful for victory, baffled by the mists, which rested on nothing, as gargantuan clouds but inches from the ground. The moonlight, the mists, and the dark blue, starry night in Gwynedd. 'Twas a scene perfect for lovers and poets; not so for soldiers.

But Arthur would nonetheless have them initiate the next phase.

Organized skirmishes.

"Use the sound of the water and the position of the stars, and not the billows of white at your feet, and harass the southeastern tip of the hill," he ordered.

"How many?" asked Cadog, who was charged to lead the tussle.

"One troop, no more. Slash and withdraw, no volleys."

Cadog, an original Round Table Knight, had executed the scheme countless times. His role was to anger the enemy, draw him out, earn a short victory, and then capture the ground the enemy vacated. When this was repeated over and over again, the high-ground position would soon be a garble of friend and foe; then the Silures would rapidly reassemble and launch a level-to-level ground offensive by longbow, followed by horseback engagements.

Caw and Llew knew what the enemy would do, yet human nature made it impossible to prevent Arthur from doing to them exactly and precisely what he aimed to do. As brains were smashed with clubs, or kneecaps exploded all around the camp, those under assault would either flee—which they could not, having the gulch and the mountain terrain behind them—or draw anger and fury, and fight back, and chase.

They did the latter, riding, else sprinting, through the fog after ghosts in the night.

Cadog was victorious.

Likewise, Cador and his three hundred provoked the same response.

Four times this was repeated, each a battle within a battle.

Four thousand from the North were slain, else scattered.

Arthur could *feel* that their discipline would break on the morrow, and that the sum of Mordred and Llew's hordes would engage them on even ground on Maes-Y-Camlan.

"We have earned the ascent point of both ridges, lord. But the fog thickens, and is wet, causing our torches to fail," Hoel reported.

"Another day is ours," rejoiced Arthur. "Let us now rest and hope my sister's fog does tomorrow lift, that we might finish this."

"Whether it abates or no, I have an idea. Would you hear of it from me?"

"Would Merlin like it?" Arthur mused, inviting to Hoel to join him for cider and to tell the king his ambition.

CAMLAN ACT IV

CHAPTER 21
The Fateful Division of the Army and Derfel's Rout of the Silures and Bretons

Merlin would emphatically *not* like it...

Hoel favored a style of attack, which had been very successful over his long career, of dividing his troop cleanly, with perfect timing, to develop a flank—and then doing so once more. If the first flank was achieved, the second was easy, and the Bretons would simply meet in the middle, ceasing to hack and thrash when seeing their own sigils before them.

Merlin disliked this approach, favoring the 'widening V' method of war. His method featured a vanguard of elite troops forming the tip of an arrowhead formation, always wider at the base than at the front. This made *being flanked* impossible. The best warriors in front would wedge through the opponent with such ferocity and precision that the opponent would scatter and try to flank both sides of the 'arrowhead' at once. This never worked, and Arthur's Silures would simply pluck and kill the dross as they spilled from the side of his arrow formation.

These were the differing open-warfare, mounted-knight methods when engaged in a field. Both were successful, and there was no dogma where war was concerned. However, Merlin and Hoel, who were great friends, did argue over this much; especially when the pride that accompanies cider was over-consumed. Because of Hoel's love for 'divide and flank', he would, as all passionate and good leaders do, contend for his method—only, this time, he advocated dividing the army and sending one third of the men to the obverse side of Craig-Y-Gamell. If it was true, as assumed and evident, that Llew and Caw would empty the mountain into Camlan below, a divided section could earn the top of the western slope (opposite of Lancelot) and reverse positions, clipping the Ravens terminally from above.

Moreover, Hoel argued that by gaining some ascent, the troop commanders could negotiate the fog, all the more increasing the advantage.

There was reason in Hoel's presentation. But it also presented risk. Morgaine's mists made an apprised census impossible. If some of the allied armies of Mark, Llew, Drest, Caw and any remaining Saxons had shifted off the mount, they could gain advantage and ambush over Arthur.

The king found himself intrigued by the idea, and sought counsel from his Round Table fellows, who were ironically, and equally, *divided over the division.*

Bedwyr ensured that he could not be found, lest he be engaged in a conference where he would be made to sit at a bench or table with the others. For the flow of red from his navel was constant. He borrowed a torch and, under the firelight, examined the severity of the wound. *A man should not see his own innards, yet Bedwyr did.* Iron was scarce, so he withdrew the seax, or Saxon longknife, from the skull of a dead Briton, heated the blade until it was nearly molten, and then seared the wound. Bedwyr thanked the Lord for the thick fog, as it allowed discretion and preserved dignity, for he could wail and screech alone.

The proposal finding equal parts favor and opposition, Arthur was empowered and encouraged to decide.

Merlin would know what to do. But Merlin is not here.

"I will go to yonder chapel, and think, and pray. And restfully consider the matter. Let us convene ere the cock crows, friends." Arthur motioned for Cai, who bled from the forearm beneath his armor.

***

The chapel of Saint Tydecho, though located in Gwynedd, had friendly ties to both Arthur and Hoel. Tydecho was the son of Amwn Ddu, the Black Knight, and his mother was Anna of Gwent, daughter of Meurig. Thus Tydecho was nephew to Arthur and Hoel. His little church had been founded during the Golden Age, a few years after the Baedan, when liberty had reigned and a new church or school had been founded seemingly every week. Tydecho lived in the church, along with his fair sister Tegfedd, and both adored Arthur, though they worshipped God after the Roman Way.

The church was empty, for surely the siblings had taken refuge in the village of Mallwyd. It featured two bedchambers, a dedicated dining and study area for the brethren, a worship hall and baptistery. There was a soft, feminine décor and feel to the dwelling, and the Iron Bear felt soothed and calm as he pondered, prayed, and slept.

***

Sunrise
June 23
AD 537

Morgaine pleaded to Ogyrfan through her looking glass. She brought her fists slamming down into the waters, hoping to reach through space, or bend time, with the might in her own tiny hands. Her mists had vanished and then reappeared around all whom she loved save Ogyrfan. He was exposed, and the hordes of Mark mixed with the Raiders of Eire, lured, angry and desperate, had spilled themselves into the field at the moment the fog had abated. *Or temporarily abated.*

"Run!" she screamed, the whole of the Castle on Ynys Enlli shaking to its foundation, its glass rafters protesting, sending dusty glass down onto the black marble floors. "Run!"

But Ogyrfan fell. Another red-silked Silure given to the soil of Cymru, who cried against the unwanted nourishment.

Lightning rained down, though the skies were clear and the morning light comely.

Seeing the field flooded with men, and gaining a brief, clear view that the Silures had gained equal ground on numerous patches of the mount above, Arthur directed Hoel to activate his plan. Instantly, and in unison, ten thousand red-silks turned their horses northwest, parading slowly to allow for spacing and proportion, and then *neigh, whinny, gallop, crackle* — and gone.

King Arthur's army was divided.

Hoel led the third that had departed, with many fabled knights joining him, Cadog, Cador, and Gwynlliw included. All were excited.

But in their excitement, an oversight.

Derfel!

The spear-wielding demigod of Brittany.

The new Lancelot.

Was he not his father's son?

'Twas he who loosed the men, giving appearance of full commitment to fighting upon the open field. And the moment the fog relented, he did dispatch ten thousand Picts to the obverse side of the mountain, where they would be waiting for Hoel, and have the double advantage of high ground and surprise over him.

Derfel would not see his brothers slain if he could prevent it, and the thought of his father's passing he put from his mind. But loyalty demanded sacrifice, and his loyalty had he sworn to Cadfan, who might also lead him to the Grail.

Seeing Arthur from afar the prior morn had filled the lad with awe, and his judgment haunted him. Therefore, Derfel deployed a tactic taught as part of those he had learned among Vivien's Martial Arts. Derfel would fight with a spear, which was longer than most and could not be used save for atop steed, allowing him to keep his distance. He would poke the upper thigh of his opponent's horse, then puncture the ankle of the rider.

Poke, puncture, on to the next. Poke, puncture, on to the next.

The new Lancelot loved animals and it vexed him to harm them, but the two-step maneuver would create injured men instead of ghosts.

The mists returned, thicker, more blinding and debilitating than before.

What Derfel meant for kindness, his mates used for easy kills, finding wounded knights, making sport in torturing them. None of the one hundred and twenty-two men wounded by Derfel survived.

And here began the *longest day of the Civil War*. The warriors from both sides fought what felt like individual battles on account of the mist. One round of combat would conclude; they would peer through the billows and find another.

And the armor began to fail.

For the first two days the Silure had been dominant, and untested. Now blows of axe and sword were making minor wounds fatal or causing hastily-made buckles to give. There was more adjusting than fighting by legions of the red-silks, and the Ravens were at last earning casualties, in large numbers, of their own.

Meanwhile, none of those who had divided off from Arthur's ranks were ever heard from again.

The Picts, vicious and skilled, rained ten thousand thousand stones upon the noble knights, which were as wasps stinging them in a haze, and by volume, killing them. The slingshot—an ancient weapon as old as man—when mastered can penetrate thick armor and crush the thickest of bones and skulls. The flat stones of the slingshots incapacitated, and Pictish clubs and spikes completed the rout, the Silures suffering the greatest loss of life in a single military exercise in their kingdom's history.

Morgaine saw this as well and became white as a phantom. God or the gods had exposed Ogyrfan purposefully, mocking her intervention. The remainder of her loved ones now fought in a blind haze, receiving no benefit of her ethereal sendings. Resigned to the fact that she could not arbitrate the wars of men, she began to do all to remove the mist, and let the free will of the Sons of Adam have its course.

CAMLAN ACT V

CHAPTER 22
Elvish Armor and War Dogs

Taliesin was conducted to the Good Court, where he was made to dance, revel, and oblige gifts to the Tylwyth Teg. This he happily did, and patiently. Every sinew of his being begged him to cry unto them to hasten and finish, but he could not. For the Fae are peculiar beings, and time for them is not as time is for the Sons of Adam. The Chief Bard continued to think on this, and not upon his kinsmen, whose battles were by now surely far advanced.

***

The Battle of Camlan was indeed far advanced.
Neither the North nor the South had established clear advantage. The first two days had been Arthur's, and this final day had thus belonged to Mordred the Traitor. He personally enjoyed kills, each of which were prepared and cleaned as freshly-caught fish by Eda.
Presently, Eda sought out Cai, that he might kill the Pendragon's lifelong companion, foster-brother, and steward.

And where Cai strove, there strove Arthur.

Lancelot the Statue peered through the fog, and was able to follow Mordred somewhat, on account of his golden skin and gold-clad horse. Even a mystical fog could not his arrogance hide.

It was at seeing Mordred's Champion draw near the king that Lancelot finally moved. At just the moment when his right hand, lifted high, was to make signal to his Hosts, the Merlin stood before him.

Lancelot paused, and dismounted.

***

"Name for me, Sir, the seven virtues of the Fae," the Elf King demanded, handing Taliesin a harp with one hand, a roasted turkey leg twice *the possible size* with the other.

Knowing that when the Fae offer, one should *take*, and do so with gratitude, Taliesin took, ate, and strummed. Seeing this pleased the Puck, Taliesin made an effort at friendly jest. "I have not eaten so well since December! May I please finish, and think upon thy riddle?"

The Prince of Pixies adored Taliesin, for he was powerful yet humble, mighty yet debased, foolish yet wise, and above all, a faithful keeper of the Mysteries. "Eat, Merlin II, eat!"

Taliesin searched his mind, filled with thirty years of bardic training. He could 'see' letters in his mind, and whole parchments could he recollect—with focus.

"Let me assist you, Taliesin; your mind seemeth too busy." If red eyes with no pupils could have a kind disposition, these did. "Are you contented with your meat?"

"Forgive me, Good King, I cannot eat another bite, but would not offend and will eat to the bursting; for it is scrumptious, and quite the delight."

"The answer of the knowledge I require of thee is already given in your responses. Ease thy mind." Other tall Faeries that had female forms took the scraps from Taliesin, tittered, and wiped his brow playfully. "With each virtue, strike one chord upon the harp. As you do this, I will draw one point of the Faerie Star, and we shall bring forth the knowledge and the wisdom already in you."

"Hospitality." *Strum.*

"Generosity." *Strum.*

"Yes, good! Go on!"

"Kindness." *Strum.*

"In our own impish way," he chortled.

"Compassion." *Strum.* "Courage!" Taliesin could see the lessons of his youth now, and finished with conviction. "Politeness and adventuresomeness!" Not only did Taliesin pair each with a chord as directed, but he then played a lovely melody and stood in victory, having forgotten the power and truth paired in these rays, which were the seven rays of Faerie virtue, and the Law of the Good Court of the Fae.

"Yes!" cried the king, clapping and pleased. "Now harken, Merlin II, and note that I also am Lord of the Bad Court, which is the contrary pole of each of these." The septogram he had drawn comprised blinking white and gold dust on the one side; when he rotated it about, 'twas hot orange fire on the other. The lesson concluded, it diminished, falling to dust upon the ground.

"I understand." The Christian Bard nodded.

Then the Faerie did something of stunning astonishment: he entered into a normal conversation with Taliesin.

"What would you have of us?" he opened.

"I understand, more than my fellows, why you cannot intervene in the all-out wars of men. That your kind will be loosed in the End of Days and battle against men is the subject of Prophecy, and easy to find in Scripture. Likewise, that you are forbidden from doing the same in this Grace dispensation is clearly detailed as well, knowing that we wrestle in the spiritual, and not the physical realm, during this time." Taliesin paused. "Easy to apprehend, impossible to comprehend." Not wanting to try the patience of his host, or the dozens of diverse creatures now gathered in what Taliesin felt was still the ring of stones (but of a certainty, he knew not), he made his questions direct. "Are there exceptions? And what happens if you try to intervene? For surely Morgaine has--"

"The exceptions are in accord with the will of the God of gods alone, in whom we believe, before whom we tremble, but whom most of us know not." First question answered. "An elect angel from above the firmament will come, and do battle with we Powers and Thrones, and could flick an unclean spirit like me into the Deep with no more effort than you would flick a fruit-fly from your breakfast." Question two answered. "Or the Most High Creator will, alternatively, intervene in some other unknown way, that His will be not usurped." Question two expounded. "Morgaine is more powerful than the whole of the Good Court and the Bad Court combined. She made as far as to change the weather for the final conflict, but could go no further."

"So she *did* intervene?" Taliesin asked.

"Somewhat, but methinks awry."

"Would God allow something, for the cause of balance, in answer to her intervention? Nothing by way of spells that stung or dashed or harmed men, but rather" — Taliesin looked for the words — "protected him to make the fight fair?"

"He is your God and your Savior, Merlin II; why ask me these things and not Him?"

"Because I am no match for an angel if the answer is 'no'." The druid smiled, and gave a longing, desperate plea with his eyes.

"Oh, little bard, knowest thou not that God hath chosen the weak things of the world to confound the mighty? One day you will judge angels, and the disaster they created down here in God's garden of Men. I am one of those disasters. One day, you will judge me. Pray you remember this gift. Now go."

Taliesin knew better than to second-guess, or ask for further explanation. Before his boot touched the border of circle, the Lord of the Elves said unto him: "Know this; one of our own did beguile your Lancelot when he was sixteen. She vexed him, planting each of the seven virtues into the lad with dark, naughty magic, that each would be extreme — a person within a person, if you will."

"Lancelot is seven?" Taliesin reacted.

"Thou forgets so soon your lesson, after

getting fat on my best bird!" The king was disappointed. But Taliesin rallied quickly.

"Polarity! Lancelot is FOURTEEN in one shell."

"Excellent, Merlin II! And she crossed them up and shook them as a jar of rocks and marbles, as a plaything for children."

"May Merlin the First balance and reconnect him, else we are all lost."

The Merlin Taliesin traversed the edge of the stones and was back near the Chapel of Saint Mary in Ynys Mon, unsure of how much time had passed. Unsure, but thankful that the Tylwyth Teg would make effort to do *something* to counter Morgaine's meddling.

***

"What will you say at this last hour?" Lancelot at last broke his cold silence. The Wizard and the Greatest Warrior to Ever Live, again nostril to nostril, that spittle and spray was exchanged. These Titans had no fear one for the other.

"Nay." Merlin was brief.

"Will you cause me to relive the seven offenses, or the three blows that brought us to this precipice of hell on earth and devastation?"

"No."

"Or tell me how that I am mad?!" Lancelot took two giant steps backwards and roared, as a lion, "I saw your Boy King's eyes when Mordred was caught in the unspeakable act. I attempted to calm him—I saw madness, and for six months after I witnessed it increase. The Madness of Maelgwn is but a small thing to the lunacy of the Bear of

Glamorgan! To slaughter his grandchildren and then goad that demon below to war—"

"He goaded him not, Lancelot," Merlin began. "'Twas I who recommended the use of shock, but to save lives, not to cause the end of more lives. The messenger Iddawg did change the message, activate the Just One in you, and cause Mordred to retaliate. The whole war is built upon—"

Lancelot found the intrigue interesting, but not overly. "The whole of the war is built upon 'I saw her first'." The two steps of retreat were retracted, the two rams' horns locked yet again. "Would we have these discussions anew, with dealings to conduct below?"

"No." Again Merlin had no desire to look to the past; rather to the future, and the present. "Do you really want to be High King, Maelgwn? It is one thing to want Arthur *not* to rule, but would you do it in his stead? If he falls, the Picts, the Saxons, and whomever else Simon has waiting in line to invade, will be full of confidence knowing he is gone. This is not about the man Arthur; this is about the legend of King Arthur. YOU are King Arthur. I am King Arthur. Camelot must live, or we will all fall." Merlin now begged Lancelot. "Do not engage in this Civil War, or there can be no reconciliation."

"There can be no reconciliation." Cold words, bereft of emotion. "Look now below, Merlin Emerys, and see the end of King Arthur."

A flat, rocky surface jutted out from the slope, a natural platform on the incline of the slope. Arthur found himself there, unhorsed and surrounded, with Eda and ten men in pursuit. Ten versus three. And one of the three's insides were burst, held in place by the nub of Bedwyr. The scene was but five hundred feet below the ridge where stood Lancelot and Merlin.

"*Where are your war dogs?* Or do you use them only to hunt women and effeminate men, like your son?!"

Arthur's exhalations and pants were so heavy underneath his helmet that he did not hear the fullness of Lancelot's invectives. But he gathered their meaning when he saw what was loosed upon him, sprinting down the hill.

The Dormarch.

Arthur had seen four-armed Giants, questing beasts that were an abominable, unnatural mixing of various animals, flying things, witches and ghouls. Yet the reasonable part of him had still thought the Dormarch, or hounds of hell, only a fable to scare disobedient children into cleaning the crockeries or attending to their studies. Yet five descended upon him.

The alpha of the pack was most swift and leapt into the air, meaning to quickly smother and torture the Pendragon, but to leave him limbless and shamed with heart still beating, that Lancelot might tear it from his chest and show it to the king as he passed into the underworld.

Arthur quickly plunged Excalibur into the rock and took up Rhon, hoping to pierce the dog like unto the hooking of a great fish. Arthur's thrust went amiss, and the demon dog was atop him. Its jaws clinched on the king's armor.

But the armor was no longer armor fashioned by the hands of men…

Vivien had tried to replicate the metal skin of the Elves, but had never dared ask for *Elvish Armor.*

In the twinkling of an eye, EVERY RED-SILK that lived was adorned in the magical armor of the Elves. Nine blows required for every one blow that would breach the chainmail of man. So light that the warrior felt as though he were sparring or at play in the kitchen with his brothers. The pieces form-fitting to the shin, to the thigh, about the loins, and upon the chest and back, the arms in three pieces and the helms a shinier, stronger version of the Corinthian fashion. Moreover, the armor glowed and caused the fog to retreat wherever its wearer stood.

The dog's gnashings were of no effect and Bedwyr, who had freed Excalibur from the stone with his good hand, did stab the beast; the Sword of Power caused it to vanish back to the underworld, leaving great pools of black bile in its stead.

Meanwhile, another factor was ebbing the tide of battle against the Round Table Knights.

Picts.

Having slaughtered Hoel and his retinue, they now poured down the mountain as locusts. Arthur, Bedwyr and Cai knew what their presence meant, and sorrowed as they readied to face them.

Derfel understood the same, not far off. Seeing the enchanted armor and the ongoing bravery of the middle-aged king continued to give the young hero pause.

Then pause turned to full repentance, for by chance Derfel caught a glimpse of Cadfan, bleeding out in an embankment.

"Cadfan!" Derfel galloped and leapt from his horse, tumbling twice in his desperation, losing his breath as he pounded upon the dirt. The Picts had pushed the whole of the conflict, save those scattered few below Lancelot's ridge, onto the open pitch of Camlan.

Recovering himself, Derfel attended to his kinsman, mentor and friend. "Red silk, Cadfan? A cunning disguise, brother?"

"My allegiance to the Council of Nine was my disguise, as was my dead Religion. I died today without my mask upon my brow, for my true self is loyal to freedom, and to—"

"Arthur of Caerleon."

Derfel held Cadfan, whose visage shone as the sun as he passed into the sleep of death, having perfect contentment about his countenance.

Derfel slowly and respectfully removed the red vest and fastened it upon his own black-lacquered, leather chest piece. The new Lancelot fought as had oft the former, with but a chest piece and leather gauntlets. A helmet slowed him down and impaired vision, and he was too quick of movement to be struck in the head besides. Knowing the battle was in balance, Derfel whispered, "I know you cherish this silk, and I promise to return it," and joined the fight — against the Picts.

Eda and Cai at last entered into single combat. Ten or more men were near, and all honored the clash. Bedwyr chased after Mordred, whilst Arthur toiled with the dogs.

After successive strikes, mirrored and blocked, Eda tackled Cai, shifting the duel to a grappling affair. Cai did well to lock one of Eda's wrists, breaking three small bones beneath the thumb. The rush of battle allowed Eda to ignore the wrist, which instantly swelled to thrice its size. Fortunately for Mordred's steward, it was his supporting hand; his strong hand still functioned well, and found a dagger stashed in his boot, which he plunged into Cai's side above twelve times.

Cai fought on, undeterred, and turned the match back into a standing contest. Cai regained advantage…until Eda the Coward kicked the Round Table Legend hard in the groin, underneath the frontal plate of his armor.

A man whose entire life, each and every day, from morning to night, had been lived with honor, was now incapacitated on account of dishonor. None can recover when kicked *there,* and there is no training to manage the pain thereof. Cai rolled upon the ground, paralyzed in pain, in vomit, in his own blood. His eyes found Arthur, and his final emotion was great disappointment in failing to be at his lord's side, vanquishing dogs and watching over the sandy-haired king. *I have failed to keep my vow, Meurig, forgive me––*

Eda raised the head of Cai high, vaingloriously boasting of his trophy.

***

"Which one of you steers the vessel, Lancelot? Who is in charge?" Merlin pressed. "You do not want to be High King. Your true love is lost, and yours she never was. You want to farm, and bed maidens, and study and live a quiet life. Do you not?"

Lancelot noted in his mind that Merlin was not wrong. He loathed politics and everything accompanied by a life devoted to it.

"Who is in charge?" Merlin reached for old magick, and sought to realign the circuits of the tormented man.

"Hospitality or unsociability?" And an ancient arrangement of words.

"Generosity or greed?

"Kindness or cruelty?" The spell continued.

"Compassion or a heart of stone?

"Courage or cowardice?" Merlin sought to tear the shards of Lancelot asunder, and reassemble him.

"Politeness or debasement?

"Adventuresomeness or recluse?" Seven multi-colored knights came forth from Lancelot, who did seize and convulse upon his steed. "Not you fellows"—Merlin charged, this time lightning and wonders discharging from his staff—"you!"

Seven more knights, void of color as shadowy ghosts, emerged. Merlin then called upon the name of the Fallen One who had done this to Lancelot, knowing that there was more work to be done.

"Dragon, Giant, Water Spirit and Man; these are all part of you, and I cannot separate them from you, old friend. The foul things I have removed, but the former are part of your being. But henceforth, methinks you will be better." Merlin did curse the witch, an entity older than the Morrigan, that had bewitched Lancelot once more, but did not tarry about that, for the time was short. Instead, he brought Maelgwn back, fully back, to awareness, to consciousness.

The Bloodhound Prince mounted his horse, quickly.

Merlin asked but one question more of he

who was yet the most powerful warrior in the land. "When it comes time to do that which you ought to do, what will you do?"

***

Arthur was taking wounds on his arms and calves, the mystical Elvish coverings saving his life—*but for how long?*

Eda continued to parade about with the head of Cai, singing aloud, "Camelot is fallen; fallen is Cam—"

A spear whistled through the air, flung from five hundred feet above. Flung by Arthur's Champion, Lancelot.

It pierced Eda between the shoulder and the heart, but was not fatal. He scurried from the scene, which was not difficult, given the erratic fog.

The surviving knights of old cried out. "Lancelot, Lancelot is with us! Fight, fight on!"

The Hosts of Maelgwn and Derfel were brilliant, noble, good, and restored.

But too late.

Lancelot personally slew King Drest, and Llew, and Arthur finished Caw, but the death count was so high that few souls remained as dusk fell; and many had fled hours earlier. Amongst these were Hueil ap Caw, and many of his brothers.

Gareth and Gaheris too were amongst the dead.

As was Gwynllyw ap Glywys, as was Cadog, as was Cador.

Arthur and Lancelot wanted to share words, but the loss of life was such that they could not speak.

The fog did diminish, beginning to recoil unto its source, which was Avalon.

And Arthur and Lancelot looked for Mordred the Whelp upon the field of Camlan.

CAMLAN ACT VI

CHAPTER 23
The Fog is Lifting
The Passing of Arthur

Some daylight remained. The sun was bright red, attempting to cut through the haze, as if helping the scant few surviving Round Table Fellows find the Traitor and finish their final stand together. The dead or dying numbered in the thousands, and the air was filled with final gasps, prayers uttered by desperate tongues.

Arthur began to panic, fearing that Mordred had fled the field and found a way, perhaps in league with the Council of Nine, to make the day for naught, bringing future devastation upon Cymru.

Morgaine of the Faeries was already upon the sea, cutting through the rough waters in a black barge, its bow fashioned as a swan. The Nine Maidens accompanied her, along with Accolon, and the boatman made twelve. The slight Faerie stood upon a platform that ran the width of the stern. Her spirit cried out to Arthur.

You are desperate, brother. But all is not lost.

"Gwyar?" Arthur ran this way and that. "Lancelot, did you hear her?"

"Nay, lord, I hear only death, and the consummation of our sins."

I was wrong, Arthur. Forgive me.

"Gwyar!" Still he could not locate the source of the voice.

The Swan Barge did not sail to Aberdaron, but rather cut directly east, making her way through the southernmost depths of the Ceredigion Bay. She would come ashore near Dolgellau, and then on to Camlan to fully restore her brother. *But I will help him ere I arrive.*

Forgive me, Arthur. Here at the end, we ALL align with you, for you are the Summer Kingdom, and the Summer Kingdom is you. Mordred shall not make the spires of Camelot to fall.

"MORGANA!!!!!" he cried, his voice hoarse, and his friends feared he was fevered, or mad.

***

Mordred hid beneath the corpses of three Ravens, fashioning a tent from their cloaks.

The mists themselves sang, a low, repetitious, brooding chant, then gave the sound of cymbals and shattered glass. Excalibur, still borne by Bedwyr, shone in response to the song, humming and vibrating, an effervescence of greens and blues. It caused the knight to point in the direction of the Whelp. The mist then fully retreated as Morgaine undid her spell and more, giving Arthur their son.

"The fog is lifting, Father." Mordred had no recourse, no way out. Drawing on the arrogance given him by the Black Pope, he slowly placed his golden helmet on, and the Divine Child approached the Pendragon.

"My lord, thy sword." Bedwyr offered Arthur his steel.

But Arthur declined. "He is not worthy to fall by Excalibur."

Arthur clasped Rhon, his fabled spear, and did the unexpected. *He attacked first.* The counter-fighter did not wait, nor plot, nor evade; rather, he attacked.

Mordred, surprised at this, fully expecting to test Arthur with the first two to three blows, was caught. And run through.

Rhon pushed through the golden armor and impaled Mordred, who gurgled, choking on an erupting fountain of his own blood. Knowing death was nigh, Mordred drew himself up on the spear, pulling it through him, drawing within striking range of the king.

This in turn surprised Arthur, who should have loosed the spear, stepped out of range, and then finished his son with dagger or, if needs be, by hand. Instead he froze and looked into *his own eyes*. Eyes that drew near, and nearer still.

Mordred swung his battle spike at the helmet of his father. It was a long weapon, and the flight time gave Arthur a half-second to recover from his startled state and avoid the strike.

Most of the strike.

The curvy-bladed hilt, fashioned to mimic Lancelot's, found Arthur's head, the force of the blow cracking the Elvish metal. The hinderside of Rhon impaled the ground behind Arthur, who would have fallen, but instead gave all of his weight to the mystical weapon. The leverage lifted Mordred from the ground, who dangled on the shaft like a freshly-speared fish, twitching, and then…lifeless.

Bedwyr ran to Arthur's side and caught him ere he fell with the full force of his weight to the ground. In the act of catching the Iron Bear, Bedwyr tore at the seam, but Derfel caught the man who caught the king.

Lancelot tended Arthur, signaling for cart and horse. Merlin was there as well.

On the field of Camlan Mordred and Arthur had fought, and Mordred had fallen.

A few moments later, the king's steely glove pulled first Lancelot, then Merlin close. The embattled lord whispered. Moments later, Britain's tallest Britons laughed in unison.

The other survivors demanded to know the meaning of such cruel blasphemy, but Merlin eased them. "Cider, lads. The old king wants cider."

"Conduct me to the chapel of my nephew," Arthur ordered, "that I might rest."

Arthur's head wound was not lethal, and the company rejoiced.

Night had fallen and Morgaine had to travel, by barge and by hired horse, eight hours more.

Bishop Tydecho returned from Mallwyd with Tegfedd. She was secretly a healer, hiding in plain sight of the Church. Arthur's niece could not heal Bedwyr, but she gave him a strong potion, that he might sleep free of pain. The company reckoned that the dearest of all Round Table Knights would pass, from blood loss or infection, in one to two days.

***

The night's rest did Arthur good, but his head wound brought nausea and early the following morning, being a discreet and private person, he walked outside, finding a place to vomit in the shade of a tree. The vomiting depleted and weakened Arthur above measure, and a hemorrhage occurred behind his eye, causing it to fill with blood and lose sight.

Derfel and Tegfedd (whose eyes had not unlocked from the moment of introduction the night before), being youthful, were first to find the king. Lancelot and Merlin slept.

"Niece and new friend"—Arthur struggled to speak—"sorrow not; I thirst."

Knowing the stream was near, Derfel bolted as a stag, leaping over brush and log, hurrying to fetch his lord water. The maiden Tegfedd was left alone with the legend, the Savior of the Cymru.

Ever looking to serve others, he attempted to ease *her* distress with light words, but she lovingly pre-empted him, wanting nothing of comedy during the tragic hour. "You shall have no cider, my lord. Only water, and herbs, and rest."

Tegfedd looked to the tree's branches, then to the sky to see what the weather might this day do; when she looked down, two thirds of a spear was in Arthur's left hand, the remainder buried deep into his loins.

Eda the Coward had thrown the spear from close range. He struck Tegfedd hard upon the jaw, that she might not spoil his stealth by screaming.

"Look how now the son hath become his father; for TWO lame kings now rule from Gwent!" Eda, himself laboring to outlast grave injuries, disappeared ere he, being unarmed, was slain.

"Merlin, Lancelot, Hosts of Gwynedd, Kernunnos, Bran, or Mabon, help me! Help me!" Derfel cried.

"Poison," the Merlin proclaimed. "A poisoned shaft hath found the loins of our king!"

Conversations with Meurig from forty and one years ago tried to invade the druid's mind, but he blocked them. The Tribes would never again accept King Arthur as Pendragon, but saving his life—not traditions or politics—was now paramount.

The cough, just a nuisance afore, now raged, and Arthur's each breath was contested. Every wound and hurt from a hundred wars worked in concert to remind the Titan of his mortality. He grabbed at his hand, clutching the scratch that Gwenhwyfar had but recently mended. Eyes rolled, and then returned only as pale slits beneath swollen flaps of burdened skin.

The hope of Britain lay nigh unto death…

CAMLAN ACT VII

CHAPTER 24
The Battle After the Battle is the Real Battle

Eda's poison was meant to render Arthur impotent, causing him to lose his office, and live out his days in shame—not to kill him. However, the head wound was causing swelling and pressure in the brainpan; in combination with the toxins, it was too much trauma for Arthur's chest and vital organs, and he began to die.

Merlin departed, hoping to find Morgaine along her way, and hasten her arrival.

Things always happen when Merlin is away.

This time, during the wizard's short absence, Arthur ordered Bedwyr take Excalibur and offer her to a still pool of water, that Arthur not die holding a false office.

Bedwyr could not receive these words—that any should reign save Arthur—but he obeyed, promising to return swiftly.

***

Dainty fingers shook the Bear's face, which had turned both ashen, and yet green.

"Brother, wake. A cart awaits, and my barge. Come now to Avalon, where I will heal you of your grievous wounds." Morgaine softly kissed his forehead; *Sister, Lover, now Mother to whom she loved, of whom she was given charge.* She gathered his boots, found his belt, shook the dried mud from his cloak. Rhon was recovered, having rolled under Tydecho's bed.

"Brother." Morgaine was exasperated, and she could feel Merlin's impatience following her. "Where is your sword?!"

***

Morgaine the Healer was in full command, and all obeyed with ready minds her decrees.

"I am not going with you, Merlin."

The wizard was agape, bewildered at the change of course.

"Bear Arthur to Aberdaron; there let him rest for an evening in the chapel near the shore. Tomorrow morning, I will meet you on at Porth Maddwy. If I tarry, my Maidens will ferry you to Avalon's shores." She was resolute. *Maiden, Mother, Lover, Goddess.* "But I will not tarry."

She then turned to Lancelot. No words were exchanged—only an embrace and instructions that he hasten unto the Old North, there to reconcile with Urien and Owain. He obeyed the Lady, asking only that he might first run to Rhun, and hold him tight once more.

"Embrace him for me as well"—she smiled—"but do so as you travel, for our world is in chaos and lies of every sort will spread. I will save the king; you save the truth about the king." Here were Morgaine and Lancelot made whole.

"And WHERE do you go?" demanded the Merlin, overwhelmed by the swiftness with which events unfolded around him—showing signs at last of great age.

"To stop Bedwyr," she answered plainly. "The king will not be without his sword, and the land not without its king!"

***

"This dreadful end is not yet." Bedwyr. "Cannot, must not, do not cast it away!"

Vivien's outstretched hand withdrew, vanishing in the like manner to which it had appeared—instant and silent—back beneath the still of the Llyn Fawr.

"I failed you, fully and completely, my friend, my best friend," Bedwyr bewailed.

"Nay!" Morgaine called, now within thirty feet of the fading knight. "I AM the Lady of the Lake now! Cast Excalibur unto me, for Vivien and I are one."

Bedwyr could see the reason in this, and trusted that Morgaine would not entreat him falsely. The fabled sword shone in his hand, giving its own low, melancholy sound, bidding him, *Cast me away*. He whispered prayers to the sword, bidding farewell to the weapon in the stead of the king. And so Excalibur was cast, flipping twice, twirling thrice in the air, now stopping of its own accord, hovering in glory above the sacred lake.

The First Knight saw Excalibur float, contrary to nature, into Morgaine's own hands: choosing her, validating her, and releasing him, having completed his last quest.

"This is not your last quest," the Lady protested. "Look around you, Bedwyr; smudge and ash, blight and barren, and yet…" A pixie, no greater than a butterfly in size, placed a dead flower upon Bedwyr's hand, which Morgaine had carefully opened, and stretched. "See how we do recover, for these are the Blessed Isles." Through her enchantment, the wilted petals were restored, and blossomed. "We need you to be our dry flower come to life again." She kissed his hand, closing it gently about the flower, and left him to the care of the Fair Folk, who promised to restore him, that the king would have his best friend upon his return.

Morgaine then gazed up to Craig-Y-Llyn, the shadowy asylum for Llyn Fawr and her sister lake, Llyn Fach. The holy mount was also a mammoth capstone for an antediluvian metropolis whose tunnels and conduits allowed those with knowledge of the Mysteries rapid passage unto sites both sacred and strategic.

And Avalon was both, being the most sacred and most strategic place in the whole of Britain.

The Sorceress made haste, arriving upon the shores of Aberdaron *before* Derfel, Tydecho, Tygfedd, the Merlin, Arthur, and their hosts from the Isle of Apples.

The king had had disruptive, intermittent sleep the prior night. His breathing patterns were irregular, his lungs filled with fluid. Morgaine and Accolon positioned him gently on the barge, situating his head upon her lap.

He spoke in broken, soft words, coughing.

"Pray for my soul."

The contrary and ruthless currents about Ynys Enlli mourned and were still, the seas about the Blessed Isles themselves sorrowing over so great a loss.

Merlin noted Excalibur and did ask the Lady, "What moved you to risk losing our friend, that he might have *that* near at the end?"

"Excalibur and Arthur are One. And the Cup and I are One. And our union is One."

Her cryptic words befuddled the wizard, for he could make no interpretation of them.

But he will. And soon…

After reaching the shores of Avalon, Morgaine summonsed another mist — this one for protection against any survivors of the North that might have followed them. Accolon and Derfel bore the king into the Glass Castle, following careful instruction on where to lay their lord. Merlin stayed at the gates of the enchanted palace. His cap removed, he scratched his head, cocking his heard to the north, working Morgaine's puzzle.

The Sorceress attended them to the castle doors, bidding them exit and await her address, which she gave from a high tower, saying, "I and I alone can do what must next be done. You beloveds can proceed no further!"

She motioned with her hand, stopping Merlin, who had unraveled her hard words and began, too late, to desperately protest. "You left me to do this alone the first time; knowest thou not that what happened in the cave was but a rehearsal? We live life in reverse order, all, for yesterday ever is a cast shadow for what we must do today. Is not the entire Old Covenant in your Sacred Book filled with types and shadows of what Christ would later do?" She lowered her hand, looking into the druid's soul. "You are vindicated—you AND the Lady Vivien, lord Merlin. You put me through the Rite IN TIMES PAST that I might be prepared for the Rite TODAY. The trauma of that perversion did not ruin my life; it readied me to save his life."

A shadow fell upon the whole of the Isle, and it was as midnight, though it were but newly morning-time.

"I am Gwyar ferch Onbrawst. I am Morgaine ferch Vivien. I am Morgana, daughter of the damned. Forbidden love captured my heart before the Flood, and by Lancelot did hopelessness yet again avenge my heart. I lost my children, again and again. But I will NOT lose my brother, my lover, my king!"

"She would perform the Sacred Rite! She is not laboring to save the king, but rather to resurrect him!" Merlin desperately tried every entrance, which were sealing and closing through sorcery before him. Though much of the Fortress itself was made of green glass, it was bewitched and impenetrable. *And her magick was greater than the Merlin's.*

When hope seemed lost, a bird appeared. *A merlin.* It appeared as if cast from the very high tower whence the witch had spoken; or, equally, as a gift fallen from heaven. Making a spiraling descent, the merlin landed on the Merlin. It plucked at his beard, then played with his ears, which were equally hairy, at last putting its pokey foot in Merlin's eye.

"What's this?" He swatted the bird away,

dislodging a piece of parchment that had been tied to its twig-like leg. Scribbled in haste was but one word, a name, in the Cymreig alphabet: "Magus."

The coned hat refitted and snug, he clutched at his heart. Feigning defeat, he, the Nine Maidens, Accolon, and Derfel retreated deep into the forest, and further still, to the Sacred Grove. Still fearing demonic ears, the druid huddled the twelve beneath a sprawling apple tree—the kind of tree that had absorbed secrets for thousands of years; a mystery for each branch.

"An evil abides in the castle made of glass. The evil that has ignited the Fall of Britain, and before us, other gilded, advanced civilizations as well. She has a plan, a strategy. We can do nought but trust Morgaine."

***

"He will die unless you perform the Rite."

"He will die even IF I perform the Rite. You would have me open a gate into the Underworld and place Judas Iscariot, or some other vile spirit, into my brother."

"I would." Magus, like Morgaine, knew the king was expiring, and durst not delay with matches of wit. "What you must do to him… happened to you. You are still yourself, but you share yourself with another, and the twain in you are now one. This is what the angels from the world that was did, and taught to man on the other side of the Flood; the Sacred Rite!" Satan's Chief Minister relished in the abominable mocking of God that was, and was to be again. "It will be the same for Arthur. The Son of Meurig he will remain. If his will as host is stronger than the *other*, I will not be able to—"

"Activate him, as you did the Giants and monsters."

"Yes, my child." Magus clapped. "You truly are the more fascinating of the famed Walles siblings. Given that your brother is the Anti-Christ, that says much, yes?" His Italian, overly-accented, ghastly cackle followed.

Morgaine rapidly sought strategies, diversions, solutions…but time waged war on her. Frenzied, she determined what must be done.

"Seven candlesticks and four of my maidens, summon." If the Black Pope would have his Beast brought from the pit, he would take a subordinate role and assist the Witch in the performance of it.

"Mandrake, Vervain, Mercury, and Wolf's Bane," she next ordered.

"Do it, do it!" He chided the Damsel with his grotesque words, seeing her priestesses arrange the necessities of the craft, and smudge the air with pungent and curious smoke.

Arthur lay in Morgaine's own bed, around which Morgaine cast the circle, and lit the seven candles. She disrobed, then bravely confronted the Masked Man, fully nude. "I assume you have the marking sticks, and *our masks.*"

"This is the consummation of my life's work! Of course I do." More Italian snarls.

Four of the Nine Maidens were positioned at each corner of the bed: a large and comely iron frame, beautifully furnished with skins and throws and pillows of every sort (*Morgaine was a dark mistress, but a lass who loved pretty décor just the same)* representing the angelic Guardians of the Four Winds. They also did mark Morgaine as the Primal Witch, adorning her as that ancient goddess who had taken lovers from the sons of Adam and, worse, her own household, creating abominations that were more part god than man. Her mask represented the Moon, the fertile earth, the feminine Light that ruled the cosmic night.

Arthur they rendered as the Stag. The Solar light, the Hunter. That old Mighty One who would lie with wicked women and beget monsters. This Rite was not about welcoming the change of the season, or celebrating the gods of harvest, wheat, creek and stone. All these were benign practices of a people that knew not the Creator God, but were thankful for their grain, the sunshine, and the health and happiness wrought by a plentiful harvest.

No; the Sacred Rite was a Mystery to the uninitiated. It was a rehearsal, or a remembrance, of those vile angels who had polluted humanity and creature-kind, established their Religion, and provoked the Creator to clean the slate, and start over with a Flood.

And the Horned One was the chief sinner, practicing more than any other in this dark act.

Now Magus would tap into those dark powers from before the Flood to raise up his Anti-Christ.

In their youth the Stag, the Sun, had been made to enter the earth, below; and so did the clumsy boy Arthur atop his sister. As Arthur lay dying, the symbolism was inverted, for the sun was *down,* and the moon climbing atop him in turn; the lesser light giving power and new life to the greater.

Morgaine used the mixture, the potion, in an effort to wake Arthur, that he might be conscious and able to perform. In his delirium she was again his *nocturnal lover, his visitor, for he too had been rehearsing this very moment for the whole of his life.*

"I do dream; the night hag doth come for my loins again," he mumbled, overcome and confused; words so forced and weak that only she could hear him.

"Hush, brother, 'tis no dream. This is why you favor the mask; don it now and hide, and I will come for thee." She comforted him, and did embrace his cheek, softly kissing her brother.

She too fitted the mask to her face. The moon responded, sending ethereal beams of moonlight through the fortress of glass. The beams burned through the mask, marking her with a crescent moon between her eyes. *The burn of the moon was more fierce than that of her male counterpart.* She let out a gasp, but the pain of it quickly abated.

The Primal Witch did speak the words of the Rite. The candles, fixed as a Faerie Star, sent lines of fire, a crosswork of red-hot flame. The flames did overcome the bed, causing it to vanish; a circle of flame encompassed the scorching star besides. Morgaine and Arthur lay in coitus on an altar of flames where the bed had once been, yet burned not.

The Maidens, filled with terror, held their positions, and the four winds did come; the rush roared with such force and noise that the six actors were as gladiators in amphitheater, deafened by cheers, by trumpets, by gusts.

BUT MORGAINE DID NOT LET THE ABUSE OWN HER; SHE OWNED IT.

There would be no sacred fornication, no incest, no dark carnal magick. All Arthur had to do was call out for the goddess thrice, and all would be set aright.

The potion rendered Arthur erect. He was disoriented, mostly blind save to shadows and forms, and felt his life slipping. And yet he was aroused by remedies.

Knowing that Magus could not see their congress through the cyclone of wind, nor approach the flaming star, she instructed her dying brother in his ruse. "You will go down, and I will bring you up again…pretend." She rolled her hips upon him and whispered once more, "Call upon me. I am here. Call upon me."

Four winds.

Seven candles to make one star.

The moon.

The sun.

The earth.

The stag.

The sword and cup!

"Now, bring me the king's sword!"

Another priestess braved the crackle and tempest, and did hand the Lady of Avalon the Sword of Power.

Here did Simon know he was to see it not ten and five feet away. The Cup of Christ! *What evils he had been empowered to unleash with this idol!*

Call forth for it she did.

"You are the sword," she said unto her brother below, holding Excalibur high with her right hand, brandishing it thrice.

"Morgana," he called, confused as ever. Fourteen again, only then with spear and no magical sword.

"I am the cup!" she cried, and the Primal Witch filled her eyes with pitch and blackened the crescent upon her brow. The markings upon her naked form were as embers; black, now orange, now white-hot, now black again.

"Morgana!" Again, as loud as his failing voice could muster.

"You are the sword of truth, I am the cup of communion. And we are One. Forget me not in the hereafter, and above all, forget not who YOU are!"

"Morgaine!" The words escaped, then were doubled: "Morgana, Morgana, Morgaine!" And now the three times three did he make, crying, "Morgana, Morgana, Morgaine!"

The Primal Goddess fully manifested, a power above four thousand years old. It changed neither countenance nor image of Gwyar, except the shadow it cast, being unnaturally tall, for it *was Gwyar*.

At the king's final utterance, the candles burst and the flames collapsed on themselves; the whirling tempest abated and the comely bed returned. In this moment, the Morrigan whispered words to the Pendragon in the tongue of luminaries.

And Arthur died, his soul falling into the Underworld.

"Good!" Simon was most pleased. "He went quickly; you did not even have to mount him much." He laughed and laughed, not knowing that Morgaine had shifted their bodies, and that no untoward act had occurred.

"Now, Walles, utter those ancient words and bring him back." The Masked Man corrected himself: "*Them*."

"You failed." 'Twas Gwyar, but the voice was that of a thousand rushing waters and ten thousand cymbals. The voice of a goddess.

"But the Rite! I saw—" Magus possessed no fear of the Witch.

"You saw with ambition and desperate hope to immanentize the End of Days. The ritual put him in the netherworld. He sleeps, but you…you die!"

The Morrigan rushed upon Magus, but an angel intervened.

Epilogue

The fleet of Prince Madoc ap Meurig discovered a new land.

A land of plenty.

The streams teemed with plump, girthy fish, speckled with every color of the rainbow. So plentiful were they that they leapt into the fisherman's net or basket, giving themselves to the grateful recipients. Eagles ruled regal skies of crystal blue and vibrant yellows and purples; so clean was the atmosphere that the sailors were awed, believing the sky to be a looking-glass.

The forests featured pools and springs filled with species of silver otters and spotted badgers of a kind unfamiliar to the Cymru. These frolicked and played, but also sang during their labor, building dams and appearing to work in union and collaboration with the native inhabitants.

There were alligators and lizards too.

Moreover, a peculiar bovine, much larger than a bull—possessing a powerful head, little horns, and a body with a singular large hump that was otherwise *all barrel and chest*—roamed free, giddy and unafraid.

So vast and majestic was this *undiscovered country* that Madoc's mind arrived at two possible conclusions:

We perished at sea and this is heaven, or…

We have reached the edge of the world and, having breached the firmament, come to the Otherworld beyond.

A feathered red man approached the prince, and offered him shelter, and wheat for bread…

Author Profile

Author Zane Newitt is an internationally recognized Arthurian scholar, folklorist and historian born on September 3rd, 1975 in Glenwood Springs, Colorado, USA. Volume One of his saga, *The Arthuriad*, was published in 2017, and six additional installments are to be published between 2018 and 2022.

Dr. Newitt is known for reviving the 'Bardic Method' – a writing style that combines epic poetry, Welsh Nationalism, folklore, theology and history in a uniquely "Druidesque" blend that conceals more than it reveals, as well as containing something to inspire and offend anyone… Just as Merlin would do.

Publisher Information

rowanvale books

Rowanvale Books provides publishing services to independent authors, writers and poets all over the globe. We deliver a personal, honest and efficient service that allows authors to see their work published, while remaining in control of the process and retaining their creativity. By making publishing services available to authors in a cost-effective and ethical way, we at Rowanvale Books hope to ensure that the local, national and international community benefits from a steady stream of good quality literature.

For more information about us, our authors or our publications, please get in touch.

www.rowanvalebooks.com
info@rowanvalebooks.com

Printed in Great Britain
by Amazon